MIDNIGHT
BABY

WENDY HORNSBY

MIDNIGHT BABY

A Maggie MacGowen Mystery

A DUTTON BOOK

DUTTON
Published by the Penguin Group
Penguin Books USA Inc., 375 Hudson Street,
New York, New York 10014, U.S.A.
Penguin Books Ltd, 27 Wrights Lane,
London W8 5TZ, England
Penguin Books Australia Ltd, Ringwood,
Victoria, Australia
Penguin Books Canada Ltd, 10 Alcorn Avenue,
Toronto, Ontario, Canada M4V 3B2
Penguin Books (N.Z.) Ltd, 182–190 Wairau Road,
Auckland 10, New Zealand

Penguin Books Ltd, Registered Offices:
Harmondsworth, Middlesex, England

First published by Dutton, an imprint of New American Library,
a division of Penguin Books USA Inc.
Distributed in Canada by McClelland & Stewart Inc.

First Printing, June, 1993
10 9 8 7 6 5 4 3 2 1

 REGISTERED TRADEMARK—MARCA REGISTRADA

LIBRARY OF CONGRESS CATALOGING IN PUBLICATION DATA
Hornsby, Wendy.
    Midnight baby : a Maggie MacGowen mystery / by Wendy Hornsby.
        p.   cm.
    ISBN 0-525-93615-7
    I. Title.
    PS3558.0689M53   1993
    813'.54—dc20   92-37883
                                                                    CIP

Printed in the United States of America
Set in Century Schoolbook
Designed by Eve L. Kirch

PUBLISHER'S NOTE
This is a work of fiction. Names, characters, places, and incidents either are the
products of the author's imagination or are used fictitiously, and any resemblance
to actual persons, living or dead, events, or locales is entirely coincidental.

For my parents, Robert and Fern Nelson—
Fifty years of the big adventure together.
Fifty years of storytelling.

CHAPTER

1

Under a full moon and sodium-vapor streetlights, the girl was all silver: her pale cropped hair, her face with its heavy trowelling of matte makeup. The parts below her face, small, pushed-up bosom, narrow hips, muscled, serviceable legs, were banded in stretch jersey and black mesh and could have belonged to any undernourished, overused hooker between puberty and menopause.

At first, I had no attitude about her. Through the viewfinder of my videocamera, she was no more than a photogenic image, good filmic contrast to the fat toddlers I had spent the day recording in Encino.

Guilt, or maybe the impulse of universal motherhood, I don't know what, took over when I learned the girl was only six months older than my own daughter, Casey. That made her fourteen and a half.

My documentary project was nearly in the can, until I met her. Over-budget and overdue as always, but under control. Until I met her.

"I'll do women," she said, trying to keep her face away from my camera. "There's no extra charge."

"What's your name?" I asked.

"You can call me Pisces."

"Where do you live, Pisces?"

"Here," she said, vaguely indicating MacArthur Park with her cigarette as a pointer. "I don't like having my picture taken. Not for free."

"How long have you been on the streets?"

She shrugged, glanced back at the red Corvette that had been following us along the curb as we walked. I couldn't see the driver; he could have been a potential date, her pimp, or her dealer. Or an undercover cop doing his job. Whatever he was, when I turned the camera on him, he sped off.

I knew better than to get involved with the girl, just as I had known better than to finish off the bottle of wine the previous night before driving home, or to put myself into debt well into the next millennium to buy a house directly atop the San Andreas Fault. Wisdom and action don't necessarily intersect on the same plane.

The street around us was a midnight carnival. Derelicts, hypes, a broad assortment of the ambulatory insane, spilled out of MacArthur Park like leakage from Pandora's box, to panhandle or rage against internal demons, to look for another fix. Among them, skittery but tolerant, were little family groups of refugees to El Norte, whose lighted food wagons sold the same spicy meat pies I had bought once in San Salvador, Coca-Cola bottled in Mexico, and dysentery on a stick—crushed fresh fruit frozen in someone's home kitchen.

It was April in L.A. The day had been warm, the usual monotonous seventy-six degrees, but the night had turned cold. My partner, Guido Patrini, had walked down to the corner to buy hot coffee from a torta vendor. I could see him leaning against the cart, practicing his Spanish while the coffee cooled. I felt impatient, not because I wanted the coffee, but because the neighborhood scared me shitless.

The girl, Pisces, wanted my attention again. Dramatically, she pulled out a dark lipstick and redid her full lips. "We can go in an alley, or there's a motel on the corner if you want to get a room."

"All I want is your face in my film," I said, dropping the camera from my shoulder. "Pisces, are you okay out here?"

"You mean, do I have a man?"

"I mean, are you okay? Does your family know where you are?"

The way she shrugged reminded me of my daughter, Casey, who, if things were going according to plan, was at home tucked in her bed under the watchful care of our housemate, Lyle. In our house that lies over the San Andreas Fault.

The same red Corvette passed us again, tight by the curb and moving slowly. Pisces moved to put me between her and the street.

"I know a shelter just off Hollywood Boulevard," I said to her. "It doesn't cost anything to stay there and they won't ask questions. If you want to get off the street tonight, I'll drive you over."

"And what do you get?" she smirked. "A free piece on the way?"

"All I get is peace of mind. I have a daughter your age. I wouldn't want her to be out here unprotected, either."

"Oh, a mother," she taunted, but she didn't walk away. "I remember mothers. They want you to wash behind your ears and eat your peas and carrots before they fuck you over."

I hefted the camera back to my shoulder. "Tell me about home, Pisces."

"I get paid by the half hour," she said. "Even if all you want is talk."

Four gunshots exploded into the night nearby—bam-bam, bam-bam, two pairs. I ducked. Everyone on the street ducked. And Pisces slipped into my arms.

Three punks in gang-banger uniform—black jeans and Raiders T-shirts—crashed through the shrubs around the park and scattered out toward the street, two of them dodging cars while the third lagged to fumble with something caught in his jacket. The police were right behind them, two sleek officers in pressed uniforms. They caught the laggard with a flying tackle and slammed his face to the sidewalk at the feet of a drunk, who didn't even notice when the batons came out to beat the kid to quiescence.

The entire show took less than two minutes. When it was over, the police raised their handcuffed quarry by the elbows and quickstepped him down the block to the police substation in the park. One of the officers held a semiautomatic pistol he hadn't had when he breached the shrubbery.

I have seen, through the lens of my camera, the conditions at home the Salvadorans fled from: chaos, hunger, war. As I looked around this carnival, I couldn't see the improvement.

Guido walked up just then with two plastic cups of coffee. I traded him the camera for one of the cups.

"Took you long enough," I said sharply, relieved to see him intact. "Did you have to harvest the coffee beans on the way?"

"I was trying to explain to this guy why he should start using paper cups." He didn't mention the shooting. "Shit, Maggie, don't they know that plastic is killing us?"

"Maybe you should start bringing your own cup, Guido," I said, blowing on my coffee, blowing off steam. "I'll get you one you can hook to your belt loops. Better yet, I'll get you a little solar-powered coffee maker you can carry around with you. You know, make your own, drink it right out of the pot. No, forget that. Just carry a bottle of water with you and some No Doz. Your body won't know the difference. I read in *Geographic* how they're burning the rain forests to plant coffee."

"Always the smart-ass, Maggie," Guido said.

"And you love it."

He raised his cup to cover his grin.

Guido isn't a very big man, about my height, five-seven or five-eight. He weighs maybe 130 pounds after a big lunch. He has that tight-wired intensity that little men often have; borderline hyper. I love having him work on film projects with me because of the energy he injects. Guido's biggest professional problem is that while he's a gifted filmmaker, he isn't much of a salesman. You have to be both if you want to get funding to do independent investigative film projects. And that is my livelihood.

So Guido found himself a decent alternative: he teaches at the UCLA film school. It's a good job, and he has made a name for himself. But he misses being out in the trenches so much that I have found him to be a bit of a slut—he never turns down my invitations to work.

I tasted the coffee, strong and bitter, and took back the camera from him. Pisces was still standing close beside me. The fireworks across the street were over. It should have been apparent I wasn't going to hire her services. So I had expected her to walk away. It surprised me when she didn't. She just stood there, eavesdropping, watching me fuss one-handed with the camera's battery pack, spilling some coffee as I fussed.

"Guido," I said, glancing up, "meet Pisces."

He nodded to her. "How's it going?"

"Well enough," she said. She had her eyes on my coffee cup, or the steam rising from it. I was cold in jeans and a wool jacket. Her exposed arms were all goose bumps. I held out my cup to her.

"Would you like some?" I asked.

"Cream and sugar?" she asked.

"Cream, no sugar."

She shrugged, condescending, but she took the offered cup. Sugar wouldn't have hurt her figure. She was skinny, but very muscular. When she moved her body had the assertive thrust of an athlete.

"So, Pisces," I said. "It's late and there doesn't seem to be much business out here. Can I give you a lift to that shelter I mentioned?"

"I don't know. It is pretty cold tonight, but I hate going to those places. Do you live around here?"

"No. I live in San Francisco. I'm only in L.A. working for a few days."

"You have a hotel?"

"I'm staying at Guido's."

She looked at Guido and waited for him to say something. He turned on me.

"Why do you always do this to me, Maggie?"

"Do what?" I asked with *faux* innocence.

"We were going to Langer's to get some pastrami," he groused. "We saw *her* on the way, so we detoured to get her on film. That's great. But do we have to do a Mother Theresa shtick, too?"

"I love it when you're forceful," I said, patting his cheek. "Pisces, you want to get something to eat with us?"

"That would be fine," she said, and smiled wryly at Guido. "Nice of you to ask."

We walked the half block to Langer's Deli like a little family group out for the evening: Mom, Dad, and baby hooker.

The restaurant is a New York–style neighborhood eatery, 1950s linoleum and glass meat cases, an institution left behind when the old neighbors moved out of MacArthur Park and El Salvador moved in. Guido claims it has the best pastrami in the world.

As soon as we got inside, Pisces excused herself to go to the rest room. Guido and I found a booth in the middle where she could find us when she was finished.

Guido pried a half-sour pickle out of the pot on the table, and took a bite. He smiled at me while he chewed.

"What?" I said.

"I was just thinking," he said. "There any kids hooking on the street in San Francisco?"

"Of course."

"And chubby little bambinos up there in model day-care palaces?"

"What's your question?"

"Just curious why you had to come to L.A. to film."

"The child psychologist who is consulting on the script agrees with me that we want to depict a broad range of child-raising experiences. You're always so cautious, Guido. I want to take the lid off on this one. I want to include some kids most people never see."

"So go to Natchitoches, Louisiana, or Bismarck, North Dakota," he said. "You didn't have to come to L.A. to film a face in the dark, or kids on a slide. You could have taken care of that shit in your own neighborhood."

"You sound like the grant coordinator. Are you asking me to defend the project?"

"Nope." He leaned forward and used the pickle as a pointer aimed at my nose. "Have you called Mike Flint?"

"Hadn't occurred to me to do so," I said, defensive. Another thing that makes Guido such a good filmmaker is his unerring insight. Sometimes I just hate him.

Guido reached into his pocket, fiddled through some change, and slid two dimes across the table toward me.

"Should I know what the dimes are for?" I asked, knowing full well.

"Make the call."

I thought about it. I had been thinking about it for six months. Mike Flint and I had started something about a year earlier that had never been resolved. As hard as I had fallen for Flint, from the beginning I knew that anything beyond *carpe diem* was hopeless. He was a detective with twenty-two years on the LAPD. A big-city dick, with a full share of the reactionary attitudes that implies. Beyond that, he was a true and loyal friend, a man with deep compassion, great thighs. He made me laugh.

I could live with his opinions—I love a good argument and he always offered plenty to argue about. The sticking point was that until he had put in his twenty-five years on the force he was stuck in L.A. And after that, he envisioned himself retiring to a cabin so deep in the woods that the sound of drive-by gunfire could only be heard on the six-o'clock news. He longed for quietude.

Simply put, Mike and I had incompatible geography. I hate L.A., but I'm not big on flannel shirts and bear meat. As I said, it was hopeless. I had had six months to get used to that reality. What I could not understand was why I kept having this running conversation with Mike Flint in my head. Why my eyes began to roll back every time I thought about the texture of the soft hair at the back of his neck.

Pisces came back from the rest room. I slid deeper into the booth to make room for her beside me. Once she sat down, I couldn't get out to use the telephone. I pushed the dimes back to Guido.

"Guido says the pastrami here is worth risking your life for," I said to Pisces. "How do you feel about pastrami?"

"It's all right," she said. "May I have some salad with it?"

"Anything you want," I said, glaring at the tooth-sucking expression on Guido's chiseled face.

"Thank you," Pisces said. "I'm really hungry now that I smell food."

Guido turned his attention to the girl, studied her with his quick intensity. In the rest room she had brushed her hair back from her face, wiped off most of the makeup, and pulled up the top of her skimpy dress to cover her shoulders. Without all the goo she was a pretty little girl with wide, dark brown eyes and good skin. She seemed to have transformed her streetwise attitude as well as her appearance.

"You have nice manners for a lady of the evening," Guido said as she spread a paper napkin on her lap. "Where you from, kid?"

"Here," she said, shrugging.

"Here, like L.A.?"

"Sort of."

"Southern California, anyway, right? You sound like a local."

She giggled a little. "You can't tell that. Everyone knows there is no California accent."

"Wrong," he corrected. "It's Brooklyn that has no accent. Unless you're from Chicago."

She laughed politely. She picked up a pickle, bit off the end of it, and screwed up her face at the sourness.

If I had felt at all protective of her before, I felt doubly so as I watched her. This was not a child raised in the streets. Guido had been correct about her manners. There was a sophistication about her, a social easiness, that comes with a certain careful upbringing. She did not appear to be on drugs. This kid was somebody's baby girl. The question that began to eat away at me was: Who had lost her?

A senior-citizen waitress came and rested her soft hip against the end of the table. She gave us a long, nosy inspection. "Have you decided?"

Guido looked at Pisces and me. "Can I order for everyone? There's an art to eating pastrami. It has to be done just right to get the full effect."

"We're in your hands," I said, and Pisces giggled again.

Guido faced the waitress. "We'll have three pastramis on rye, with yellow mustard—none of that gray poop. Three cream sodas, and one dinner salad, not slaw, on the side. And that's all."

"A man who knows his mind," the waitress said. "Be right back with the salad."

She was true to her word; the salad came immediately. While Pisces ate, Guido and I talked about the footage we had shot in Encino at a model day-care center. I couldn't get very excited about it. I knew the real story about children was sitting on the banquette next to me.

"What's the schedule tomorrow, Maggie?" Guido asked.

"The Florence Crittenton Home for unwed mothers in the morning, then Pop Warner cheerleader practice out in Orange County in the afternoon. Think you can get us to Yorba Linda?"

He curled his lip. "I'd rather go to Natchitoches."

"Maybe next time," I said.

The waitress set pastrami sandwiches in front of us that were at least five inches high, no exaggeration. As she set a squeeze bottle of yellow mustard in the middle of the table, she smiled maternally. "Can I get you anything else?"

"Yes, please," Pisces said with a smile. "A doggie bag."

The waitress drew back, disapproving. "You haven't eaten anything yet, honey. You pile into that sandwich, and when you're finished we'll talk about a doggie bag."

I started to laugh at the nerviness of the waitress, but stopped when I saw that Pisces was not amused. I guessed she might have later plans for her meal. The way she had devoured her salad, I knew she was hungry. In her position I would have mouthed off to the waitress. But Pisces docilely followed instructions and began to eat. At first, she only nibbled at the edges of the sandwich. In the end, there was nothing on her plate except a few strips of gristle. I couldn't even finish half of my serving, and neither could Guido.

When the waitress came back with the check, she picked up Pisces' plate first. I could have smacked the smug look off her powdered face. She said, "Well, young lady, I guess you were hungry after all."

"I guess so." Pisces seemed subdued. She seemed to have a lot on her mind. Maybe the end of dinner meant the beginning of whatever came next. I could not imagine seeing this child go back out onto the street. I was also powerless to stop her if that's what she decided to do.

I handed up my plate to the waitress with its half sandwich. "May I have a doggie bag? Guido needs one, too."

As the waitress walked away again, Pisces said, "If you take the bread off the meat before you put the sandwich away, it won't get all soggy."

"Thanks for the advice," I said. "It's a lot of food. You know, Guido and I probably won't have a chance to get to it tomorrow. We'll be out all day. Be a shame to let it go to waste. Would you like to take the bags home with you?"

"Yes, thank you." She looked into her lap when her chin quivered. "Thank you for dinner. It was very good."

"Pisces." I touched her hand, and saw her tense up. "Please let me take you to a shelter?"

She shook her head. "I'm all right. I have an okay place to sleep."

"What does 'okay' mean?" Guido challenged. "You have an apartment, a room, what?"

"This shelter," she said, raising her face. "They don't ask a lot of questions?"

"As long as you're fourteen, there are no questions," I assured her.

"What if you're nine?" she asked.

Guido snapped to. "You're nine?"

"No. I told you, I'm fourteen. But what happens to a kid who's only nine?"

"If she's that young," I said, "Child Protective Services has to be called. A kid that young shouldn't even be crossing the street alone. Not that you should, either."

The waitress came back with change and two doggie bags. "Thank you." She smiled. "Have a nice evening."

Pisces wiped her hands on her napkin and sat forward on the seat, ready to go. She seemed resigned.

"What about the shelter?" I asked.

She shook her head and frowned. "There's someone I have to look after."

The implications of her soft statement were not lost on Guido. When he looked up at me with dew in his eyes, I knew he also was doomed where this girl was concerned.

"I just thought of another place you might go," I said as we slid out of the booth. "A good friend of mine. You'd like her. You wouldn't have to say anything to her that you didn't want to."

Guido looked more hopeful than Pisces. "Really? Who?"

"Let me call her first, just to make sure it's okay."

Guido fished out two dimes again. There was a telephone booth in the back by the rest rooms. I walked back alone and placed the call to Sister Agnes Peter, an old friend, a professional easy touch.

"Pete," I said. "It's Maggie MacGowen."

"How nice to hear from you." Her voice was hearty, like a PE teacher's. "Are you in town?"

"Yes. I'm working on a film, and I've run into a situation with one of my subjects. I need your help."

She laughed. "Dare I ask?"

"Do you have a couple of extra beds for the night?"

"Certainly. You know the address. The front light is on."

"Bless you. We'll be there within the hour."

I walked back to Guido and Pisces, smiled at their expectant faces. "All set."

The girl wasn't ready to accept anything yet. "Your friend said we could come?"

"Yes. She's waiting. I told her there will be two of you."

Pisces' chin began to quiver. I put my arm around her, and this time she did not flinch.

"Did you tell her who I am?" she asked.

"I don't know who you are," I said.

She pulled at her tight skirt self-consciously, and sniffled a couple of times. "I mean, what I do."

"You can tell her anything you want her to know. Or tell her nothing. She'll like you, don't worry. That's what her job is."

Pisces was working on the possibilities when I explained, "She's a nun."

"What about this other kid?" Guido asked. "Where is she?"

"He," Pisces corrected. She turned toward the glass front door and pointed outside. "He's right there."

I followed where she was pointing, but I didn't see anything except the straggly shrubbery lining the sidewalk. He must have been crouching there behind the low planter. When we opened the door, he stood and revealed himself. When he turned toward us, the light from the full moon hit his small face the way high beams catch roadkill.

CHAPTER

2

The boy was a foul-mouthed, evil-smelling little wretch. Pisces said he was nine, she called him Sly. He looked old, not like a wizened old man, more like a small animal. Something feral.

Pisces handed him the bags of leftover sandwiches. He ate quickly, standing hunched over the food protectively while he tucked it in. I was trying to visualize a few frames of his dirty freckled face edited among some spick-and-span Little Leaguers I had in my film files when he looked up and caught me staring.

"What the fuck you watching?" he demanded through a mouthful, spewing crumbs. "Get outta my face."

Pisces snapped, "Shut your mouth when you chew."

"Fuck that. Fuck them," he sneered. "What they hangin' here for?"

"They're all right," Pisces assured him. "They have a place for us to sleep tonight."

"We already have a place," Sly snapped.

"I want a shower," she said. "And you need one."

"Do not."

"Do too."

Guido put a hand between them before they came to blows. "You two related?"

"Related to this whore?" Sly sneered. "Fuck that."

"Wipe your face," Pisces admonished the boy. "You eat like a pig."

Sly obeyed her by wiping his face. I was having some difficulty sorting out this relationship. In the restaurant Pisces had said there was someone she looked after. After meeting the boy, I had to wonder who actually looked after whom. She seemed to be trying to mother him, but on matters of street survival, I suspected that he was the pro. He had doubtless scripted her hooker routine. All by herself, the little girl I'd had dinner with would not have been able to come up with the line of garbage she had fed me.

"So?" Guido said, gathering up the boy's sandwich litter from the sidewalk. "Are you coming, or what?"

Sly eyed him. "You cops?"

"Nope."

"If we go to this place, what do we hafta do there?"

"Take a shower if you want," I said. "Eat. Go to sleep. That's all."

"Eat?"

"If you're still hungry," I said.

"Sly's always hungry," Pisces said. "Must have worms."

"What'll it be?" I asked.

"Clean sheets," she said.

Sly reached for Pisces' arm. "Okay. Just for tonight. But we gotta get our stuff first."

Pisces let out a long breath. I thought she seemed relieved.

"Where's your stuff?" Guido asked.

"On the other side of the park," she said. "We'll show you."

"Fuck that." Sly pushed her away from Guido. "Don't show them nothin'. I'll go get the stuff by myself. Meet me at the liquor store."

Sly gave us no time to argue. He ran off toward the park like a rabbit let out of a bag. As soon as he was across the street he somehow merged with the night and disappeared. A good trick, considering how much light there was.

"Sweet child," Guido said.

"He used to be worse." Pisces shrugged. "Where's your car? It's better to drive around the park than walk across it. Too many bizarros hang out in there. The liquor store is on the other side. I'll show you."

Sly surprised me. I have been single long enough to have recognized the I'll-call-you-tomorrow tone in his voice before he took off. Apparently, however, I had misread him. We found him waiting for us exactly where he'd said he would be. That meant that, A, he was fast, and B, the place where he kept his stuff was close by.

When Sly climbed into the backseat of Guido's Jeep beside Pisces, he was clutching a brown grocery bag against him that contained something about the same size and shape as a leg of lamb. Since it didn't smell or leak, I didn't ask.

Sly and Pisces sat quietly in the back. She seemed apprehensive, while he appeared to be somewhat awed. He tried out the windows and fiddled with the seat belts and dome lights.

"You got a CD player?" Sly asked.

"No. Sorry," Guido said.

"Yeah." Sly nodded sagely. "It just gets ripped off, don't it?"

I began to have second thoughts about what I might be delivering to Sister Agnes Peter. Troubled kids, certainly. A nightmare, possibly. From his fidgety silence, I suspected that Guido was having similar misgivings, though he didn't say anything. Despite the potential for disaster, I could not come up with another alternative.

What I'd told Pisces was true. Taking people in was part of Agnes Peter's job description. She had doubtless dealt with tougher cases than these scrawny kids. I just hated being the bearer of grief. But in the end, I knew that if Agnes Peter couldn't handle them, she would know who could.

Sister Agnes Peter lived with about a dozen other nuns in a large bungalow on Griffin Avenue in Lincoln Heights. The house belonged to the church. It wasn't a convent and none of its residents could be bothered wearing a traditional habit. Most of them taught at Sacred Heart High School in the next block. The rest of them were doers of the good work, like Agnes

Peter, whose vows of poverty made them wards of the church.

All things considered, the bungalow was a good place to seek sanctuary. The resident virgins wouldn't take shit off anybody. Even the local gangs paid their respect: the walls of the house were the only flat surfaces for miles that weren't tagged and scarred with gang graffiti.

Agnes Peter was watching for us from the broad front porch, huddled in a wicker rocker under a crocheted afghan. She rose as we got out of the Jeep and came down the front steps to greet us, striding with the athletic assertiveness of a drill sergeant. I could not judge her age, fifty-something judging from the context of various conversations we'd had. There seemed to be a little more gray in her short brown hair than the last time I had seen her, though it could have been a trick of the silver moonlight.

"Maggie MacGowen!" Agnes Peter beamed, crushing me in a bear hug. She always smelled of Zest soap. "Good to see you."

"How have you been, Pete?"

"Flourishing. Just flourishing." She stepped back and surveyed the others. "So, you've brought me some company?"

"You remember Guido Patrini?" I asked.

She offered her hand. "Nice to see you again, Guido."

"How are you, Sister?" he said, lowering his eyes, nervous as if she had caught him chewing gum in church.

"Pete," I said, "I want you to meet Sly and Pisces."

"Pisces, hmm?" Agnes Peter smiled, focusing on the girl. "Astrological sign of the fish. Your birthday's in the spring, then?"

Pisces shrugged.

"It's freezing out here. Come inside." Agnes Peter took both kids in hand and moved with them toward the house. "Have you eaten?"

"Yes," said Pisces.

"No," said Sly.

"You have too," Pisces scolded.

"Have not."

"Perhaps not enough," Agnes Peters said. "I think we can find something to tide you over until breakfast, Sly."

Guido and I, ignored by the others, trailed up the steps and into the house.

I was greeted by warm house smells, of dinner, furniture polish, and fresh flowers. The furnishings were old and the rugs were a bit threadbare. Just the same, there was a gracious air about the old place, a sort of well-tended, if impoverished, gentility. A house full of women.

The old floorboards complained as we walked across the large foyer. But no one seemed to notice us. This house was filled with activity, and newcomers in the night weren't cause for special notice. The chorus of conversation rose and fell as we passed each open doorway: women in the living room talking back to Arsenio on TV, others around the polished dining-room table grading papers, sharing a liter of diet Coke and a bag of Oreos.

Gripping his bag of "stuff," Sly clung close to Agnes Peter as we made our way toward the back of the house. Pisces seemed more at ease, openly curious about the place. Without seeming forward, she stopped as she passed a nearly antique baby grand piano and picked out the first few bars of "Für Elise" with her right hand. Casey had been struggling mightily with the same piece for weeks.

Pisces caught up to Agnes Peter. "The G is flat."

"I thought so, too," Agnes Peter chuckled. "So, Pisces, Sly, how did you two meet?"

"He was in trouble," the girl said with a smug grin on her face.

"Was not." He gave her a token shove. "She was the one in trouble. Any asshole knows you get busted panhandling inside the market."

"Shoplifting is any better?" She returned the shove. "And who got busted?"

"Both of us." Sly finally smiled, an economic little crook at the corner of his mouth. "And we both got away, didn't we?"

"I'm glad you're here. Both of you," Pete said. She glanced over her shoulder at me. "Maggie, will you be staying the night?"

"No. I'm at Guido's for a couple of days."

Guido gave me a sharp jab in the back and a mortified glare. Like me, he had been raised a good Catholic.

"Calm down," I said. "Pete knows we're just friends. Friends can stay under the same roof and not go to hell for it."

Agnes Peter laughed. "I saw Mike Flint last week, Maggie. He looks fine. Does he know you're in town?"

"I haven't had a chance to call him," I said.

"Uh huh," she said. "There's a phone in the kitchen. Mike's number is in the directory under F. You know, F as in 'friend.' "

In the kitchen we interrupted two women who were seated at the enormous kitchen table poring over a ledger and a stack of bills. They looked up and smiled as we came in.

"Mary Grace, Mary Catherine, we have some hungry guests," Agnes Peter said. "Would you please see if we have anything in the refrigerator that might interest Miss Pisces and Master Sly? I want to see Maggie and Guido out."

Sly snapped his face up at me. "You leavin' us?"

"It's late, kiddo," I said. Sly had big, moist brown eyes that reminded me of a sickly puppy I had found dodging traffic on the Embarcadero a few years back. He had been a panic-stricken mess. Like any good citizen, I had taken him to the animal shelter. When I left him, his pathetic cries had followed me all the way out to the parking lot. He now weighs about fifty pounds and sleeps on the antique brocade sofa my grandmother bequeathed me. He still has big, moist brown eyes, and he still cries every time I leave the house.

Pisces clutched the back of a chair, her eyes wide and steely. "Are you coming back?"

"You're in good hands here," I said, wishing I didn't feel so rotten about going away. "Just behave yourselves. If you need anything, tell Agnes Peter."

I watched Pisces swallow back panic. My impulse was to be a hero some more, promise her something. I just had no clue what that something might be. We had already done the Prince Charming thing and rescued her from the woods. Now what? I had no castle to offer her. Nor any happily ever after. Whether we left sooner or later, the pain for all of us would be the same. So I did what I hoped was the sensible thing. I followed Agnes Peter's lead and walked out.

When we were again out of earshot of the kitchen, Agnes Peter turned to me. "What do you know about them?"

"Very little," I said. "They seem to have been working the streets around MacArthur Park. She's a nice kid. But Sly? You should lock up the silver tonight."

Pete smiled. "He'll be fine. Did they say anything about family?"

"Nothing specific," I said. "Certainly nothing I could repeat without going to confession after. They both were very clear that they did not want to answer questions. I only got them here by promising that there would be none."

"You know I can only keep them here for so long, Maggie. I prefer to begin by making some contact with their families, determining whether that situation is redeemable before we call Child Protective Services. The kids will have to give me some background."

"Good luck," Guido said. "They won't talk."

"Don' vorry, *mein Herr*." Agnes Peter narrowed her eyes. "Ve haf our vays."

"I'll call you tomorrow, Pete." Fighting back tears, I handed her all of my cash, maybe eighty dollars. "Anything you need . . ."

"We'll be fine, Maggie." She wrapped a reassuring arm around me. "You've done all that you reasonably can. Sly and Pisces have troublesome problems. Their own problems. Remember that, Maggie, and don't feel guilty about leaving. Your hands are full taking care of Casey. And Guido here. Don't beat yourself up about what you can't do."

"I'll call," I said.

She shrugged. "That's up to you."

"I'll call."

I felt miserable all the way to Guido's house. I think he did, too. He was very quiet, for which I was grateful. He took the long way home, driving through the hills of Elysian Park instead of going straight to the Hollywood Freeway.

The park road offers one of the best views of the city. As the night was exceptionally clear, the city below shimmered like a movie version of fairyland. It was spectacular. I wondered what had happened to Cinderella after she moved out of her stepmother's small house and into Prince Charming's big one.

When we were blasting north on the freeway, I turned to Guido. "Who said they lived happily ever after?"

"Who?"

"Cinderella and Prince Charming."

"The word probably came down from his public relations people. Why? What's on your mind?"

"I'm not sure."

He rolled his eyes. "Please, God. Give me strength."

"For what?"

"I know the signals. You're cooking something, Maggie. I'm afraid to find out what it will be this time."

"Right," I said. I was in the strangest mood, very antsy, and I couldn't figure out exactly why. I slumped back against the seat to watch the lights go by, trying to clear the clutter from my mind.

Guido lives in an inherited cottage that overlooks one of the canyons behind the Hollywood Bowl. The house is small but comfortable, an unpretentious ornament set on a million-dollar lot. When we turned up his street, we were less than two miles from the peak insanity of Hollywood Boulevard. Cradled deep among the canyons, we couldn't see or hear anything except the sounds of wilderness around us.

Guido pulled into his drive and parked in front of the garage. We have worked together many times, and have fallen into a comfortable routine for sharing the load. He's a modern man, I know he respects me professionally. Still, his name is Patrini, of the Sicilian Patrinis, and I am a woman. The pain he goes through when he sees me carry anything remotely heavy is pitiful to behold. So when he hauled out the big aluminum camera cases and the insulated bag of videotapes from the back of the Jeep, to spare him grief, I reached for no more than a tripod and a half-full bottle of Evian. He wrestled his load up the incline toward the front door, while I strolled behind. Don't tell Gloria, but we were both perfectly happy.

The evening air was perfumed with dry eucalyptus and night-blooming jasmine. Somewhere in the woods above me, an owl hooted and set off a rustle of small creatures through the undergrowth.

Guido stopped to listen to the owl before he went inside and turned on lights. Through the open door I could hear him rattling around.

I lingered outside, enjoying the cold breeze on my face, the soft rustle of leaves. Below me, the rugged canyon was too deep for the moonlight to reach the bottom. I felt very small looking over the edge. Not small in the sense of feeling vulnerable. Rather, I felt invisible. Safely insignificant. The sensation helped put the events of the day into perspective.

The film I had been working on had been a problem for me from the beginning. There was a guideline of sorts written into the contract I had with WGBH in Boston and some health consortium. I had spent a lot of effort accumulating footage as if I knew where I was headed. But, truth told, I hadn't a clue what the thing was really about. From the beginning, I hadn't been able to find its essential core. Child-raising—what about it?

As I peered into Guido's canyon, I finally heard the mental click. Behind my eyes I could see the finished film, frame by frame. And the face of Pisces in the moonlight. It was a sad film I saw, but I still felt the exhilaration of discovery at last.

Guido came out of the house and put a glass in my hand with about an inch of Glenlivet scotch in it. I knocked it back and held out my glass for a refill.

"Thanks," I said.

"Message on the machine from Lyle. He says Casey has a slight fever, but don't worry."

"Too late to call her tonight," I said. "I'd just wake her up."

"Are you planning to stay out here much longer?" Guido had an evil little expression on his face. "It's cold."

"What's up?" I asked.

"I have something to show you."

"What?"

"Just come. You may be a genius."

Who could resist a line like that? I went inside with him, sipping the second drink on the way. By the time we reached the living room, I was ready for thirds. Guido handed me the bottle and I carried it to the sofa. I pried off my boots, stretched out on the cushions, and waited for him to show me what he was talking about.

Guido squatted in front of his big-screen TV and slipped one of the day's new tapes into the VCR.

"This is Encino," he said. He fast-forwarded cherubic little preschoolers at play in the sunshine of their day-care center's garden until he came to a pudgy little girl. She pranced across the lawn in mommy-dress-up gear: high heels, long dress, pearls, feather boa, big hat. She stopped by the paint easel to daub her cheeks with red tempera paint, then strutted on, feeling elegant. I followed her with the camera until she turned and noticed me. She stopped and dropped her head shyly.

"What's your name?" I asked her.

"Mrs. Unicorn."

"Where do you live, Mrs. Unicorn?"

"Here." With a languid hand she indicated the beautiful playground behind her. A band of little boys on tricycles had stopped in the background to eavesdrop. She turned her back on them and gestured me closer. She whispered into the lens, "I don't like having my picture taken. You have to call my nanny and make an appointment."

"Cute, huh?" Guido ejected the tape and slipped in another. "Now MacArthur Park," he said.

I had hoped that the silvery tones of Pisces by moonlight would be caught on the tape. Instead, she was a deathly blue-gray. The flat screen made her seem even younger, as if she too were a little girl playing dress-up with makeup and sexy clothes. She tottered on heels that were both too big and too high for her.

I heard my voice: "What's your name?"

"You can call me Pisces."

"Where do you live, Pisces?"

"Here." She gestured toward MacArthur Park, averting her face from me. "I don't like having my picture taken. Not for free."

All the time I was recording Pisces, my eyes had been focused only on her face and her body. I had not noticed much of the background then. On Guido's big screen, what I now saw happening around Pisces as we talked I can only describe as a nightmare version of the scene on the Encino playground.

In the frame to the right, a few yards behind Pisces, a derelict sat vomiting in the gutter. Frame left, an old woman with an aluminum walker began a slow and painful progress across the screen. In a flash of lights and sirens, a black-and-white police car blasted out of the station in the middle of the park and sped toward us, its speed and noise a wild contrast to the stillness of the derelict and the old woman. It was great choreography. I wished I could take credit.

On some level, I had noticed all of it as it happened. The city is always noisy. The destitute are everywhere. Who hears sirens anymore?

The one image that really stood out against the blue-tinged scene was the red Corvette that had followed us along the curb. An eerie counterpart to the little Encino boys on tricycles.

"Want to see it again?" Guido asked.

"No," I said. I tapped my forehead. "I've got it here."

"Infuckingcredible, isn't it?" Guido took a slug of scotch straight from the bottle. " 'What's your name and where do you live?' Next time I complain when you want to stop and film something, just slap me across the face, will you? It's brilliant, Maggie. The parallels, each scene a visual metaphor for the other. Fucking brilliant."

"Uh huh," I said, getting to my feet. " 'What's your name

and where do you live?' How else do you start a conversation with a kid? The really big question is, 'Does your mommy know you're here, or has she lost you?' "

Guido was watching me as I began gathering up the tapes and stuffing them into the insulated duffel.

"Need something?" he asked.

"If you're still sober."

"I am. More or less."

"Will you drive me to the airport?"

He yawned. "Now?"

"As soon as I can get a flight," I said. "Unless you want to drive me all the way to San Francisco."

"Whatever. But why?"

"You were right. I'm doing nothing here that I can't do in San Francisco. I want to be home before my daughter wakes up."

CHAPTER

3

Casey's fever had amounted to nothing. She was already at school before I managed to get home.

I felt like shit. For more reasons than fatigue.

I had always been a working mom. For the last two years I had been a single working mom. It was a fact of Casey's life that I was not often at home like the Beaver's mother, with fresh-baked cookies and milk waiting for her after school. Because of the nature of my job, sometimes it was necessary for me to be gone for weeks, and occasionally for months at a time. Casey accepted my time away from her with various degrees of grace, as I accepted it with various degrees of guilt.

During my absences over the years I have been accused of going to extremes to make sure that Casey was not only well tended, but well loved. If that's true, it's a sin I can live with. For the last couple of years the privilege of being with my daughter in my stead had been bestowed upon Lyle Lundgren.

Lyle used to be our back-fence neighbor in the Marina District of San Francisco. When the big quake of recent memory hit, my family was lucky. All we lost was the rear wall of our restored wood-frame Victorian house, while the block behind us, Lyle's block, was completely leveled. The afternoon of the quake we found Lyle out on the street and took him in. And we kept him.

We have evolved a very happy arrangement. Lyle is our housewife. He works at home as a free-lance copywriter. I charge him some rent for his Bay-view room, but not nearly the going rate. To compensate, he does most of the cooking and cleaning and errand-running. He deals with the workmen who are still making repairs on the house. When I travel, he takes charge of Casey. We adore him. We cannot imagine life without Lyle.

When I called Lyle from Los Angeles before I boarded my plane, he reminded me that it was his day to volunteer at the hospice. He said that on the way he was dropping our beloved dog, Bowser, at the groomer's to be flea-dipped.

All the way in from the San Francisco airport, I looked forward to having the house to myself for a while.

As soon as I got in the door, I began the ritual of homecoming. First, I put on a pot of coffee—not fresh-ground espresso or caffè whatever, just auto drip stuff out of a can, the way I like it. Then I toted my bag upstairs and unpacked, dumping my dirty clothes down the chute into the basement laundry room. By the time I had finished that, the coffee was ready. I poured a cup and carried it into my workroom. I sorted through the mail and the telephone messages, catalogued the new videotapes, and put the rolls of 35mm stills I had shot into preaddressed processing mailers and set them out for the mailman. It was all very ordinary and, in its way, very comforting.

The next order of business was checking on Sly and Pisces. I picked up the telephone and dialed Agnes Peter.

"How are my kids, Pete?" I asked her.

"They took off, Maggie. Right after breakfast."

"Did something happen?"

"No. I think they sensed the inquisition was about to begin. They had clean clothes and full tummies, and they just scooted right out the front door."

"I guess I'm not surprised," I said. "But, damn, I wish they hadn't gone."

"Pisces is a bright little girl. She has our phone number. If she needs us, she'll call."

"I hope you're right. What do I owe you?"

"Whatever you can spare. Walk down the street and put it into the nearest poorbox." She paused, and I waited. "Are you okay, Maggie?"

"Me? Sure. Why wouldn't I be?"

"Just asking. You have my number, too. Anytime you want to talk."

"I appreciate the offer," I said. "Thanks for everything."

I hung up and poured myself a second cup of coffee. I had a lot on my mind. My project needed to be refigured. I thought that while I was at it, maybe my entire life could use some refiguring.

Herman Melville said that when a man's mind turns to contemplation, his feet naturally lead him to water. I did the next best thing. I went up to the third, and top, floor of the house and leaned against the tall front window. From there the view of San Francisco Bay was the stuff of postcards.

The sun shone on the water. Across the Bay, a few dark clouds hovered near the peak of Mount Tamalpais. I watched the ships in the harbor, the ferry crossing to Sausalito, yachts at full sail passing under the Golden Gate. The carillon of Grace Cathedral over on Nob Hill marked the hour. It was better than therapy.

All day, no matter what else I happened to be doing or thinking about, at the back of my mind the film project kept percolating. I saw Pisces as the focal point. Not as a prostitute, but as a child who had somehow lost her family. The title I thought I would use was one of her tough lines, "I remember mothers." Almost as good was something the pretty little preschooler in Encino had said: "Make an appointment with my nanny."

I had to redo the working outline and schedule new locations to shoot. The small crew that would help me do the actual filming needed to be booked. The grant people had to be dealt with.

I went back downstairs to my workroom on the first floor and got out my primary resource book, the Metro telephone directory.

In the Yellow Pages I found baby-sitters: live-in, live-out, court-order monitors, nannies. Then I looked under child care: before and after school, latch-key program, swing-shift hours, early mornings, overtime available, vacation day camp, in-home care for sick children, drop-off center for sick children, breakfast, lunch, and dinner. Bible stories.

I had a fair list of numbers to work with before I closed the book.

By then it was just after three o'clock, time to start watching for Casey. I pulled a camera battery off the recharger, slipped it into a videocam, and went down to the sidewalk in front of my house. I searched around a bit for the right background, and played with angles to get the light just right. Then I waited.

The primary-grades children in our neighborhood school get out about half an hour before the older ones. At three-fifteen, the parade of children heading home began.

There are many young families on the block. Lots of kids. As real estate in the neighborhood comes dear, there aren't many single-wage-earner families. When both parents work, someone still has to raise the kids.

The women escorting the predominantly towheaded tots home from school were a fair representation of solid peasant stock from both Asia and Latin America. Now and then a Nordic-looking au pair came into view with a little charge held firmly by the hand.

Visually, the scene was good—happy little faces, crisp hair bows, and thick-soled sneakers coming into view over the crest of the steep hill. The sound was also wonderful. I had the volume input control on my camera turned all the way up:

"María," I heard a little redheaded boy say to the tiny dark woman who carried his Ninja Turtles lunch box and Benetton school bag, "I'm real thirsty. *Quiero* lemonade."

"*No, mi hijo*," María responded, "only *leche*."

I was still chuckling when my Casey came into view. The little ones were cute, but Casey stole my eye. She strode down the hill, swinging her jacket from one hand and her book bag from the other, a magnificent, graceful creature. I have a whole wall of tapes and films I have made of Casey, because I love to watch her. Casey is singular. Maybe every mother feels that way. In my case, it's true.

My sister Emily is six feet tall. There's a good possibility that my daughter will top her. I kept telling Casey, who had just turned fourteen, that one day she would love her height. Casey wasn't ready to accept it.

Her one true passion since she was old enough to walk had been ballet. She had indeed become a beautiful, long-legged ballerina with real career potential. The sad thing was, there were rarely boys in the City Ballet tall enough to partner her. Odds are, no matter where she might go, there never would be.

Casey saw me following her with my camera. Ever the ham, performing for her most adoring audience, with a big smile on her face she executed a series of gazellelike leaps for me, incredible legs fully extended, toes like arrows, book bag and jacket whipping through the air as she flung her skinny arms. It was a good show. I am always relieved when I come home to find her intact.

She ended with a showy jeté at the base of our front steps, where she dropped her things. She took the camera from my shoulder and turned it on my face.

"What are you doing here?" she asked, grinning so wide I could see all of the bands on her teeth.

"I live here," I said, grinning back. I reached out and switched off the camera. "Aren't you home early?"

"I'm ditching study hall. Mr. Stemm isn't there today. No one will notice."

"I noticed," I said, failing to sound stern. I picked up her things as we walked up the steps to go inside. "I'm going to call the school right now."

"Yeah, sure," she laughed. She set the camera on the parson's bench in the entry and took her heavy book bag from me. I had so much to talk to her about. But she pulled out a small paper sack and yelled up the stairs:

"Lyle, Lyle, crocodile!"

"He isn't home yet," I said.

"Rats. I brought him a treat. He helped me with my English paper and I got an A."

"Good girl," I said, stretching up to kiss her cheek. My voice sounded forced. I admit I was a little jealous. Casey hadn't brought me a treat. She turned a bright smile on me, though.

"Where's Bowse?" she asked.

"Getting a flea bath." I was beginning to feel pouty. I was happy to see her. "Isn't it time for you to say 'Hi, Mom, I missed you'?"

"Hi, Mom, I missed you."

"That's better. Want to go do something together?"

"Like what?"

"I don't know. Exploratorium? Ghirardelli Square?"

She curled her lip. "With the tourists? I don't think so. Anyway, I told Madame Semanova I would tutor some little girl this afternoon. She's getting ready to audition for a mouse part in Cinderella."

Casey bounded off toward the kitchen.

"Let's drive up to Squaw over the weekend," I called after her, still trying. I felt dashed. Rejected. Fully pouty. "We haven't been skiing all season."

She turned and looked back at me as if I had lost my mind. "I'm flying to Denver this weekend. Remember?"

"No, I don't remember."

"Oh." Her attitude de-escalated quickly. "Didn't I tell you? Dad and Linda are baptizing the baby Sunday. I'm the godmother."

"You are your baby brother's godmother?"

"Weird, huh?" She headed off again, talking with her back to me. "Maybe you can get someone else to go skiing with you. Janet or Grandma or someone."

"Maybe." I followed her to the kitchen and leaned against the counter while she poured herself a glass of juice and slathered cream cheese on a bagel.

"What are you doing home, anyway?" she asked. "You said you'd be in La-La Land till Monday."

"I missed you. I worry about you when I'm away."

She had her mouth full, so she could only nod.

"I have a new direction for my project," I said, filling airtime. "It took me a long time to figure out what was missing. But I have it now."

Casey looked as if she had something to contribute, so I waited for her to wash down a mouthful of bagel with juice.

"Did you and Mike have a fight?" she asked.

"Of course not. I didn't even see Mike."

She seemed dubious. "I thought that's why you went down to L.A."

"I went down to work."

"So why are you back?"

I sighed.

Casey dumped her dishes into the dishwasher and wiped off the counter. She kissed me as she sped past.

"Glad you're back, Mom. I gotta go."

That was Thursday.

Friday I hardly saw Casey. In the morning I kissed her good-bye and saw her off to school as on any other weekday.

I spent most of Friday talking to the staff at a drop-off center for sick kids. It was a nice place. They served chicken noodle soup and soda crackers for lunch. It was probably better than some of the alternatives: staying home alone, Mom staying home and therefore not earning the rent money, going to school sick.

Several anxious mothers and fathers dropped in during their lunch hours. I talked to them, too. They seemed to be far more upset than the children, who by all appearances were generally accepting of the arrangements. I would have preferred being

sick in a quieter place, that is, in my own bed with my own
TV remote. With the Beaver's mother bringing me milk and
cookies.

I ran into a woman I had met at some charity auction earlier
in the year. She was expensively sleek, a decorator or a gallery
owner, I couldn't remember. I couldn't remember her name,
either.

"Maggie," she said, kissing the air somewhere around my
head. "Do you have a sick little one?"

"Just visiting," I said. "Doing some background research."

"You must interview my Rachel." She carried a bag from a
downtown food boutique. "I always bring her favorite soup
when she's sick. Anything to make my million-dollar baby feel
better."

I had nearly asked if she was visiting a grandchild. Even
with her face stretched, she couldn't hide sixty years of sun on
her hands. The director had told me they accepted children up
to the age of fourteen, but I thought the oldest there that day
was around ten. The math didn't work for this woman.

We found million-dollar Rachel in the television room, re-
clining on a beanbag chair and wrapped in a small comforter.
She had her thumb in her mouth and a stuffed cat in her arms.
Her dark eyes were glassy with fever, but she perked up when
the woman knelt beside her.

Rachel was about three years old. A pretty child, as dark as
her mother was fair. My guess was she came from Indian stock
in Central or South America.

"My baby feels better?" The glossy mother hovered over
Rachel, fussing with the blanket and kissing the little girl's
damp face. She looked up at me. "Isn't my Rachel a sweet ums
thing?"

"Very sweet," I said. "Your million-dollar baby?"

"Not really a million. But plenty. And worth every penny
and peso." She hovered over Rachel with a spoonful of soup.
"Aren't you, my precious baby angel?"

I could see she had more than a million-dollar emotional

investment in the girl. I was happy for her. I wondered how long her child dream had been deferred.

I left them snuggling together in the beanbag chair.

Early Friday evening, Casey left for Denver to attend her new half brother's baptism. When I got back from driving her to the airport, the house was far too quiet. I didn't know what to do with myself. Lyle had a dinner date. That left Bowser and me to entertain each other.

Bowser is nothing much to look at, uneven masses of medium-brown fur over a body built by a genetic committee. But he is an affable fellow. I have had worse dates. He loves two things above all others: sleeping and running. He was beside himself with doggie glee when I pulled out his leash and snapped it to his collar.

We took a long run through Marina Green and Fort Mason, over Russian Hill, then back home by way of Lombard Street. I hadn't run for over a week, so the course I had set out was much too ambitious. The last mile was sheer torture, all uphill. Even Bowser was flagging.

Halfway back up our own hill, my legs gave out. I stumbled into the neighborhood video store. I wasn't so much interested in renting a movie as I was in finding a place to catch my breath with dignity before I collapsed. To have his master collapse on the sidewalk might humiliate a sensitive fellow like Bowser. And Bowser is sensitive. Anyone as ugly as he is has to be.

I was choosing between the original *Invasion of the Body Snatchers* and *Aliens* when someone brushed against me.

"Hot date tonight, Maggie?"

I turned and found my neighbor, Felix Mack, with two John Wayne movies under his arm. I like Felix. He's a great talker—a quality I admire in a man. He teaches neurosurgery at the University of California because his mother won the big argument. His ambition was to play sleazy sax in nightclubs. Now and then he jams with a group from the medical school that is equal parts Ivy League surgeons and jive-wise janitors. I love to tag along.

"Bowser is the hottest date I could come up with," I said to Felix. I tapped his cowboy movies. "Planning a romantic evening at home tonight?"

"Do you like John Wayne?" he asked.

"No," I said.

He stuffed his tape boxes onto the nearest shelf. "If Bowser won't mind, you want to go get something to eat with me? No sense both of us soloing on Friday night."

"Love to," I said. "Give me half an hour to get presentable."

I limped home, showered, slipped into wool slacks and a blazer with spangles on one sleeve. Bowser was snoring on the brocade sofa when I passed him on my way out.

Over frittata at Balboa Café, Felix and I solved an amazing number of the world's problems, if none of our own. In no time at all we found the bottom of a bottle of very good cabernet.

It was still early when we finished eating, so we took a cab to Kimball's, a jazz club over by the Civic Center. We stayed through three sets, another bottle of wine, and a snifter of brandy. Maybe two. By the time our shared cab pulled up in front of my house, I was full-on mellow; equal parts good wine, good music, good company.

"Come in for coffee?" Felix asked as the cab drove away.

The question had undertones that made me uneasy. I really liked Felix. We had had a wonderful evening, one of several over the years. In the cab coming home, because it had seemed to be only a companionable gesture on his part, when he took my hand I hadn't pulled away. On the sidewalk, with him looking into my eyes, I began to think maybe that had been a mistake. Then again, maybe I was reading a lot into nothing. It's just that I didn't want to move our relationship beyond the comfortable point where it had been before we left Kimball's.

I gave Felix's arm a firm squeeze.

"This evening was a great idea," I said. "Thanks for suggesting it. It's late and I think I've reached my limit."

"Me, too. I guess." He leaned forward and gave me an awkward hug. "Let's do it again. Soon."

It was nearly one o'clock when I opened my door, according to the hall clock. Lyle takes good care of himself and usually goes to bed early. He had left lights on for me, always considerate.

As I locked up and turned out the lights, I tried to imagine Felix as a love interest. I had no success with it. Felix was great. Few better. His only flaw was, he wasn't Mike Flint.

When I thought about how Mike Flint might be spending his Friday night I went suddenly cold all over. I knew how we used to spend Friday nights. And every other night of the week when we were together. I tried to shake away the images; they made my chest feel tight.

I was so confused. Calling Mike, I knew, could lead to dangerous complications. Not calling him hurt too much. I hated feeling indecisive. I was glad I was a little tipsy so I would fall right asleep.

Bowser was snoring in the living room. After thinking about Mike, I wasn't going up to bed alone, even if it meant sleeping with the dog. I went in to fetch the old fellow.

Bowser wasn't in his usual place on the brocade sofa. I couldn't find him at first in the dark room. Then I saw that the big leather wingback chair that usually sat in the far corner of the room had been pulled around to face the window that overlooked the street. All that I could see of Bowser was his tail hanging over the arm of the chair.

I walked around the chair to rouse him.

Bowser was sound asleep, all right, but it was Mike Flint who was snoring. I looked at him for a moment, making sure that I hadn't conjured up Mike's image out of those bottles of cabernet. Booze coupled with lust can do stranger things to the mind.

If I had conjured him, however, I knew I would never have put so many clothes on him. Nor would my erotic fantasies include the dog that was sprawled over him, with his muzzle in the crook of Mike's neck where my muzzle should have been.

It was a sweet scene, dog and man together, man snoring with his mouth open. Mike is tall, with a distance runner's slenderness. He is only in his mid-forties—he lies about which zero he's closer to—but his hair is already silver. He may not be Cary Grant, but he is very striking.

As soon as I saw Mike, I knew I was doomed. I had been almost proud of myself for not calling him, the way a recovering drunk takes pride in avoiding the block where his favorite gin mill sits. Seeing his cheek all pushed out of shape where it rested against Bowser's skull was like putting a drink in an alcoholic's hand.

Call me weak. I succumbed. I wrestled the mutt to the floor and took his place on Mike's lap before either of them had both eyes open.

"Hi, sailor," I said when Mike smiled at me sleepily. "Looking for company?"

"Mpfh," he said.

His front was deliciously warm from the dog. I snuggled into him and kissed his forehead, his cheek, his chin, found his mouth.

"Maggie," he moaned. God, I loved to make Mike moan.

Full dress for Mike Flint included tie, suspenders, belt holster and gun, a beeper, and a detective shield as big as his fist. I began to undo him, keeping his mouth busy with mine while I worked to open the tie, buttons, buckles, clips, and, at last, zipper.

When I got to the point of sliding my hand into his open fly, he grabbed my wrists and held them.

"We have to talk," he said.

"So, talk," I said, and leaned around to take a nip of his earlobe.

"Maggie, this is serious," he said sternly, though he didn't resist when I kissed his bare chest, starting at the hollow at the base of his neck. I licked and bit him gently, moving slowly all the way down his flat belly to the elastic band of his blue boxer shorts. His erection peeked through the open flap, and I kissed the tip of that, too, with a little tongue.

He began to writhe under me.

I straightened up then and faced him, smiling like the cat who lapped the cream. "So, what did you want to talk about, Mike?"

He laughed and let go of my hands so he could wrap his arms around me. His lips found the place at the back of my neck that sends chills all the way to my knees.

There is something incredibly sexy about kissing someone for the very first time. The joy is discovering a whole new set of textures, smells, and flavors. But the first embrace in no way compares to the sheer, sensual power of being held once again by someone you have loved and lost and thought you might never be able to touch again. I hadn't lost Mike, exactly. Just mislaid him.

"Will you stay the night?" I asked.

"If you'll have me."

I got to my feet and gave him a hand up. With my arm around his solid waist I started moving him toward the stairs. "Where's your bag?"

"I don't have one. I wasn't planning on coming up."

I laughed. "You just found yourself on an airplane?"

"Sort of. Look, Maggie, we really have to talk. I was going to call, but some things are better said in person."

I had that cold feeling again. I stopped at the foot of the stairs. "Is there someone else?"

"Jesus, no. Look, just sit down a minute." He switched on the light over the stairs and we sat on the bottom step. His clothes still hung open, so he fumbled a bit to find his trouser pocket. He took out a color photograph and handed it to me. It was a Polaroid of a very disheveled Pisces. The camera had caught her with her eyes closed.

"She in trouble?" I asked.

"Depends on your theology. Sister Pete tells me you know something about the kid."

"I know very little. Guido and I found her on Alvarado Street by MacArthur Park. She tried to solicit me while I filmed her."

"Pete said you picked her up."

"I don't like the way 'picked her up' sounds. We bought her some dinner. She's only fourteen, same age as Casey. It made me feel sick to see her on the street. She was a nice kid, Mike, once we got past her routine. So we fed her and took her to Pete's."

I handed back the picture. "There was a nine-year-old boy with her."

"We got him," Mike said. "He's in MacLaren Hall."

"What did they do?" I asked.

"In a minute," he said. "Tell me everything you know about the girl."

"She was careful about not saying too much." I shrugged. "I can only give you my impressions. She is well-spoken, well-mannered. Plays the piano. Probably comes from the West Coast. Doesn't have anything nice to say about mothers, but she took to me right away. She was pleasant with Guido, not seductive like many sexually abused kids I've met. I got the feeling she's new to the street. She doesn't like to be dirty, and the park scares her. And that's all I know. Now, your turn. What happened?"

He was in no hurry to share anything. He puffed out a few deep breaths and absently stroked my back.

"You liked her?" he asked.

"I guess I did. I worried about her. The other kid, Sly, is a little pip, though."

I tugged on his open shirt front. "Is it that bad?"

"Yeah," he sighed. "She had Pete's phone number in her bra. And this."

He handed me a thin gold ring with a tiny opal stone. Engraved inside the band was "Hillary" and a heart.

"Mean anything to you?" he asked.

"Nothing." As soon as I saw the ring, though, I knew. "Is she dead?"

"Yes."

"Oh, damn." I choked back what felt like rage but came out as tears. "Why didn't she stay with Pete?"

"That's what Pete wanted to know."

"Tell me," I said.

"A Rampart Division patrolman found her in the park Thursday night. Looked like a routine prostitute slaying. Detectives assigned to the case found Pete's number on her. Pete referred them to you. And, of course, because you were involved, she called me."

"So it's not your case," I said.

"It is now. I went to the lieutenant and told him I wanted it. He sent me to Rampart for clearance with their detectives. I told them I knew some of the players in the case. They have so many murders down there they were just real happy to let me have this one.

"Besides," he said, "they generally give me all the murder cases that fall in two categories. The first category is anything with your name on it."

"You're sweet, Mike."

"The second category is anything that's totally weird. Often as not, it amounts to the same thing."

I buried my face against him. "Don't tell me it was really awful for her."

"No. I think her passing was easy and quick. Her throat was slashed, something very sharp, like a straight razor. It severed her jugular. She would have had time to be scared. But not enough to hurt."

"You said this case was weird."

"Your prostitute," he said, "died *virgo intacta*."

CHAPTER

Mike held me all night. I'm not sure whether I slept. We didn't make love until dawn. In the dark, the specter of young Pisces and her violent end lay between us like a fevered child who slips into the parental bed at night.

When the first light filtered through the bedroom shutters, I opened my eyes and found Mike looking at me with a worried crease between his pale brows. I kissed his shoulder, and what followed was very sweet, unusually tame for us.

The carillon at Grace Cathedral was chiming nine when we finally walked downstairs.

Lyle was in the kitchen, drinking coffee over the *Examiner*. He wore his uniform, that is, a starched dress shirt open at the neck, chinos, and loafers—no socks. His thin brown hair was still damp from the shower.

"Morning," he smirked, and popped up for two more coffee mugs. "You children hungry?"

"No," I said.

"Starved," Mike said. "I missed dinner."

"Why didn't you say something when you got in?" Lyle scolded. "We don't do room service in this house, but the kitchen never closes."

Mike pulled me against him and kissed the top of my head. "Guess I wasn't thinking about food."

"Maggie always says she's not hungry in the morning, but she eats breakfast like a lumberjack." Lyle talked on as he got eggs and milk from the refrigerator. I found his abundant energy exhausting. "Mike, you're so skinny. You look like a little cholesterol packing won't hurt you just this once. I'm thinking fluffy crab omelettes with Parmesan and tomatoes, toasted corn bread on the side. Some fresh papaya. Sound good?"

"Sounds good." Mike ran his hand down my back. "But what did you say about room service?"

"Mike, honey," Lyle laughed, "from the moaning I heard coming from that bedroom this morning, you'd better eat something, take a little rest before she gets your ass back up those stairs. I don't want no white-haired guy dyin' in my house."

"Lyle, Lyle, crocodile," I mocked, pulling out a chair and sitting. "Whatever can you mean?"

"You know what I mean, missy." Lyle waggled a finger at me. "And drink your juice before you get started on coffee."

I poured juice for us from the pitcher on the table and handed a glass to Mike. "Is there a plan?"

"I hope." Mike sat down. "I told you we took in the boy who was hanging with the victim. Problem is, we can't get him to talk to anyone. Even Pete had no luck. He's a scared little rabbit. Who can blame him? He might have seen the killer. I thought, you being a civilian and someone familiar, he might open up to you. Will you go back to L.A. with me this morning?"

"You know I will, Mike," I said. "All you had to do was call. You really didn't have to fly all the way up."

"Stupid, stupid," Lyle exploded, eviscerating a steamed crab with his cleaver. "Go ahead and slap her, Mike. Or you want me to do it for you? Jesus H., Maggie. Who didn't have to fly all the way up? Look at the pathetic shell of a man sitting across the table from you. Then go look at your own pathetic self before you say another word."

"He doesn't look at all pathetic," I said, reaching for Mike's hand.

"Sure. Not now. Not after you spent all night blowing life back into him. Shit." Dramatically disgusted, Lyle slid sliced papaya in front of us. "Eat your fruit."

"You're getting awfully bossy, Lyle," I said. "You're even beginning to look like my mother."

Lyle laughed. "Wish I had her legs. So, anyway, Maggie, your laundry is folded. Eat your breakfast, then go pack your bag. It'll be nice to have the house all to myself for a couple of days."

While Mike had a third cup of coffee, I went about the house gathering a few essentials: some cameras, film, extra tapes, two battery packs, a few clothes, and the blue silk nightgown I had bought for Mike's birthday the year before. All of it fit into a carry-on duffel.

The commuter flight between San Francisco and Los Angeles normally takes barely fifty minutes. But you always have to figure an hour on either end of the flight to shuffle through the airport. So it was early afternoon before we got out to MacLaren Hall in El Monte, where Sly had been taken.

MacLaren Hall is L.A. County's only juvenile detention facility for nonoffenders. The kids who find their way there have generally been abused or abandoned, or both. It is supposed to be a safe place for youngsters to wait until the courts figure out what should be done with them. From the street, it looks thoroughly institutional, acres of county-beige stucco, high fences, wired windows. Externally, it is not my idea of homey, though inside a good effort is made with limited means to make the surroundings pleasant.

Saturday is visiting day. As it was a lovely, sunny Saturday, the campus grounds were crowded with family groups and children at play on the patchy lawn. Considering the size of the crowd, it was oddly quiet.

Mike and I signed into the reception area and were shown through to a small conference room furnished with a worn sofa and several mismatched easy chairs. The room was Spartan, but a big-hearted, low-budget attempt had been made to brighten the place. There were a few cheap framed pictures on the walls, some kiddie artwork stretched between thumbtacks, a hand-crocheted afghan tossed over the back of the sofa. It wasn't *House Beautiful*, but it was a giant improvement on a cardboard box in an alley.

We had to wait a few minutes. The bag of burgers and fries we had brought with us was beginning to leak by the time the door opened. Sly came in, escorted by a professionally cheerful-looking caseworker.

"Wayne Cofeld." The caseworker thrust out his hand. "Pleasure to meet you, Miss MacGowen. I've seen your films. Gripping reality. Intensely moving."

"Thanks," I said. Everyone's a critic, but I don't mind. At least they're watching. I got my hand back from Cofeld and turned my attention to Sly.

Sly had been processed into hygienic respectability. He looked scrubbed and cleanly dressed. His hair had been trimmed and slicked to the side from an uneven part. I thought he seemed frightened, though he was trying to cover his feelings behind a sullen scowl. Tight against his chest, he held the leg-of-lamb-shaped package of stuff he had retrieved from hiding the night we took him in. Even the stuff had been spruced up, in fresh brown wrapping paper.

"*Qué pasa*, Sly?" I said, moving toward him.

Sly shrugged.

"Miss MacGowen asked how you are, Ronald," Cofeld said, patronizing.

"I heard her," the boy snapped.

"Ronald?" I said. "Is that you, Sly?"

"Fuck that." He turned his head away.

"Ronald Allen Miller," Mike said. He offered his hand to Sly. "It's nice to meet you. I'm Mike."

Sly stepped back. "You're a cop."

"He's okay, Sly," I said. "He's a friend of mine. He wants to find out who did that to Pisces. So do I. Please help us."

"I ain't talkin' to no cop."

"Will you talk to me?" I asked. He didn't answer. That meant he hadn't said no.

I looked up at Mike. "Mike, will you excuse us?"

He hesitated.

Cofeld opened the door and held it. "Detective, if you don't mind. I'd like a word with you in my office."

"Sure," Mike said, accepting the graceful out. He touched my sleeve. "Holler if you need anything."

"We're just down the hall." Cofeld flashed his dry smile and led Mike away. They had left the door open behind them.

I sat down on the sofa. "So, who are you, Sly or Ronald?"

"Don't matter."

"Sure it matters. It's your name. What do you want to be called?"

"Like I give a fuck?" he sneered. But he sat down at the opposite end of the sofa, with his stuff tucked in beside him.

"You look like you're okay," I said. "Are you?"

He shrugged, avoiding eye contact. He had no expression at all on his face, not even dumb shock.

"Getting enough to eat?"

Again a shrug.

I passed him the bag of burgers. "Thought you might be hungry."

He fished out a drippy cheeseburger and, staring blankly at a point in front of him, wolfed it down in four huge bites.

"Sorry the food got cold," I said.

"Doesn't matter." There were two more burgers, a jumbo order of fries, and a chocolate shake still inside the bag. He rolled the top of the bag closed and set it on the floor between his feet.

I took a deep breath. "Can you talk about her, Sly?"

He said nothing, but a single tear finally rolled down his cheek. I moved closer to him and put my arm behind him, not touching him. When he didn't shy away, I let my hand rest on his shoulder.

"Did you see it happen?"

He nodded.

"Tell me about it."

"Why should I?"

"Because I want to nail his balls to a tree. Don't you?"

Sly's chin quivered, but he held on to his composure. He also pulled himself out of his stupor to speak to me. "She picked up this guy."

"What did he look like?"

"Just a guy."

"Short, tall, fat, skinny, old fart? What?"

"Tall, I guess. Big fucker. Not real old like that Mike dude."

"Would you know him if you saw him again?"

"Yeah. Like, I seen him around before. Just cruisin'."

"He had a car?"

"Real sweet car." He perked at the mention of the car. "Red 'vette. Someday I'm gonna get me a car like that. So sweet."

I also perked at the mention of the car. If it was the same one, I had it on videotape.

"So," I said, "he picked her up. Then what?"

Sly squirmed around uncomfortably.

"You know, Sly, you can tell me anything and all that will happen to you is you'll get a pat on the back and maybe some more burgers. Whatever went down, it's not your fault. You're a kid. You're not going to jail, no matter what you think you've done. Do you understand that?"

He thought about it. Then he turned in his seat to face me. "No shit?"

"No shit."

"Okay. Here's the deal," he said. "Like, Pisces wasn't really no hooker. She'd pick up some guy and talk like she was going to do him. They'd go someplace and she would get his pants down, get him all hard talking to him. Then I'd come out, make like I took their picture, and tell the guy how old she was and he better pay us or we'd give the picture to the cops."

I smiled. "You're a little blackmailer."

He had a self-satisfied smirk on his pinched little face. "It worked real good. You shoulda seen those guys. Scared the shit out of 'em."

"It was a very dangerous game, Sly."

"Better than fuckin' 'em for real. Most the time, the guy paid off. If he got real weird or real pissed, we just took off. Fuckin' fast. Mostly you should see her run. She told me she used to be this like really big swimmer and shit. It could be pretty comical, these assholes runnin' after two little kids with their pants all fallin' off and their limp old dicks flappin' around.'"

I had learned two important things about Sly. He liked cars and he liked making adults look like fools. Both pleasures could get him into a lot of trouble.

"Night before last, Sly, something went wrong with the scam. What happened?"

The question unnerved him. He spoke to me staring ahead again, but this time I had the feeling he was seeing beyond the space in front of him, searching deep into his mind's eye.

"That guy?" he said slowly. "He was different. He'd been cruisin' us for a coupla days and she was scared of him. She took him into the park, like she does a lot of the time, but she told me to hang real close. The guy didn't want her to touch him. He wouldn't let her get his pants down. She has to get his pants down right off, in case we gotta get away. But he pulls her up by her hair and says to her, 'Give me a little kiss.' And she yells for me. I get out from where I'm hiding and he's got her head all the way back. He sees me and he turns her and he goes . . ." His finger slashed his throat. "I never saw no knife. He just did like that with his hand. And she kind of looked at me scared and fell down and he ran away."

"She fell down?" I meant to prompt him, to get him to finish the story. Then it hit me that that was the end. I saw the boy standing there in the park, felt time stop because what had happened was so horrible it could not have occurred, had to be something like a scratch in an old record that played its distorted screech over and over until you gave the arm a push. I hugged Sly and gave it a push. "And she was dead?"

He scooted up against me, but he did not cry.

"Oh, Sly." I hugged him.

"I wasn't fast enough," he said.

"It wasn't your fault."

"I shoulda been faster."

"I'm sorry you saw it happen." I was crying, as angry as I was sad. "I wish I could take it all away. But I can't, any more than you could have changed what happened."

"Fuck that," he whispered.

"You going to help us get this asshole?"

He nodded.

"Good. We'll be a team, okay? You and me and Mike."

"Yeah." He gave me a limp five and a grim smile.

"Know anything about her family?" I asked.

"Usual assholes."

"Do you know where they are? They need to be told."

"I don't know where, down by the beach. When her mother was fucking her boyfriend and making a lot of noise, Hilly used to run down and sneak onto some boat till it was over."

"Who is Hilly?"

"That's like her real name. You know, like Ronald."

"Hilly what?"

"Don't know."

I took out the little opal ring Mike had found on Pisces. "Was this hers?"

"Yeah. Her old man gave it to her."

"What do you know about him?"

"Nothing, except he's not gay."

"Why do you say that?"

"She always says, 'My mother fucks at home and my father fucks a broad.' So I guess he does girls."

I tried not to laugh. I gave his shoulder a squeeze and stood up.

"You're a good friend, Sly Ronald. For the next couple of days, while you're hanging here, try to remember everything that happened that night. And while you're at it, think about everything Hilly ever told you about herself and her family. Will you do that?"

"I guess." He got up and gathered his package of stuff in one hand, his leaky bag of burgers in the other.

"You comin' back?" he asked. "Not that I give a fuck."

"I'll try to come by every day. If I can't come, I'll call you, okay?"

"I guess."

"Mike Flint is a good friend of mine, Sly. He's going to be coming to see you, too. I know you don't like cops. Just remember that you haven't done anything you should be worried about. You can talk to him. Finding people like the guy who killed Pisces is what he does. Help him out."

Sly narrowed his eyes at me. "You fuckin' him?"

"None of your business."

He chuckled wisely. "If you're fuckin' him, I'll talk to him."

"Then talk to him." I went with him to the door. "Where's your cage?"

"Cottage three. You don't have to take me. I know the way. Shit, I've been dumped in this place lots of times."

"Talk to you tomorrow," I said.

"Yeah." He started down the corridor, looking very small and vulnerable, clutching his stuff and his food close to his skinny chest. "See ya."

"Hey, Sly," I called after him.

He turned.

"What's in that package, anyway?"

He grinned. "None of your business."

CHAPTER

5

I talked, Mike listened, all the way downtown to Parker Center, the Los Angeles police administration building. For Sly's sake, I hoped that something he had told me about Pisces and about the man who had killed her would make a difference. It was too late to do anything for Pisces. But I had a feeling that finding the man who had killed her would help Sly a whole lot more than all the efforts of an entire phalanx of county-hire shrinks.

We pulled into Parker Center's covered garage. Mike found a space to park his plain-wrap city car among maybe a hundred other similar nondescript, superannuated American-made wrecks.

"If you can get Lyle to locate the videotape that shows the Corvette, I'll have a courier bring it down."

"I'll call Lyle right now," I said.

We got out and walked away from the plain cars and between rows of black-and-white units, working toward the underground entrance to the building. Mike had long legs and I had to stretch mine to keep up.

I looked over at him. "I'm really afraid that the footage I shot with the Corvette isn't going to help much. I panned to the right from the girl to include the hood of the car because it was bright and glossy and it boosted the sleaze quality of the scene. I'm not sure I got the driver. When I closed on him, he took off. He gave me good sound for maybe eight seconds, but probably no face."

"Whatever you got, it's a hell of a lot better than nothing. The thing is, if we bring the asshole in and Sly IDs him and we tell him we have him on tape, odds are better than even he'll cop to it."

"You have to catch him first," I said.

"I always get my man," Mike said, nudging me with his shoulder. He held the door for me and we walked through the back passage to the elevators. I had never been in the bowels of headquarters before. From the general scruffiness, I guessed that nothing had been refurbished since Jack Webb retired.

Next to the elevators there were two wide, jagged cracks in the plaster. With a pencil, someone had labeled the cracks "Whittier Narrows Quake" and "Sierra Madre Quake," and dated them. When the elevator door opened I was reminded that disasters always come in threes. I stepped inside anyway.

"What are we going to do here?" I asked.

"Get some real coffee." Mike pushed the button for the third floor.

"And after that?"

"Start working on the girl's ID."

Mike was forever telling me that assignment to the Major Crimes Section of the Los Angeles Police Department was the ultimate any detective could hope for: high-profile murders, serial shit, VIP details, all the good stuff. He said the detectives who worked majors were America's crème de la crème of big-city dicks. He wouldn't lie to me. Then again, Major Crimes was where Mike worked.

When we walked into his office that late Saturday afternoon, things were fairly quiet. A couple of detectives were cleaning up paperwork from a shooting in the Valley they had rolled on the night before, four members of a Korean family found dead in their home. A second two-man team had tickets for the evening game at Dodgers Stadium and were just hanging out

until it was time to go. I don't know why they didn't find someplace more comfortable.

The Major Crimes Section has space within the Robbery-
Homicide bull pen. The office is a long, narrow room badly in
need of paint and housekeeping. There are the requisite ranks
of gun-metal filing cabinets lining the walls. Two dozen or so
detectives work literally shoulder to shoulder at old library
tables and scarred metal desks set in two parallel rows down
the length of the room. Each detective's work territory is
marked off by a plastic blotter and some essential clutter: family snapshots, potted plants, trophies, personal computer ter-
minals, telephones, case files.

Densely packed on the floor around the city-surplus chairs,
and under the tables, jutting into the narrow aisles, balancing
on every flat, nonmoving surface, are cardboard file boxes
crammed with case files.

I sipped my coffee and looked up at the wild African boar
head mounted on the wall over Mike's work area.

"Family member?" I asked.

"My first mother-in-law," he said. "Number two is down in
the locker room."

"Uh huh." His chair squeaked when I sat in it. "Now
what?"

"You're going to make a list of everything you know, or think
you know, about Pisces. There are probably a couple thousand
missing juveniles in the state computer system. Anything you
can think of that will narrow down the list will help."

While Mike called the county coroner and ordered a dental
workup to be done on Pisces, I started writing: female Cau-
casian, age fourteen, five-two or -three, ninety-five pounds, eyes
brown, natural hair unknown, first name may be Hillary, possibly from Southern California, right-handed, played the piano,
athletic build, pierced ears, mother may have lived at the
beach. Virgin.

Mike called Sacramento and talked his way through the
switchboard until he got the state investigator working juvenile records who was on call for the weekend.

"Detective Mike Flint, LAPD Major Crimes," he said. "Who am I talking to?"

He listened and gave me a thumbs-up.

"Hell yes, Art, I remember you," he said into the telephone. "That particular homicide convention was the end of my marriage. Your wife ever speak to you again?"

He laughed a whole lot louder than I suspected the joke from the other end merited.

"I just hope you weren't so drunk you forgot you owe me a big one."

More male-bonding laughter.

"You got it. Now I'm calling in the debt. You ready? Okay, I got me a female juvenile Jane Doe at the county coroner's office. I've ordered the dental workup. They promised me they'd do it now and get it sent out to you ASAP. In the meantime, this is what I have."

He read off my list, exactly as I had written it.

"I don't know how long she was missing," Mike added. "So give me some variety in the height and weight, age maybe a year or so either way. If you could do a computer Tab run and get me a list of all possibles, and get it to me overnight, I might consider your debt paid in full. Besides, it's Saturday night. I know you've got nothing better to do."

Mike's smile gradually died as he listened to Art on the other end. He seemed all seriousness when he responded.

"Don't think about it," Mike said. "We were all over with a long time before that. Guess we just needed a kick in the pants to realize it. Good talking to you, pal. I'll be watching for your report."

He cradled the receiver.

"Do you know everybody?" I asked.

"Everybody who counts."

"What do we do until Art's report comes back?"

"Track down the ring," he said. "Go over the field interviews from the crime scene. Make passionate love."

"In which order?" I asked.

"Take your pick."

I got up and started clearing a space on his table. "Let's do that last item first. Right here. Right now."

He laughed, but I saw the cast of doubt in his eyes. He wasn't sure how far I would go. I liked knowing that he didn't have me all figured out. When I began to tug at his shirttail, he grabbed my hand.

"Let's go talk to the Bunco-Forgery guys," he said. "That little manufacturer's symbol stamped inside the band of the ring is probably registered in their book."

"Whatever you say," I said, and put his desk back in order.

We spent about an hour poring through a registry of copyrighted jewelers' symbols, comparing each one to the sketch Mike had made of the stamp inside Pisces' ring.

"What does the symbol look like to you?" he asked.

"Could be an R or a G," I said. "Or maybe a Greek omega. What do you think?"

"Just keep looking. If the ring came from a large chain store or wholesaler, figuring out who made it probably isn't going to lead us anywhere."

My eyes got tired from using a big, scratched magnifying glass. I wasn't very hopeful.

Mike was far more patient, meticulously looking back and forth between possibilities in the book and the sketch, and back to the ring. He made notes of a few of the more likely candidates. Finally, he handed the ring to me and pointed to a listing in the book.

"Got it," he said. "It's no Greek whatsis. It's a rainbow."

The listing he showed me was for a custom jeweler down in Long Beach, Rainbows.

"Custom jeweler," I said. "That's a break."

"We'll check it out."

"What happens when we identify her, Mike? We still won't know who killed her."

"Maybe not," he said. "It's just part of the drill, Maggie. Don't you want to know who she is?"

"Of course I do," I said. "But it seems to me that we're looking for two different girls. One of them was a middle-class teenager who took music and learned how to set the table. The other was Pisces, the street urchin. Which one of them was murdered?"

"Good question." The pager on Mike's belt sounded, and he unclipped it from his belt. "The thing is, they're both gone."

He put his reading glasses back on, held the pager against the light, and flashed the readout of the caller's number.

"Coroner," he said, frowning. "Wonder what, huh?"

He reached for the telephone and dialed.

"Mike Flint returning your call," he said. He listened, gave me a look of absolute puzzlement. "Thanks for alerting me. I'll be right there."

Mike grabbed his jacket off the back of his chair.

"What is it?" I asked, following close on his heels.

"Someone has come to the morgue to claim the kid's body."

"Who?"

"Get to steppin' and we'll find out."

Officially, Mike's city car was on a salvage list. When it reached ninety-six thousand miles or so, it was supposed to be scrapped. But because there was no budget for a replacement, he had never turned it over. Most of the cars in the police lot were on the same list.

Even though on that day Mike's heap was forty thousand miles beyond the city's definition of junk, Mike made it move. We blasted out of the Civic Center with all eight geriatric cylinders pinging, and roared down Mission Road toward the county morgue in Lincoln Heights.

I rolled down my window and took in all the fresh air I could, wishing I could save it up somehow. This would be my second trip to the morgue with Mike. What I remembered most vividly was the smell. Once you have been there, you never forget the smell.

Mike bounced through the potholes in the asphalt drive of the massive County–USC Medical Center campus and jerked to a stop in a no-parking zone right beside the front steps of the morgue. He bounded out of the car, his jacket flying out, his holstered automatic bouncing on his hip. I was right beside him.

To my great relief, we were headed for the front door. Last time I had gone in through the back way, through guest reception. That had been surreal, a charnel house. The front was mauve marble and mahogany office doors. The only stiff was a bureaucrat snoring at his desk.

Inside one of the offices that opened off the lobby, I could see a man and a woman sitting together. He was grim-faced and pale, she wept softly against his chest. They were in their early forties, I guessed. Except for their grief, there was nothing remarkable about them, a couple in ordinary Saturday clothes: jeans, sneakers, windbreakers. The woman was thin and blond, probably pretty under better circumstances. The man had a fair-sized sports-fan gut; a big man who worked with his hands.

They looked like nice, careful people. Not the sort who might mislay a daughter.

"Mike?" A small Oriental woman came out of the office where the couple sat. She wore business attire, a lightweight wool suit and low-heeled shoes. Clipped to her lapel was a coroner's investigator badge.

As we walked to meet her, Mike whispered in my ear. "Act like a cop. You're probably not supposed to be here."

"How does a cop act?" I asked.

"You know." He grinned. "Pushy, like you own the place. Just let me do the talking."

He offered his hand to the investigator.

"Sharon Yamasaki," he said, "this is MacGowen."

She smiled at me and reached for my hand. Her eyes lit up, as if a light bulb had come on inside. "You're Maggie MacGowen."

"Guilty," I said, and nudged Mike with my toe.

"I'm very pleased to meet you," she said. "I saw you interviewed on PBS last week. Program about reporting from a war zone. It was very interesting."

"It's nice to meet you," I said.

"Is Mike helping you with research for a project?"

"In a way," I said, and smiled at him.

"When you two are finished?" Mike tugged on my arm.

I pulled away from him and moved closer to Sharon Yamasaki. "Who are those people?"

She glanced at the couple inside. "Mr. and Mrs. Metrano. They say that someone called and told them that our young Jane Doe is their missing daughter."

"Did you call them?"

"No."

"Have they viewed the body?" Mike asked.

"Yes. On video."

"They ID her?"

Yamasaki held up her hands. "People sometimes see what they want to see. Why don't you talk to them. I promise you, it's a puzzler."

We walked into the office, and Yamasaki did introductions all around. "George and Leslie Metrano, Detective Flint, Maggie MacGowen."

I rolled their names over in my mental Rolodex a couple of times. Nothing came up right away, but I knew the card was there.

Then I looked at them both closely, rudely I guess, trying to match their features to Pisces. I saw no obvious likeness, but they seemed to be within the range of possibility.

"How long has your daughter been missing?" Mike asked them.

"Ten years, five months, twelve days," Leslie Metrano said, her voice breaking.

"Ten years is a long time," Mike said. "Kids change pretty fast when they're growing up. What makes you think this girl is your daughter?"

"A mother knows."

"Possibly." Mike looked very uncomfortable. "But we'll need something more concrete before we can release the body to you. Do you have dental records?"

"She was only four years old when she was taken from us," George Metrano said. "She had never been to the dentist."

Mike nodded. "We can draw samples from you and run a DNA match. The results from that are damned near hundred-percent. Problem is, results will take anywhere from a couple of weeks to a couple of months. Is there anything you can offer in the meantime, fingerprints we might match with Jane Doe?"

"She has a name," Leslie cried out. "Amy Elizabeth Metrano."

"Jesus Christ." Mike sat down on the closest chair and stared at them. "Amy Elizabeth Metrano."

I remembered the little blond with big brown eyes. There had been posters with her pretty round face everywhere for over a year. As I recalled the story, little Amy had disappeared during a family picnic in the mountains around Lake Arrowhead. I couldn't remember all of the details. She had been playing hide and seek in the woods with older siblings and various other children. She hid and they never found her again.

There had been a lot of speculation about what had happened to her, from kidnapping to consumption by the local wildlife. Other than a pink sweater hanging on a bush, she had vanished without a trace.

"I have pictures," Mrs. Metrano said. She laid out the familiar poster snapshot, and then a series of computer-generated sketches that projected what Amy might have looked like at various ages, had she lived. I picked up two of the sketches, one labeled age twelve, the second age sixteen. The artist had assumed that she remained healthy and well-fed, and round-faced. Pisces' features had been gaunt.

I put the sketches down and looked over at Mike.

"What do you think?" he said.

"She was a pretty little girl." I shrugged.

He nodded. "When we get your videotape down, we'll get a forensic anthropologist to make a bone-structure comparison."

"What videotape?" Mr. Metrano asked.

"I filmed part of my conversation with the girl who called

herself Pisces. I'm sure you'll have a chance to see it. Just
remember, she was lying to me. She was a little scam artist,
but she wasn't a hooker."

Mrs. Metrano began to weep, "My baby, my baby."

I thought poor Mike would have to leave the room. I have
watched Mike follow an autopsy from Y cut to final suturing
without flinching—unphased even when the skull popped open
like a champagne cork. But this weeping woman was another
matter.

Mr. Metrano held his wife against him and patted her back
rather hard.

"Mr. Metrano," I said, "if this girl is your daughter, where
do you think she's been for the last ten years?"

He had turned a sickly pale. "Right at the beginning, we got
a report from this private investigator that Amy Elizabeth had
been sold into a sort of white slavery ring. He told us they were
always looking for little blond-haired girls. We went up to
Montana where this ranch was supposed to be, where they took
these girls. But we never found it. I took out a second mortgage
on the house, and we kept on looking until the money ran out."

"You believed in this PI?" I asked.

"Well, he kept at it after the police and sheriffs said there
was no hope. No one else was giving me anything. And he
showed me pictures. Awful pictures of grown men and little
girls."

"Was Amy Elizabeth in the pictures?" I asked.

"I couldn't tell. A father sees his princess doing what they
had those babies doing, you think he could make himself recognize her?"

"Did you see the pictures, Mrs. Metrano?"

"I wouldn't let her," George jumped in. "No mother should
see that."

"This girl, Pisces, was never used that way," I said.

Metrano took a deep, shuddery breath. Color began to return
to his face.

"I ask again," I said. "If this is Amy, where has she been?"

Mike cleared his throat, and I looked over at him.

"Sorry," I said. "Was I messing in your territory?"

"You're doing just fine," he said. "Nice of you to bring me along."

"Now what?" I asked.

Mrs. Metrano sat upright. "We want to take our baby home. She's never even had a memorial service."

"I'm sorry," Sharon Yamasaki said. "I can't release her until we have investigated further. You understand our need for caution."

"We've waited so long," the mother sighed.

"You have to understand," Mr. Metrano said, tears in his eyes as well. "We accepted a long time ago that our Amy might be dead. But until we know for sure, we can't move on. If my wife feels in her heart that we have found Amy, then I believe her."

"We haven't eliminated any possibilities, sir," Mike said. "But I caution you not to get your hopes up too high."

"Mr. and Mrs. Metrano," Yamasaki said gently, "why don't you go on home now. I'll call you personally if anything comes up."

Mr. Metrano lifted his wife's chin and tenderly kissed her. "She's right, Leslie. The kids are waiting for us."

She nodded and rose with him. They started for the door.

"One more thing," Mike said. The Metranos stopped and turned to face him.

"Who called you?" Mike asked.

"Someone from the coroner's," Mr. Metrano said.

"I'm certain you are mistaken," Yamasaki said. "Our office called no one."

"That's what he said," Metrano insisted. "A man called about three o'clock and said he was from the county coroner's office. He said we should come and identify our daughter. We used to get a call like that every week or so in the beginning. But it's been a long time."

Mike made a note in his case book. "He actually said, 'Come and identify your daughter'?"

"Yes. That was different, come to think of it. They used to

drive over with a snapshot and say, 'Do you know her?' or 'Can you identify her?' Now and then they would have us drive all the way up here, just to make sure. They're real careful about what they say."

"You drove up here from where?" Mike asked.

"Where we live. Down in Long Beach."

CHAPTER

Long Beach. If I had ever given Long Beach a thought, and I
cannot imagine why I ever would, I would have assumed that
the city was to Los Angeles what the flats of Oakland are to
San Francisco. That is, a backyard in which to stash some less-
than-lovely utilities: harbor, shipyards, downscale housing. I
was right. And I was very wrong.

After some telephone tag, Mike had managed to locate the
owner of Rainbows Jewelry. It was late, nearly ten o'clock, but
the man had agreed to meet us. He gave Mike directions to his
shop in the Belmont Shore section of Long Beach.

All the way down from L.A., Mike told me cop war stories.
They were good stories, well told; he kept me laughing. I knew
what he was doing, though. Sometimes when he has something
on his mind that might be difficult for him to say, he busies
the air talking about other people until he feels ready to get
to the real stuff. I was in no hurry to hear what was on his
mind.

Until the night before, I hadn't seen Mike, or spoken to him,
for six months. I needed some time to get over the initial physical hum of being with him again before we got into "So, now
what?"

We exited the freeway and drove along a dazzling oceanfront

city skyline of post-moderne high rises, posh hotels, a new concert center, and a vast yacht harbor. Downtown ended in a strip of million-dollar mansions with a million-dollar view across the water toward Catalina Island.

Belmont Shore was a few miles farther down the beach, a quaint neighborhood and shopping area surrounded on three sides by water. Something like a flat version of Sausalito.

Second Street, the main thoroughfare, was jammed with Saturday-nighters. The crowd assorted itself into thickets: around the Keg and Panama Joe's, rowdy youth in need of gutters to barf in or dark nooks for some postgrad Anatomy 1A spilled into traffic; toward the east a more sedate, upscale parade convened around Café Gazelle and Belmonte, and strolled in and out of trendy boutiques.

We found the jewelry store easily enough, but a place to park posed a challenge. After ten minutes of cruising, circling around through alleys and trying again, Mike spotted a Porsche about to leave a choice space in front of the sports bar across the street from our goal. He got into position and, with the skill born from years of city living, wedged the big Ford into the tight space. I was impressed.

Rainbows was closed for the day, but as we crossed the street, we could see a light inside and the owner watching for us behind the window. Mike showed his ID through the glass, and the man unlocked the door to let us in. And bolted it again after us.

"I'm Dennis," the man said, switching on more lights. "I was afraid my directions had led you astray."

"Directions were fine," Mike said. "Nice of you to come out so late."

"My pleasure." He smiled. "You saved me from a rather dull dinner party. It took some persuading to keep them all from tagging along. They made me promise to come back for dessert and give a full report."

I liked him right away. He was tall and slim, soft-spoken, very intellectual-looking but with a flash of humor in his eyes.

The jewelry cases he leaned against were empty for the night.

Mounted on the walls there were enlarged photographs show-ing wonderfully imaginative pieces, unusual combinations of gemstones and precious metals.

"Is that your work?" I asked.

"Most of it is," he acknowledged with the quiet pride of a person who knows he is very good at what he does. "How can I help you?"

Mike brought out the opal ring that had been found on Pisces' body. "Do you recognize this?"

Dennis nodded as he took the ring. "It's my design. A nice piece for a young person. We made it up in several ways, various stones, different finishes on the metal. I had to rework the prongs to set an opal in it, cast them up higher to protect the stone. Opals are relatively fragile. They can shatter."

"Do you know who bought the ring?" Mike asked.

"I can look it up."

We followed him into his office at the back of the store. Sketches and jeweler's tools littered the desk. He pushed aside a box of purple wax sticks and turned on a computer. When he punched in a code name from memory, a short list scrolled on the screen.

"We sold four of this design with opals. I have the names and addresses of three of them." He looked up at Mike over his wire-rim glasses. "If a customer pays with cash and declines to give a name or address, I don't push it."

"I understand," Mike said, with a just-us-guys grin on his face. "The ring is engraved to Hillary."

"That helps," Dennis said.

He opened a drawer of file cards and thumbed through them. Then he wrote a single name and address on a notepad, tore it off, and handed it to Mike.

"For Valentine's Day this year, Randall Ramsdale bought two rings from me: an opal for his daughter, engraved 'Hillary' with a heart, and a two-carat, emerald-cut diamond engraved 'Randy Forever.' He paid with his American Express card."

"Do you know Randall Ramsdale?" Mike asked.

"Not well. He's something of a neighborhood character. More

money than brains." He tapped the card and smiled. "But obviously fine taste. I haven't seen him around for a while. Maybe a couple of months. He was supposed to have gone off to Europe with a waitress from the bar across the street. Something must have happened, though, because she was in here shortly after he bought the ring, trying to sell it back to me."

"You wouldn't know her name, would you?" Mike asked.

"Oh, sure. Lacy. I see her all the time. She still works over there."

I asked, "Was the diamond an engagement ring?"

"Maybe a premature one. Randy already has a wife."

"What about Hillary?" I asked. "What can you tell us about her?"

He frowned as he thought about it. "To be honest, I can't answer that with any certainty. The Shore is a fairly close-knit community. A lot of kids hang out on Second Street. I don't have the sort of store they cruise through, but after a while you come to recognize faces. You see the same ones in the ice cream stores, or looking around in The Gap, renting tapes at the Wherehouse. I might recognize Hillary Ramsdale as a familiar face, but I'm sure I couldn't point out a girl on the street and say that's her, that's Hillary."

Mike took out the Polaroid of Pisces that had been made in the morgue. I stayed his hand before he could turn it over. It didn't seem right to me that this nice man should be exposed to her dead face. Not that the picture was especially grim: she had been hosed down, and her hair combed back from her face. The slash across her neck looked like no more than a thin black cord. I guess I thought that showing her face in death was an invasion of both her privacy and his peace.

"I can make a better still from the videotape," I said. "Can't it wait?"

Mike looked at me as if I had lost my mind.

I said, "Lyle sent the tape. It should be delivered first thing tomorrow. As soon as it comes, I'll take it over to Guido's and get some nice full-face prints made."

"I don't get you, Maggie," Mike said. "We're here now."

"Please," I said, looking up into his eyes. That was taking cruel advantage. Every time I looked up into Mike's eyes his jaw sort of went slack and his cheeks took on a glow.

"I don't mind taking a look," Dennis said. In fact, he seemed eager. I backed off and Mike showed him the picture.

Dennis studied the pale, scrubbed face, then shook his head. "Sorry. Maybe with her hair done . . ."

"We'll bring you a better picture later," Mike said, sounding a bit grumpy. And sarcastic. "A nice still made before she got all mussed."

I patted his arm.

"What about Mrs. Ramsdale?" I asked Dennis. "Hillary's mother, that is."

Dennis shook his head. "Again, I've seen her around. The Ramsdales are part of the yacht-club set. You might ask over there."

"Do you know the Metrano family?" Mike asked.

He thought that one over, too.

"Amy Elizabeth Metrano," I said.

"Ahh." He nodded. "I haven't heard that name for a long time. And the answer to your question is no. That I would have remembered."

"Thanks for your help." Mike extended his hand to the jeweler. "We may be back."

"Anytime." Dennis smiled at me. "Next time, come during business hours so I can show you my work. I'm especially proud of my rings."

"Bye," I said. I wouldn't even look at Mike. I have a good nose for danger zones, and we were fast approaching one. Things had been going so well between us. Why mess it up with the old argument? I walked straight to the door and waited for it to be unlocked.

When we were back outside, Mike caught my arm and turned me to face him. "He mentions rings, you get all panicked. You have a phobia maybe? Ringaphobia? How about bellsaphobia?"

"How about shut up?" I said.

"I like this." He grinned. "It's like finding a new tickle spot."

I glared at him. "Are we going to try to talk to this Lacy person now?"

"Yeah. You going to let me show her the picture?"

"Of course. I'm sorry about that, Mike. What can I say?"

"Forget it."

We elbowed through the crowd on the sidewalk around the sports bar and made our way inside. The bar was dark, noisy, and full of cigarette smoke. A baseball-game replay ran on several large screens, but no one seemed to be paying much attention to it. The clientele was a mix of singles on the make, heavy-duty drinkers, casually dressed couples out for the evening.

"Need a bullhorn to talk to anyone in here," Mike yelled in my direction. He signaled to a passing waitress, a young, buff blond dressed like a basketball referee.

"What can I get you?" she asked. She had to shout.

Mike showed her his police ID. "Is Lacy working tonight?"

"No, sorry. She called in sick."

"Know where I can find her?"

"The boss does. Is she in trouble?"

"I don't know."

Mike pulled out the morgue Polaroid and handed it to her. She held it up to the light reflecting from the closest TV screen and looked at.

She looked up at Mike. "It's Hilly. Is she back? My God, she looks sick."

"Back from where?" he asked.

"Somewhere in Europe, I think. Ask Lacy."

Mike put the picture back into his pocket. "Hilly is Hillary Ramsdale?"

"Yes." The big smile was gone. "Is Hilly okay? God, she's such a sweet kid."

"Where's the boss?" Mike asked.

She pointed toward the back of the bar.

Mike put his lips close to my ear. "Wait for me. I'll be right back."

The waitress stayed with me.

"Where is Hilly?" she asked.

"How well do you know her?" I asked.

"Just through Lacy. Hilly used to drop in sometimes when she needed someone to talk to."

"You're close to Lacy?"

She raised a shoulder. "We work together, that's all. She doesn't party much."

"I thought she partied with Randy Ramsdale."

"I don't know what was going on with those two. My guess is Lacy likes Hilly a whole lot more than her father. He can be a real dweeb. And he's old. Forty at least." She had to be at least twenty-one to serve beer. If I had been a cocktail waitress, I would have carded her. She asked, "Is he back, too?"

"I don't know. No one answers the phone."

"Well, if you see Hilly, say hi for me." She was ready to go back to work. "Tell her to drop in."

I put my hand on her arm. "Hillary died two days ago."

"*Died?*" she gasped. I saw tears in her eyes before she lowered her head and ran off into the crowd.

The smoke and the happy din had become oppressive. I went out into the cool night to wait for Mike. I was standing beside his car, watching for red Corvettes, when he came out five minutes later.

"Did you call Lacy?" I asked.

"No one's home." He unlocked the car door for me. "No one seems to know where Ramsdale is, either. I called his ex-wife again and got the machine. I'll do some checking around, come back later." He nudged my shoulder. "When I have more socially acceptable photographs, right?"

"So what are we going to do now?" I asked.

"Too late to do anything more tonight. How about we go home?"

I didn't argue. I sank into the car seat wearily, yawned when he yawned a few times.

Traffic headed north on the San Diego Freeway was heavy and slow, an endless river of taillights in front of us, headlights behind. Mike had a condo in Sherman Oaks, a relic from his

second marriage. The decor was a little heavy on black lacquer
and gray leather for my taste, but it was nice. I only wished
it weren't so far away. I was having trouble staying awake.

"You'd make a pretty good cop," Mike said, startling me from
a stupor. "Good police do more listening than talking."

"I keep thinking about those poor people, the Metranos. It
just doesn't seem right. Here are good people, love their kids,
do the right things for them, invest their hopes in them. The
very worst thing that could happen to them is to have one of
their children taken away. Then I think about old Sly. Would
anybody even notice if he got snatched? Where's the justice
here? We're one kid short on one hand, one kid left over on the
other. But the equation will not balance."

"Which cliché do you want, Maggie? Shit happens? Life ain't
fair? Go figure?"

I looked over at him. "So we know Pisces was Hillary Ramsdale. Do you think Hillary could have been Amy Elizabeth
Metrano?"

"Anything's possible. Not likely in this case, but possible."

"Too bizarre, though. That equation doesn't seem to work,
either."

"You sound tired," he said. "You okay?"

"It's been one hell of a day, hasn't it?"

"What do you want for dinner?" he asked. He had dark circles
under his gray eyes. "We can go out or stop at the market for
something to cook. Barbecue some chicken if you like."

"Whatever you want. I'm not very hungry. It's too late to
eat."

"We haven't eaten since breakfast."

I had been fiddling with the set of handcuffs Mike always
had dangling from his turn indicator. They were tarnished, a
little rusty at the hinges.

"Things been slow at the office, dear?" I asked. "From the
look of these cuffs, you haven't arrested anyone for a while."

"I don't use that set for arresting people," he said, playful
malice shining from his narrowed eyes. "You like to play with
handcuffs?"

I laughed. "I wouldn't know."

"You really need two sets to do it right, though. I think I have some more in the trunk."

"Keep them there."

"You might like it, Maggie. Cuff you to the bedpost tonight, I could have my way with you all night long. Make you scream in ecstasy fifty times in a row. If I wanted to."

"You don't need cuffs for that, cupcake." I was laughing, though I wasn't quite sure whether he was serious. All right, so I didn't have him completely figured out yet, either.

"Think about it," he said.

"Right."

Mike winked lewdly at me and flicked the handcuffs to set them swinging. "So? What'll it be?"

I took the handcuffs off the turn indicator, opened them, and snapped one over Mike's right wrist.

"Real funny," he said, nonplussed. The empty cuff dangled from his wrist.

"Hope you have the key," I said, and locked the second cuff around the steering wheel. "Now you're trapped. I can do anything I want with you."

"Jesus, Maggie," he laughed, but he was nervous, pulling against the chain. "Get them off me. The key is on the ring in my right pocket."

"The key ring's in your pocket?"

He stretched up from the seat so I could get my hand into his pocket. I put my hand into his pocket all right, but I didn't bother with the key ring.

My hand was cold and his pocket was deliciously warm, so I just felt around inside there. Rubbed his flat tummy, reached all the way down to the pocket's bottom seam, squeezed his thigh, worked my way down into his groin.

"Maggie," he said, rattling the cuff against the wheel. "Knock it off. Unlock these damn things."

"Hell, no. I'm having fun." I stroked him through the fabric, felt him rise under my hand. "And so are you."

"I am not. Now stop."

"Your lips say no, no, no, but your hard-on says yes, yes, yes."

He threw his head back and laughed. "You're going to make me hit something."

"Then pull over." I took my hand out of his pocket and started to work on his belt. I opened his fly. Up to that point, I had only been teasing. The fun was all in making him wonder—okay, worry—about how far I would go. Keep him off guard. As soon as I touched his bare skin, the game changed.

"Oh, for God's sake, baby," he said, feigning shock when my fingertip grazed him. But he tilted his hips forward and helped clear his belt away with his free hand so that I could get to him more easily. He caught my hand for just an instant. "What are you going to do?"

"I'm going to make you scream with ecstasy fifty times in a row." My hand was inside his shorts. I ran two fingers down his smooth, firm length, circled his balls, started up again. His breath was coming in deep, regular sighs.

A greaseball astride a Harley roared up beside us on Mike's side, looked in, figured out what was going on, gave me a grin and a raised-fist salute, then roared off screaming "Yeeha," or something close to it.

"People are watching," Mike said.

"Let them." I cuddled up against him, kissed the side of his neck, ran my tongue around the rim of his ear while my hand stroked him. With my lips against his five-o'clock shadow, I said, "What do you want me to do?"

He shrugged, smiled shyly. "I swear, you'll make me run into something."

"Just give me warning when you see it coming," I said.

"I promise," he said, and sighed again.

I opened his suit pants as far as I could, and went down on him. He was a very sweet man, lovely to behold. I took as much of him into my mouth as I could. I licked him, sucked on him, worried about bumps in the road, but gently bit him anyway. Never in my life had I imagined doing such a thing on the freeway, in traffic—cars zipping by on either side. Just thinking about where we were added a certain dimension to the pleasure. Weird, maybe. An antidote for fatigue, absolutely.

I couldn't see Mike's face, but I could hear him. And I could feel the car's movement. I think we made a couple of unplanned lane changes, accompanied by irate horn honking. The horns lent appropriate background for Mike's version of "Yeeha." Then we rolled over a lot of lane-divider turtles, swerved sharply right, and the car began to slow.

"Maggie," Mike moaned hoarsely. He grabbed my collar and tugged me up. I thought he was just being fastidious. But when I raised my head I found we were on an off ramp, on a direct collision course with the stop sign at the bottom. When the front bumper met the stop-sign post we were hardly moving. Still, there was a bump.

I looked up at Mike's face. His teeth were clenched, but he was smiling. I started to laugh.

Mike began to tuck himself in one-handed. I reached into his pocket, found his key ring, and unlocked his handcuff.

"What do you think?" I asked.

"It's a good way to die." He wrapped me in his arms and gave me a lovely long, deep kiss. When he finally looked up again, he said, "Do you have any idea where we are?"

"Not a clue," I said, as he bumped down off the curb and accelerated into traffic.

CHAPTER

7

Sunday morning, the doorbell rang while Mike was in the shower. I pulled on one of the sweatshirts from the assortment of clothes littering his floor and answered the door.

A courier handed me a large package addressed to Mike in Lyle's extravagant scrawl. I forged Mike's name on the delivery register, shut the door, and opened the package as I walked toward the kitchen. Inside the box I found the videotape we needed. Lyle had also tucked in my vitamins and a dozen of his homemade bran muffins. He is such a fuss.

I poured two mugs of coffee from the Mr. Espresso on the kitchen counter and carried them with two muffins and the tape back to the bedroom. I turned on the TV, slipped the tape into the VCR, and sat down on the end of the bed to watch it.

Mike came out of the bathroom, all fresh and smooth-faced, smelling of baby powder. His blue boxer shorts complemented his eyes.

"What are you watching?" he asked. "*Debbie Does Reseda?*"

I paused the VCR. "The Pisces tape arrived."

"Good. I want to see it."

Mike brushed bran-muffin crumbs off the spread and reclined on the bed beside me with his chin resting on my knee. He was as close to me physically as it is possible to be, but as soon as he restarted the tape, I lost him to the image moving across the screen.

Concentration drew his face into a deep frown as he listened to Pisces run through her line. He watched the entire tape through once, then rewound it and started it again. At the point when Pisces invited me to a motel, Mike picked up the remote, pushed the slow-motion function, and went over to the TV. Pointing to a red smear on the right edge of the frame, he said, "See the Corvette here?"

"Yes."

He fast-forwarded, hit play, and pointed as the Corvette cruised up to us a second time.

"How many passes did he make?" Mike asked.

"I don't know. I was concentrating on her. Whenever I bring out a camera, an audience gathers. Bunch of jerks trying to get famous. You know, they wave, mouth 'Hi, Mom.' I don't pay any attention to them unless they screw up my scene. So when I first noticed the car, my only worry was what he was doing to my sound levels, not what the driver was up to."

He nodded thoughtfully. We watched the entire tape in slow motion, tracking the red car, which was for the most part a glossy blur at the edge of the frame. Now and then I had caught some of the windshield. I strained to see the driver's face. Because the streetlights reflected against the tinted glass, the driver was nothing more than a stationary pale spot behind moving reflections.

At one point I had turned the camera full on the driver. I remembered having felt annoyed at him because the man was a pest.

Now and then in filming there is a serendipitous moment, like Mr. Zapruder's moment in Dallas in November 1963. My moment was certainly on a lower rung, but it made my palms sweat and my heart pound. I couldn't see it except in slow motion: at the instant the driver was in the center of my view-finder, the car passed into the gulf of darkness between two streetlights. For a fraction of that instant, the windshield was black. Behind it I could discern features on the driver's face.

"I think I got the bastard, Mike. Did you see that?"

"Yeah, but it goes by so fast. Will the lab be able to make a decent still from that short bit?"

"You mean the police lab?"

"Any lab."

"If you're asking my professional advice, I'll tell you to take the tape to Guido. A, he's a genius. And B, he has access to the right equipment."

"The tape is evidence, Maggie. We have to be careful with it. I'm real damn sure that Guido can do better things with it than our guys, but I'll still have to get authority to release it to him."

"I haven't been served with anything like a subpoena," I said, trying to remember what I had done with the wrappings addressed to Mike. "Until I release the tape to you, sweetcakes, it's still my tape. Right?"

He laughed. "I really love the way your mind works, Maggie. What do you want to do?"

"Take this to Guido, get him to dub a copy for us to play with. Then you can have the original back."

"Not strictly kosher. But expedient." He kissed my knee and got up. "When are you going to do it?"

"If Guido's home, as soon as I get a shower and get dressed. His house is only fifteen minutes from here. I'll show you how to dub."

"The thing is," Mike said, "it's Sunday. I always spend Sunday with my son. I was thinking maybe the three of us could go to breakfast together. It's about time you met him."

"Mikey Junior?" I said, feeling my palms start to sweat again.

"It's Michael. When you're seventeen, it's Michael."

"You two go ahead with whatever you had planned, Mike," I said. "I don't want to interfere. Besides, I have a lot of work to do."

"Maggie," he said with sudden heat, "what's the big deal? Just meet him. He's a great kid. You'll like him. He'll like you."

"Later," I said. "Okay?"

"If you say so." He slid a pair of Dockers off a hanger and

put them on. I could see that he had something more to say.
But he just sighed.

I walked over and put my arms around him. He resisted me
for a moment before he put his arms around me, too.

"Mike," I said, "we've been over all of this. I know I'll love
Michael; he's your son. So, what if he and I get to be really
close? And Casey develops something with the two of you? Then
you and I don't work out in the end? What happens to the
kids?"

"Maggie . . ."

"Or you and I do work out, but Michael hates me? What do
you do then? Casey can't stand her father's new wife. We can't
expect the kids to turn their feelings on and off to suit us. They
can be so easily hurt."

"Dinner," he said with some force, holding me away by the
shoulders. "Just dinner. Could you commit to dinner?"

It was my turn to sigh. "If it's that important to you."

"Meet you back here around six?"

"Fine."

He smiled. "Fine, then."

I watched him as he walked over to his closet, pulled out a
shirt. I thought he looked terrific without one. That was in
large measure where the problem lay. The physical thing between us had been atomic from the beginning. But beyond that,
the gap between what either of us was ready for was enormous.
In some ways, my divorce was still a bleeding wound. Mike
didn't want to live alone anymore.

Mike turned around and caught me staring.

"I'll stop by the station and see what juvenile records has
come up with," he said. "Whether she's identified as Hillary or
not, we still have to address the Amy angle. I'll start a birth-
certificate search."

"I need a car," I said.

"Take mine. I'll use my official poh-leese vehicle. You have
my pager number. Call me if anything comes up."

"I will." I walked over and zipped up his fly. "But if anything
comes up with you, how will you contact me?"

He smiled wickedly. "What? You think you're the only woman in town?"

I laughed as I turned away toward the bathroom. "Honey, after last night, you won't pose much danger to the female population for a long, long time."

"Says you," he called after me.

"Damn right," I said. I pulled off the sweatshirt and tossed it to him on my way through the bathroom door.

Mike left while I was still in the shower. I dressed quickly in jeans and a sweater, repacked my duffel, and stowed it in a corner of his closet. I called Guido, who told me he would be happy to help if I could hang loose for a couple of hours. He had a tennis date.

I hadn't spoken with Casey since Friday night, when she had called to tell me that she had arrived in Denver safely. It was eleven o'clock Denver time when I dialed her father's number.

Casey answered.

"Have you been to the church yet?" I asked her.

"Just got back."

"How did it go?"

"Baby Scotty cried when the priest got his head wet."

"Babies always cry," I said. "Did you make a little speech, godmother?"

"Sort of. It's so weird, Mom. Linda has me promise to look after Scotty's moral education, but she says I'm still too young to baby-sit him. She hardly lets me touch him. Or Dad. She is such a bitch."

"It isn't easy to be a stepmother."

"Sure. Defend her," Casey snapped. "Like it's any fun being a stepchild? You know what I figured out?"

"What?"

"When I was born, Linda was eight years old."

"Definitely too young to baby-sit," I said.

"It's not funny, Mom."

"Lighten up, Casey. You'll only be there a few more hours."

"Thank God." I heard her let out a long breath. "I gotta go.

All these people are coming over for lunch and I'm supposed to help Linda. I can't baby-sit, but I can peel carrots."

"Go to it," I said. "I'm back in L.A. for maybe another day or two. Lyle will pick you up at the airport tonight. Call me when you get in."

"You staying at Guido's?"

"No. Tell you what. I'll call you. Now, go be helpful."

"Bye, Mom. Say hi to Mike for me."

Smart-ass kids can complicate your life.

On my way out to the garage, I stopped in the kitchen to pick up the rest of Lyle's carefully boxed muffins. I had plans for them.

The CD system in Mike's Blazer was truly state-of-the-art. I put k.d. lang's "Big Boned Woman" on repeat, and had the tricky chorus nearly down pat by the time I got through the snarl of freeway traffic around Dodger Stadium. By L.A. standards it wasn't a big snarl, so I made it to Lincoln Heights in fair time.

On a Sunday morning, one would expect to find most nuns on their knees counting rosary beads. I found Agnes Peter on her knees scrubbing the kitchen floor.

"We don't cook on Sundays," she said, stretching the kinks out of her legs. "It's the only day the floor can dry before it gets all tracked up again. Did you wipe your feet?"

She led me out to the small backyard, where she dumped her mop bucket under a desiccated fruit tree.

"I figured you would be back as soon as you heard about our girl," she said, wiping her hands on her jeans. "What have you learned?"

"Quite a lot, actually. I just don't know how it all hangs together yet. Her name was Hillary. Hillary Ramsdale. I thought you'd want to know that."

"Hillary. The name suited her." She shielded her eyes against the bright sun behind me. "What's the rest? I know you didn't drive all the way over on Sunday morning just to tell me her name."

"I want to check in on Sly," I said. "I thought you might like to ride along."

She gave me a wise glance. "And?"

"I'll be going home soon. He needs a friend in town, Pete. Someone who will be a constant for him."

"Where is his family?"

I shook my head. "From what he told his caseworker, even if we could find his family, Sly is better off without them."

Pete leaned her mop against the back wall. "Okay. I'll go. The little bugger kind of grew on me. Like a wart on my butt."

"You have a big heart, Pete."

"And absolutely no sense. Lead on, before I change my mind."

We stopped at a market for some juice to go with the muffins. I also grabbed a bunch of bananas, a pack of bubble gum, a small playground ball, a balsa glider kit, some baseball cards, and a couple of comic books. The kid was, after all, nine years old.

We found Sly sitting alone on a bench in a corner of the MacLaren Hall playground, hugging his bundle of belongings to his chest. He seemed drawn into himself, oblivious to the children running around him. He brightened when he saw us. Or when he saw the big brown grocery bag.

"How's it hanging, Sly?" I asked. "You remember Sister Agnes Peter."

"What do you want?" he asked.

"Nothing. Just came to see how you're doing."

Pete was close beside me. "This looks like a nice place, Sly. How's the food?"

"Food?" Sly made a face. "You mean shit, don't you?"

Shit or not, he had been able to choke down some of it. His face had filled out considerably since the first time I had seen him. His stomach looked rounder, too.

I sat down on the bench beside him and watched a group of younger kids playing foursquare. "It's warm today."

He turned to me. "That faggot cop get the guy in the 'vette?"

"Not yet," I said. He hadn't said "fuck" once since we had been there. Something was happening.

"What's in that bag?" he asked.

"A few things you might need," I said.

He reached for the bag, looked through its contents, rolled the top closed, then set it between his feet.

"Anything else I can get you?" I asked.

He shook his head. "I'm pretty well set."

Pete touched his shoulder. "I've never been here before. Feel like giving me a tour?"

He looked away. But he gathered his things and stood up.

"Maggie," Pete said, "I can get a ride home."

That was the second time she had dismissed me. And the second time I obeyed her. I stood up beside the small boy.

"I'll see you, Sly," I said.

He glanced at me and shrugged his thin shoulders. "Later."

Sly and Pete began walking across the lawn. I watched them for a moment, silently blessing her for the generosity of her spirit. Just as I was turning away to leave, Sly broke away from Pete and came tearing back toward me.

"Hey, camera lady," he panted.

"What is it?" I said, stooping to his eye level.

He held out to me his ragged bundle of stuff.

"Look after this, will you?" he asked. "Some of these assholes in here keep trying to take it off me. Just give it back when I get outta here, okay?"

"I promise. I'll take good care of it."

He aimed a grubby finger at my face. "Don't open it."

"Wouldn't think of it." I clutched the bundle against my chest. It felt softer than I had expected, and weighed almost nothing. There wasn't much substance to the sum of Sly's stuff.

"See ya," he said, and ran back to Pete.

I carried the bundle back to Mike's Blazer. I started to toss it into the rear deck. When the import of what I had been entrusted with hit me, I carried it up front and buckled it into the passenger seat beside me. Sly took the keeping of his stuff with deadly seriousness. I thought it was incumbent upon me to do the same.

CHAPTER

"You look different, Maggie." The intensity of Guido's gaze made me squirm like a prospective in-law. "What have you done to yourself?"

"Not a thing." I handed him the videotape as I walked past him out of the bright, eucalyptus-scented day and into the dark cool of his living room. Guido still wore his tennis whites.

"There is something different." He followed me in and shut the door. "Your hair? You cut your hair."

"Nope. I got a good night's sleep. Maybe that's it." I continued through the house with him to the studio and darkroom he had built onto the back.

"If it's okay with you," I said, "I'll go ahead and run a dub."

"Go ahead. I'll get the camera set up."

Making a copy of the tape took no time at all. When it had run, I rewound the original, took the dub out of the recorder, and was sticking a label on it when I noticed that Guido hadn't made much progress with his tripod and 35mm camera. He kept watching me until I felt intensely uncomfortable.

"Knock it off, Guido," I warned.

"You lost some weight," he said.

"Since you saw me Thursday? Not likely." To speed things

along, I took the camera from him and loaded it with black-and-white Plus-X pan film. As I screwed it onto the tripod, I said, "Maybe the difference is with you. Did you clean your glasses? Smoke something funny or put something up your nose?"

He crossed his arms over his chest like an aged professor, and studied me through narrowed eyes. "No. It's you. But I can't put my finger on it."

"Will you stop?" I pushed his shoulder hard enough so that he had to uncross his arms to keep from falling over. "Can we just get this finished? I want to drive down to Long Beach today and I have to be back in the Valley for dinner at six. So could we cut the shit, my friend, and get to work? And nothing about me is any different."

"Whatever you say."

He dutifully bent to the task at hand. As I had told Mike, Guido is a master. If there is a manipulation that can be made with raw film or videotape, Guido can do it. He is fun to work with, and I would have enjoyed this little project thoroughly, except that he kept watching me.

A few hours later, we had a work table covered with eight-by-ten glossies, all different angles of Pisces' face.

Stills made from videotape always have streaks and fuzzy edges. Considering that we had been filming at night using available light, Guido had wrought several small miracles of quality and clarity. We selected the four prints that showed the girl's most typical expressions. These I put into a stiff mailing envelope and stowed in my bag.

Guido had also made a second set of stills, close-ups of some of the people who had been in the background that night. If they were neighborhood regulars, they were potential witnesses. Again, because the camera had been trained on the girl, the background extras were generally out of the range of focus, amorphous shapes gliding through the shadows. The quality was better than I had expected it to be, though I had doubts about how useful they would prove for Mike.

A bigger disappointment for me was the enlarged print of the Corvette driver's face. Guido's best effort came out looking more like the moon and its craters than a human.

He studied the print under a large magnifying glass. "What I want to do, Maggie, is give this to someone I know who does computer enhancements. Maybe he can get you something better."

"Then do it."

I had been stacking things together to pack into my camera bag. I stopped to look at one of the rejected full-face shots of Pisces. She had high, well-defined cheekbones, a small dimple in her chin, rather prominent ears. Just for comparison purposes, I wished that I had kept a copy of one of the later sketches the Metranos had shown Mike and me at the morgue. I knew I wasn't going to solve the ten-year-old case of Amy Elizabeth Metrano by comparing two electronically generated pictures of dubious quality. It's just that I was awfully damned curious.

"Tell me about computer enhancements," I said.

"What do you want to know?"

"Are they worth anything?"

"Depends." Guido frowned over the shot of the driver. He was going to talk apples when I was thinking oranges. It was all right with me. Somehow, I knew, all of it would end up in the same salad.

"Depends?" I said.

"Depends on the data available and how good a guesser the technician who interprets it is. A lot depends on luck. There's a techno-nerd on campus who does this sort of thing, usually from information sent back by space probes. What we'll do is give him what we have and tell him it's a man's face. So he'll use statistical averages and some voodoo and give us back a man's face with more details defined. If we gave him the same shit and told him it was a monkey, he'd give us back a bald monkey."

"So they're worthless," I said.

"If it's all you've got, though, go for it."

"I told you about Amy Elizabeth Metrano," I said. "Some

computer wiz took a picture that had been made of her when she was four and projected from it what she might look like as she aged. Would you put any faith in the images he generated?"

"Hard to say. That's different voodoo from the other situation, but it's still voodoo, Maggie. Again, most of it is based on statistical averages. You know, how fast the nose grows, how dark her hair might get using family history. The problem is, there are so many variables.

"Why?" he asked. "I can hear the wheels turning, but I can't see which way they're headed."

"Right now they're turning toward Long Beach. It's a nice day. Want to come along?"

"I would, but I have too much shit to do." He began unscrewing his camera from the tripod. "You said you had dinner plans?"

"Yes. I'd invite you to come along, but it isn't my party. I'm meeting Mike's son."

"Mike?"

"Yes," I said. "I told you, I'm staying at Mike's."

"No, you didn't tell me. Is everything cool between you two again?"

"I don't know yet."

He thought about that as he put the camera into its case. I picked up my bag and slung it over my shoulder.

"You do good work, Guido. Thanks for everything."

"Yeah." He was staring at me again.

"Bye, Guido," I said.

"I'll walk you out."

My eyes were tired after hours of close work. The sun outside dazzled them, made them sting. I shielded my face with one hand while I rummaged in my bag for sunglasses. I put them on and turned to give Guido a hug. His eyes were all squinty, but I could see that he was still looking me over.

"Stop it," I said.

He seemed to shake himself. He smiled at me as we walked down his long drive toward Mike's Blazer. "You be careful down in Long Beach, hear? I've been hangin' with you for a lot of years, Maggie. I know how easy it is for you to get into trouble."

"I'm just going to the beach," I said, all innocence.

"Duck if you hear gunfire."

"I always do," I laughed. "But, Guido, if I don't make it back?"

"Yeah?"

"Make sure Casey gets my grandma's rubies."

"Will do." He held my arm. "Be a hell of a shame if you died on us, Mag. But if you do? Can I have your cameras? You wouldn't be needing them."

"Sure, Guido."

"And that brass iguana you picked up when we were in Honduras?"

"Sure, Guido."

He continued with his wants list all the way down the hill.

I opened the car door and leaned toward him to kiss his cheek. He started to meet me, but then he suddenly drew back, his face bright as if the flash had exploded.

"I've got it." He grabbed me by the shoulders and gave me a wet smooch full on the lips. "It started coming to me as soon as you said 'Mike.' I know why you seem different."

"Dare I ask?"

"You got laid. After months of celibacy, Maggie MacGowen finally got laid."

"Jesus Christ, Guido." I pulled away from him and climbed into the car.

He held the door so that I couldn't shut it. He was positively bubbly. "That's it. I know it is. So you gotta tell me about it, Mag. This is major. I mean, I figure Mike probably joined the police sometime early sexual revolution: post-Pill, pre-herpes and pre-AIDS. We all know what those guys did. What's it like to hop into the sack with a guy who must have fucked his way through half of the female population of L.A.?"

I turned on the engine, slipped it into drive, and eased off the brake. The car started to roll, but Guido still clung to the open door.

"Shit, think about it," he said, jogging now. "L.A.'s like the third-largest city in the country. What's that, like the twelfth-largest city in the world or something? That's a lot of tutors. The things he must have learned how to do. God, I hope you kids are being careful."

"Close the door, Guido," I said. My toe tapped the accelerator. The car leaped forward, forcing Guido to drop back. I reached for the door and slammed it just as I turned out of his drive and onto the twisty street below. Through the rustle of eucalyptus, I heard him yell:

"Way to go, Maggie."

Just for academic reasons, I glanced at myself in the rearview mirror. I seemed no different. It was just me, with mussed hair. And roses in my cheeks.

The canyon below Guido's house was dappled with patches of deep shade and bright sun. The sky above was the hard, artificial blue of a Beverly Hills swimming pool. A day of rare beauty. To waste any part of it slogging along a grimy freeway seemed sacrilege. I thought about finding a place to pull over and go for a walk down to the narrow creek that ran along the canyon bottom, breathe some real air, scuff the dry earth, clear my mind.

Watching Pisces over and over, hearing her voice, hearing my voice talking to her, had left me feeling haunted. Like spending the morning with a ghost. I peered again into the darkness at the bottom of the canyon and kept moving along.

CHAPTER

I took the most direct route south, skirting along the blighted eastern fringe rather than traveling down the more genteel Westside. Not that it mattered; from the freeway, all neighborhoods look more or less the same.

When the freeway ended, I followed the signs toward Long Beach. As soon as I crossed the bridge over the cement gash labeled the San Gabriel River, the air freshened and the sky was clearer than it had been downtown. The ocean was only two or three miles farther on. I could see it on the left, a flash along the horizon.

The first public telephone I spotted was at a bus stop in front of the large state university. Parking was by permit only. So I stopped in the bus zone and left the motor running while I got out to use the directory attached to the phone.

The night before, Dennis, the jeweler, had told us that the Ramsdales were part of the yacht-club set. I wrote down the listed address for the yacht club, then flipped to the M's.

There were two listings under Metrano: George and Leslie, and Amy Elizabeth. Both gave telephone numbers only, no address.

Out of curiosity, I called Amy's number first.

A recording kicked on after the first ring. A soft, woman's voice, sounding very nervous, said, "Thank you for calling the Amy Elizabeth Metrano Search Foundation. Correspondence may be mailed to . . ." A post office box was given. "Messages are checked regularly. If you have *any* information about our Amy, please wait for the tone and speak clearly."

I wondered how often the message phone rang. Anytime that phone rang, I knew it must sound like a fire bell in the night to the family.

I dialed the second listed number. The same soft voice answered. Live this time.

"Mrs. Metrano?" I said.

"Yes?"

"This is Maggie McGowen. We met at the morgue yesterday."

"Oh." A response with new energy. "Are you the one that said you have videotape of Amy?"

"I have videotape of the girl in the morgue."

"That's what I meant to say. The girl in the morgue." She seemed chagrined.

"We made some stills from the tape. Would you like to see them?"

"Oh! Yes. Oh, thank you," she said in a breathy rush. "I have to go to work right now. I have to be there when the shift changes. But I could get away right after. Where do you want me to come?"

"Maybe we could meet. I'm in Long Beach right now. At the university."

"My job isn't so far from there. I need about forty-five minutes or an hour."

I said fine. She told me she worked at an outlet for Bingo Burgers, and gave me directions.

"Mrs. Metrano," I said, "would you bring along some pictures of Amy?"

She hesitated. "All right. If you need them."

"Thanks."

I saw a bus approaching fast up the street behind Mike's car.

I said goodbye to Leslie, scooped up my notepad and change, and made a dash. I didn't peel rubber when I pulled away, but almost.

Bingo Burgers sat on a corner across from a large city park, an ideal location. As it was a beautiful Sunday afternoon, the place was humming. Dodging kids and minivans, I managed to get inside unscathed.

The menu was the usual fast-serve bland-in-a-bun the several thousand Bingo Burgers restaurants sell nationwide. This particular outlet had evolved a long way from the sticky plastic-and-linoleum places Casey used to drag me to when she was little. If Ronald McDonald and Walt Disney had done it in the dark, this place would have been their offspring. I walked into a two-story fantasy of tropical birds and giant aquariums, of ten-foot palms and tables in imitation grass shacks. A long spiral slide connected the upper dining room to the lower. The racket of overstimulated children and squawking birds merged into a steady, high-decibel roar.

My thought was that whoever owned this franchise saw life in the big picture.

I found Leslie behind the service counter, directing a couple of dozen adolescent employees. She wore slacks and a blazer with the company's clown logo on the breast pocket. The manager's blazer. She was pretty, trim in her uniform, but there was a hardscrabble edge about her. Leslie was a working woman, not a mom with a weekend job.

When Leslie saw me, she grabbed a manila envelope and two large drink cups and came around the counter.

"Maggie?" She handed me a cup. "Get yourself a soda. It's a little quieter in the back. We can talk there."

We filled the cups and I followed her into a beachless cabana with a view of the street in front. When we sat down, we did show and tell, lining up both our sets of pictures on the table.

I gave her a minute to look them all over.

"What do you think?" I asked when she sat back.

"I just don't know." There was some country twang in her speech. "I really hate it when I get told that Amy would have changed a lot by now. Like I didn't already know that? I look at my older girls." She glanced up at me. "Did you know I'm a grandma now?"

"Congratulations," I said.

"Don't congratulate me. I didn't have anything to do with it. It was just one of those things. Or that's what my oldest told me at the time." She smiled, resigned.

"What I mean to say is," she continued, "they look so different when they start to fill out. Amy had real fair hair when she was little. I suppose it darkened up some. Like mine did. I never was as blond as she was. The last time I saw my natural color it was sort of lightish brown."

Her hair that day was about the color of honey. She held one of the Hillary pictures at arm's length to study it. Hillary's hair had been bleached white. "What color do you think her real hair was?"

I shook my head. "Maybe the coroner can tell us."

She had to swallow hard, and I regretted having said that so baldly. She shook it off. "I've been going through this routine for a lot of years. You'd think I would get used to it by now. But I just don't seem to."

"I think that's normal," I said.

"I guess so." She dropped her eyes and busied her hands unwrapping her straw. She stuck the straw into the cup.

Some people have about them an appealing mantle of vulnerability. You are drawn to them because you think they need protection. They make you feel like big stuff, strong and capable. Leslie made me feel that way. Until she took a drink through her straw.

Leslie pushed her cup aside and roughly grabbed the arm of a passing busboy. Her expression was severe enough to scare the boy.

"Tell Arturo to come over here," she ordered. "Tell him I said move fast."

I turned to watch the boy scuttle away. "Something wrong?"

"These kids. Just when you get one trained right, they go quit on you. It's just constant aggravation." She softened again.

"I'm used to it, though. I always said I had six big babies, five kids and George. Now I have about ten times that many. Believe me, you gotta know how to handle them."

A tall, lanky boy about seventeen sidled over. He had dark, close-cut hair and a single stud earring. If I'd had to choose which of them, him or Leslie, needed a protector, I would have taken the boy. His knees shook.

"You want me, Miz Metrano?" His voice changed register twice.

She handed him her cup.

He paled as he took it. "I forgot."

"Arturo, your job is recharging the soda base. There's nothing in this cup but fizz and water."

"The fry timer went off when I was standing right there. I had to take care of the fries."

"Are fries your responsibility?"

"No, ma'am." He looked weepy.

"Were the fry people around to take care of their job?"

"Yes."

"Your job is the soda dispensers. You come on in the middle of the lunch rush, Arturo. The soda base is gettin' real low by then. If you don't do your job, what happens when the customers get their drinks?"

"I'm sorry, Miz Metrano." Arturo was backing away. "I won't forget again."

"You got that right," she said. "Go back to work."

I did a quick reevaluation. The woman was no creampuff.

She turned her attention back to me. "Sorry. Where were we?"

"Mrs. Metrano, do you know a family named Ramsdale?" I asked.

"Ramsdale?" She ran it over in her mind. "Commonish name, I guess. I can't think of anyone in particular, though. Why?"

"They had a fourteen-year-old daughter named Hillary." I tapped a Pisces picture. "She has been identified as Hillary Ramsdale."

"Did she run away?" Leslie asked.

"She ran or was pushed away."

"Dammit, though," she said in her soft voice. "If I'd known how hard it is to hang on to your kids, I would have had them all tattooed."

"Amy has something better than a tattoo. She has her parents' DNA. Did you and your husband give samples to the police so they can run a DNA screen?"

"I did." She emphasized *I*. I couldn't read her. All she had to do was give a small amount of blood. It was neither scary nor painful. Nothing to be embarrassed about. "They only needed one parent. Might as well be me. George doesn't like needles."

"My pictures haven't helped, have they?"

"Tell you the truth? They only make things more confusing."

I gave her my card with Mike's home number written in below mine. "Call me anytime. You can leave messages."

As I gathered up Guido's pictures, Leslie Metrano gathered hers. She handed them to me. "You might as well have them. You never know what will help."

"I'll keep in touch," I said. "I'll let you know what happens."

Following Leslie Metrano's precise directions, I approached Belmont Shore from the east end this time. I crossed the bridge onto Naples Island, passing over the ski boat basin and the channel to the open sea. The scenery on Naples was more boats, more yacht harbor, more million-dollar houses.

I had looked up the address of the yacht club in the Thomas Guide map book I'd found in Mike's car. The area was a maze of narrow streets and intersecting waterways. I got lost a couple of times, stymied by one-way passages and dead ends, before I found the right path.

I drove around a horseshoe-shaped bay and over a two-lane bridge. Past a swimming beach with an opalescent boat-oil veneer shimmering on the water, and past the Sea Scout headquarters, I found the yacht club.

The main building sat on a promontory that bulged out into the boat channel. A spiky collar of naked masts defined the contour of its water side. The clubhouse looked something like a Polynesian restaurant left over from the sixties, a long arc of heavy wood and fieldstone shaded by shaggy-leafed banana trees and leggy coco palms.

Though everything looked well tended, I wouldn't have described the club as posh. It was the boats out back and the cars in front that defined its status. Here were Mercedes station wagons, sleek Jags, more Cadillacs and Lincolns than I had seen in one place outside of Detroit, and litters of Volkswagen convertibles—the California teenager's car of the moment. What this said to me was that there were at least three generations of the affluent playing in the same sandbox.

I walked in past the brass plaque on the door that said "Members and guests only," crossed the parquet entry, and headed straight up the stairs toward the sound of voices. Not a soul said boo to me.

On the second floor, I found the bar, a large, cozy lounge walled by glass. Terraces overlooked the Olympic-size pool on the deck below and ranks of moored boats beyond. Through the open windows a brisk breeze blew in off the water, smelling more of bait and petroleum than sweet ocean. A dozen fat brown pelicans rocked in the wake of a passing harbor patrol boat. A peaceful place.

I stood to the side, next to a popcorn machine, and surveyed the crowd, looking for an opening wedge. The atmosphere was friendly, the wealthy at ease among their familiars. My father, who teaches at Berkeley, would have described the group as Establishment. Even worse, Republican.

I don't know why I was even thinking about my father. Actually, I do know. I say the same little prayer of gratitude every time I am in an opulent environment and I do not find my father. It's a knee-jerk sort of thing.

When I was immediately postpubescent, my mother enrolled me in a cotillion at the Claremont Hotel in Berkeley. All the better sort from our area sent their little future ambassadors to learn to dance, bow, and curtsy so that they wouldn't disgrace their families should they be invited to dine at the White House. The boys had been okay, and the dancing instruction wasn't so bad. It was my father's presence that caused me pain.

My father, who has never missed a meal without intending to, or lived in a house with fewer than five bedrooms, carries a tremendous load of guilt for the comfortable circumstances of his birth and upbringing. So, while I box-stepped and cha-cha-chaed, he sat in the parents' gallery, double bourbon in hand, and did his best to convert the local matronage to the virtues of socialism. Some of the mothers instructed their sons not to ask me to dance, lest I taint them. I heard enough pinko jokes that I will never wear pink again as long as I live.

As much as I love Comrade Dad, I made a quick sweep of the yacht-club bar to make sure he wasn't there before I made my move. One can never be too cautious.

A pair of elderly matrons with tight butts and champagne-colored hair brushed past in an aureole of perfumed air. The smaller of them smiled at me.

"Hello, dear," she said. "Beautiful day."

"Lovely," I said, and fell in behind her. They walked out to a table on the terrace. I found a vacant stool at the bar and sat down.

The bartender in a private club is almost always the keeper of the real scoop. For the price of a drink, maybe a flash of cleavage, chances were he could be mine. As a source of information.

The bartender was at the far end of the bar from me, in the middle of what appeared to be a good joke. There was no hustle in him. I was in no hurry. I didn't mind having a little time to figure out my opening gambit. The first problem was that drinks were being signed off to club accounts rather than paid for. I had no account. I could always ask for water.

The stool behind me changed ownership. I swiveled around and found myself eye to eye with a middle-aged man with a good tan and smooth hands, doctor hands. He was spare in his frame, in his movements, and in the smile he gave me. He pushed his sweat-stained yachting cap back on his blond head and leaned toward me.

"Nice nose," he said. "Good workmanship."

"Thank you," I laughed. "I paid a lot for it."

"Chicago, late 1970s."

"Dallas, 1981."

He took my chin in his hand and turned my face so he could inspect my nose from the side. "Maybe the work was done in Dallas, but the surgeon trained in Chicago."

"Could be. Even a snake from Chicago can buy lizard-skin boots in Dallas." I refrained from touching the itch at the bridge of my nose where once there had been a hump. A hump like my father's. "Are nose jobs some kind of hobby for you?"

"Noses make the payments on that Bayliner tied up in slip fifty-two." He offered his hand. "Greg Szal. I don't remember seeing your nose around here before. Or any of the rest of you, for that matter."

"I've been up in the Bay Area," I improvised.

"What are you drinking?"

"Diet Coke," I said.

He caught the bartender's attention. "*Dos Cocas*, Sammy, *por favor*. Tall skinny ones."

I filed the bartender's name for possible future use.

Greg Szal sat forward so that his shoulder almost touched mine. At five-seven I am no giant. His eyes were just about level with mine.

"How come you aren't out there racing with the big girls?" he asked. "Isn't this the last day of qualifying?"

"Racing isn't my thing."

"I know what you mean. Sabots are kid boats."

He brushed my hand with his as he reached for one of the glasses Sammy the bartender set in front of us. I couldn't tell whether Szal was coming on to me or just being friendly. Not that it mattered. What I wanted from him was conversation, and he seemed to be a willing donor. I could worry about his intentions later.

I took a sip from my glass and smiled at him.

"I've only been back in town since yesterday," I said, trying to sort out the essentials of the information Dennis the jeweler had given to Mike and me. "I haven't connected with the Ramsdales yet. Have you seen them lately?"

"Which Ramsdale, him or her?"

"Either of them. Or Hilly. Hilly is the same age as my
daughter."

He frowned. "Your daughter goes to Rogers?"

"No," I said, thinking fast. "As I said, we've been up in the
Bay Area for a while. You know Hilly?"

"Sure. My son is on the club swim team with her."

"When did you see her last?"

He was looking at me sideways, thinking about something
hard enough to put a crease between his nearly white brows.
I took another sip of Coke for something to do.

"How long did you say you've been gone?" he asked.

"Quite a while."

"And no one told you about the Ramsdales?"

"No," I said. "I'm afraid I haven't done a very good job of
keeping up. Has something happened to Randy?"

"Something's always happening to Randy," he chuckled.
"You know how he is. Old Ramsdale can be a royal pain in the
ass, but to tell you the truth, I kind of miss him. He's a pushy
son of a bitch, but he has a good heart."

"Where is he?"

"I don't know. He and Elizabeth split up. It seems to me one
day he was here, the next he was gone. If you really want to
know the gory details, why don't you check with information
central?"

"Where?"

"Come with me." He slid off his bar stool and waited for me
to follow him.

He took me to a cluster of low sofas arranged around a massive stone fireplace. Two women about my age lounged there,
feet up on a free-form granite cocktail table. They were an
attractive pair, unaffected, casually dressed, obviously loaded
—between them they wore enough rocks to ransom Aladdin.
The taller woman, an aristocratic blonde, held a swimsuit-clad

toddler sprawled across her lap. The child slept with his mouth open, dried Popsicle streaks staining his chin.

The second woman was her opposite, a small, voluptuous brunette. She was pretty in a romantic mold, dark curls, long lashes, pouty valentine-shaped lips. When she raised her manicured hand to brush a stray strand of hair from her face, I saw flecks of green fire in her brown eyes.

The pair were whispering back and forth as Greg Szal and I approached, sharing a few private nudges; curious rather than catty.

The brunette looked up at Szal through her lashes, and I saw a tremor pass through him. She saw it, too, and milked it a little.

"Greg?" she cooed.

He took a gulp of air and turned to me. "You remember my wife, Regina."

There was something about the way she looked at me, a wry, smart-aleck appraisal, that made me like Regina Szal immediately. More steel town than steel magnolia. I offered her my hand.

"Maggie MacGowen," I said.

"Maggie MacGowen," Regina repeated for the benefit of her friend.

"No." The woman shook her head. "That isn't it."

"Isn't what?" I asked the blonde.

"Your name. Actually, I suppose, it is your name if you say so. But that isn't who we decided you are."

Regina smiled. "We were just trying to remember where we met you. I know it wasn't PTA. Cynthia suggested John Tracy Clinic volunteers."

I felt my face grow hot, and I knew I was blushing. There was a time everyone in town—whatever town I might have been working in—knew my face. I left network broadcasting in the mid-eighties, and being recognized on the street is getter more and more rare. Almost the only on-camera work I do anymore is promos for PBS. Even with my expensively edited nose, I feel more comfortable on the back end of the camera. I always have. Still, I am around enough so that now and then people who watch public television recognize me on some level.

I had had this who-are-you conversation and variations on it dozens of times. I did what I always do: I just shrugged my shoulders and smiled innocently.

"I was asking Greg about the Ramsdales," I said. "He thought you might be able to help me."

"What about them?" Regina asked.

"For starters, where are they?"

"Why?" Regina seemed skeptical. And smart.

"I want to talk to them about Hillary."

"Is she in some sort of trouble?"

I nodded. "Big-time trouble."

"What sort of trouble?"

"She ran away from home," I said. "I want to know why."

"Are you a social worker?"

"No," I said. "I'm a mother."

"Well, then." Regina looked up at her husband and batted her eyes again. "Greg, on your way out, please tell Sammy to send over another bottle of Moët. And keep them coming. We have some serious talking to do. I want to hear all about Hilly. But I have a feeling I need to be about half blind first."

"On my way out?" Greg asked, gazing at her with a hangdog longing. "I just got here."

She pressed his arm. "I said, this is serious."

As he sloped away, dejected, I had a feeling Regina had already been served a few by Sammy. She was certainly willing to talk.

I turned my smile on her. "It's wicked what you do to that man."

"I know," she purred. "And after all these years. It's the ultimate power, you know, to hold a man's balls in the palm of your hand that way."

The blonde snorted. I guffawed.

Regina grabbed me by the wrist and pulled me down beside her. "Maggie, meet Cynthia."

"Hello," I said.

"Nice to meet you." Cynthia sounded as highbrow as she looked, very long vowels, very Vassar. The grubby child on her lap didn't quite suit the stereotype. But he suited her. "What nature of trouble is Hillary in?"

I took out the stills of Pisces again, and silently asking the girl for forgiveness, handed them to Regina. This wasn't the same as showing them to Leslie Metrano. Hillary would have been mortified if either of these women had seen her on the street.

Regina held the prints so that Cynthia could look on and leafed through them twice.

"Do you know this girl?" I asked.

"It's Hillary Ramsdale." Regina grimaced. "Do they dress this badly on the Continent, or were these taken on Halloween? She looks like a little whore."

"That was her intention," I said. "I filmed her in Los Angeles just a few days ago."

"Ah-ha." Cynthia raised a slender hand. "Now I have it. Maggie MacGowen. *Aged and Alone.* We showed your film at a Junior League seminar about the sandwich generation. You know, adults raising children and caring for elderly parents at the same time. You remember, Regina."

Regina still seemed confused. She held up one of the pictures. "Hilly was in makeup for a film?"

"No," I said. "That's how I found her. Hillary was a working girl."

The frozen horror on Regina's face melted to mortified tears as she leafed again through the stills. She turned the stack facedown on the table before she wiped her nose on the sleeve of her sweater. The valentine poutiness was gone from the gaze she turned on me.

"You said 'was,' " she said.

"Hillary is dead."

"An accident?"

"No. She was murdered."

"No." Cynthia drew the sleeping toddler tight and buried her face against him. Regina reached out and grasped the child's hand. The gesture was very tender, but the green in her eyes sparked with her wrath. It was the right reaction. It showed genuine concern. I liked her even more. Why hadn't Hillary turned to people like these when she was in trouble?

Sammy came over with champagne and tall flutes and began pouring. Glasses were passed from hand to hand in just the way Kool-Aid was being passed among a group of youngsters down at the pool. As long as Sammy was present, no one said a word.

Sammy draped a white towel around the neck of the half-full bottle and went away.

"To all the bastards." Regina tipped her glass toward mine.

"Hear, hear," Cynthia intoned. She arched her long neck back and took a hefty slug from her glass. The price of Moët being what it is, I figured her intake to be about a dollar-fifty per swallow.

"Where is Hillary now?" Regina asked.

"County morgue," I said.

"All alone?" Regina seethed. She reached for the bottle. "That goddam fucking son of a bitch Randy."

"What did he do?" I asked.

"All his brains are in his prick. He all but abandoned Hilly. When Elizabeth caught him screwing his latest bimbo, she tossed him out. Literally. Dumped all his shit into the canal. The neighbors watched her do it. Then he took right off, left the country, and left Hilly behind."

"Left her with her mother," I said.

Cynthia sneered. "Elizabeth is not her mother. By my count, she's wife number three."

"Then where is her mother?"

"She died." Regina turned to Cynthia. "Was it five or six years ago?"

Cynthia shrugged. "I'm not sure. Five or six years and two wives ago, anyway. It was a terrible shame. Hilly's mother was such a lovely person. You can see her influence in Hilly."

"Hold the phone," Regina snapped, draining the bottle into her glass. "Hilly ended up a streetwalker. How lovely is that?"

Cynthia looked down her narrow nose. "You know what I mean. Mother and daughter were both gracious and well-spoken. They kept a bit to themselves, but they were very charming. If Hilly ended up on the streets I would look to Elizabeth before I placed blame on Hanna."

"Why?" I asked.

Regina summoned me closer so she could whisper. "Because Elizabeth is a tramp. Any idiot could see right from the beginning what she wanted from Randy. Everyone except Randy."

And what did she want?"

"This." Regina's gesture swept the room. "And the Virginia Country Club membership, a house in Naples. For a little waitress who grew up in Northtown, she did all right for herself."

"Nasty Reggie," Cynthia reproved.

"But it's true." She sat back. "Randy must have a thing for waitresses. Look at his latest conquest. What's her name? Lacy? Apparently he likes them young and deft at juggling hot dishes."

"Richard likes Lacy." Cynthia was beginning to slur her words. "He says Lacy's awfully intelligent. More like Randy's first wife than Elizabeth. She's working on a teaching credential at State. And she's good with Hilly. He thinks maybe Randy is beginning to pull himself back together."

"Who is Richard?" I asked her.

"My husband," Cynthia said as if any idiot should have known.

Listening to them, I was beginning to feel like a spectator at a tennis match. The wine and bouncing back and forth between them was making my head buzz.

"Wait a minute," I said, holding up my hands. "Where can I find Elizabeth?"

"Haven't seen her for a while. Have you, Cynthia?"

"No."

"She still has the Naples house," Regina said.

"I'd like the address," I said. More than that, I wanted an introduction. I hoped Regina was up for a Sunday-afternoon social call. "I'm sure the police have already contacted Elizabeth. But I want to talk to her."

"Why?" Cynthia challenged. "Seems ghoulish."

"Research," I said, perhaps defensively. Maybe she was right.

Regina had an impish smirk on her face. "You want to do the Nancy Drew thing. Snoop around. Get into some trouble."

I laughed. "Exactly. Want to come with me?"

"Seriously?"

"Elizabeth will be more receptive to a chat if I'm introduced to her by someone she knows. Like you."

"True." Regina got to her feet. "Besides, she lives right on a canal. It's a tricky place to find. Be easier if I just drove you. Cynthia, are you coming?"

"I pass." Cynthia's sleeping child was beginning to stir. "David needs lunch."

Regina gave little David's leg a pat. "Keep an eye out for my boys. I'll call you later."

"My car's out front," I said.

But she shook her head. "We'll get there faster by water."

On the way past the bar, Regina scooped up a second bottle of Moët and tucked it under her arm. At double-time march, she led me downstairs and out the back way to the ranks of moored boats.

When Greg Szal mentioned his Bayliner, I had assumed big. It wasn't. It was a behemoth. There was enough gear on the fishing tower to go into the tuna business if his nose-job practice failed.

A craft that size would tear up the open water, but in narrow passages like the boat channel or the canals of Naples it would be a nuisance, a shark in a goldfish bowl. I was thinking it might be faster to swim to the Ramsdales' than go through the bother of bringing the beast out when Regina ripped a tarp off a four-man Zodiak raft that was tied alongside.

"Give me a hand," she said. We untied the raft and pushed it through the slip until we had cleared the Bayliner's stern. Regina jumped in, heedless of her white linen slacks, and I followed, gracelessly, bouncing on the rubber bottom. I had just managed to get to my knees when she fired up the powerful outboard motor and blasted out into the channel, knocking me flat.

The bottle of Moët rolled against my leg. I grabbed it and slid into the bow. With my legs stretched out front, my back against the inflated side, I was thoroughly comfortable. Wind snapped through my hair, a fine sea spray chilled my face. I popped open the wine, let the foam spew over the side, then took a big swallow.

"Beautiful," I shouted over the ratchety motor noise. I passed the bottle into Regina's outstretched hand.

"Cheers," she shouted back, and took a slug herself.

With practiced skill, Regina maneuvered the Zodiak through the channel and then cut into the wide bay instead of continuing out toward the open sea.

Both sides of the bay were lined with dense-packed houses, everything from tiny cottages to three-story confections of glass and wood. There was an East Coast feel about it all: old money, restricted entree.

Regina powered up to pass a black-and-gold gondola that was being poled by a striped-shirted, opera-singing gondolier. His passengers were snuggled together drinking red wine. Very romantic. Regina raised our bottle to them and they waved back.

At the mouth of a narrow canal, Regina cut her motor to an idle. We glided into a shady canyon between rows of big houses. The cross streets that had been so confusing to me earlier were charming arched bridges from our perspective. The bridges trailed dusty green ivy and bright bougainvillea from either end. The air was rich with the smells of moss and salt water and star jasmine. The atmosphere was just short of exotic. A secret place discovered.

The houses we passed were magnificent. They faced the canal as they would a street, shamelessly flaunting their graces to passersby. Sunday strollers filled the walkway at the edge of the canal on both sides, festive in the weird clothes Southern

Californians wear near water. Altogether it was like a Disneyland ride, a sort of Pirates of the Upper Middle Class. I was having fun.

Every house we passed had a small dock in front. And almost every dock had a boat of some sort, or evidence of a boat: lines, tarps, chains. Some of the docks were furnished with patio chairs and tables, here and there pots of geraniums or trailing succulents.

After the second bridge, Regina killed her motor and coasted to an empty dock. She tossed her line over the metal stanchion and pulled us in close. The house before us was an Italianate mansion with a pink marble terrace overlooking the water. Tall windows along the front must have filled the house with southern light.

It was a warm day. Had it been my house, at least some of the tall windows would have been open. That was my first reaction; a nice place, but stuffy.

I clambered out of the raft and pulled Regina up after me.

"Looks awfully quiet," I said.

"The boat's gone. I know the neighbor. I can ask her when it sailed."

"Let's try the front door first."

Regina was edgy, excited, definitely high. I wondered if she needed more adventure in her life. As adventures go, the one we were on was so far tame stuff. I let her ring the bell.

When no one answered, I stepped to the first set of terrace doors and brazenly looked inside.

I saw a professionally decorated living room, good antiques, polished wood floors, original artwork on the walls. Everything in order. I went to each set of doors and saw more of the same in different rooms. The message was lots of money, knows how to spend it.

"Maggie?" Regina walked across the terrace toward me waving a gray business card. "This was in the door. Should I just leave it?"

I took the card from her and read: Los Angeles Police Department. When I saw the name next to the gold-embossed detective shield, I got a knot in my stomach. Detective Michael Flint, it said, Robbery-Homicide Division, Major Crimes Section. There was a note on the back in Mike's careful hand: "Mrs. Ramsdale, please call immediately."

Patience is a virtue. Unfortunately, it's not one of mine. In my rush to find out about Hillary, I had neglected some of the essential groundwork. That is, it was not my place to tell Elizabeth Ramsdale that her stepdaughter was dead.

Mike has told me that the most important part of a murder investigation is the first twenty-four to forty-eight hours. The physical evidence is fresh, and that's nice when he gets the case into court. But it is usually more important to him to have fresh emotional evidence. When he questions someone, he listens to the body language as closely as he does the verbal answers: an inappropriate laugh, eyelids that drop before an answer, any reaction that catches the liar. For me to spring the news on Elizabeth would be evidence-tampering as egregious as tramping through the murder scene would be.

It was time for me to back off. I went over to the front door and tucked Mike's card back into the space above the deadbolt where Regina had found it.

I started down the slick marble steps. "Want to take me back now?"

Regina stayed her ground. "While we're here, let's talk to the neighbor. She's such a dear old thing. I'm sure she's seen us. She'd think it rude if I didn't stop in to say hello."

I hesitated. An old lady next door wasn't the same as talking to the family, but they can be wonderful sources of information.

I smiled at Regina. "Lead the way," I said.

The neighbor's house was a slate-gray Cape Cod with white trim and a lot of polished brass. Standing alone it would have been a charming beach cottage. But sandwiched between a *faux* English Tudor manor house and the Ramsdales' palazzo, it seemed as contrived as a movie facade.

Regina banged the huge knocker a few times and we were let in by a maid wearing blue jeans and a flowered tunic.

"Have a seat in the living room," the maid said. "I will tell Martha you're here."

"Martha knows they're here." The voice was estrogen-deepened, the woman behind it ancient. She came down the stairs leaning heavily on the railing, as wrinkled and fragile-looking as an orphaned baby bird. She offered her crooked hand to Regina, to hold not to shake. "So nice to see you, dear. How are the boys?"

"Getting big," Regina said, planting a kiss on the powdered cheek. "All except Greg. He keeps hoping, but dammit, Martha, he's just not going to grow anymore."

Martha laughed. "Who's your friend?"

"Martha, this is Maggie MacGowen. She's a filmmaker and she's interested in the Ramsdales."

Martha turned her bright eyes on me. "Whyever would you be interested in the Ramsdales? Unless you're doing soap opera."

"Are they good soap-opera material?" I asked.

"Good Lord, yes. Much better than most television. I never rent videos on weekends. So much more interesting to just sit on my terrace and snoop." She patted Regina's hand. "Let's go in and sit down. May I offer you some refreshment?"

Regina rose to the offer. "I wouldn't mind a double something, on the rocks. How about you, Maggie?"

"No thanks," I said. "I'm well past my limit."

I looked at my watch as I followed them into the living room. I needed to be on the freeway within the hour if I was going to be in Sherman Oaks by six. The time wasn't my problem. The wine was. I was in no shape to drive. I had known even as I accepted the first glass of champagne that I should stick with soda.

I'm a funny drunk. Charming even, according to my friends. I had never had a problem with booze, really. But I had had a rough year or so, and a little chemically induced happiness had helped me get by now and then. I was beginning to be aware how many evenings over the last few months I had been funny and charming by bedtime. There had been nights that without the help of a bottle of wine or several stiff scotches I wouldn't have had the courage to go to bed at all.

For the first month or so after my ex-husband moved out, I went upstairs every night with the sense that an onerous burden had been lifted. There is nothing worse than going through the motions night after night out of habit, because you haven't embraced the inevitable alternatives, with someone you wish had missed his freeway off ramp. Had gone over the side, maybe. Into the cold, unforgiving waters of the San Francisco Bay, perhaps.

Anyway, the relief wears off after a while and you begin to notice that one person can't warm a king-size bed. Mike had helped warm the sheets for a while. Then, when he was gone, medium-priced chardonnay and Bowser had now and then sung my lullaby. I preferred Mike.

"Martha," I said, "would you mind if I used the telephone?"

"By all means, dear," she said graciously.

While Martha and Regina uncapped a new bottle of bourbon at the wet bar, I called Mike's pager and programmed in Martha's number. If he was still in Long Beach, there was no point in both of us driving all the way back to the Valley for dinner. Separately. I was thinking about his handcuffs when I rejoined the others.

Regina made room for me beside her on a velvet settee. "Martha knew Hillary's mother."

"Tell me about her," I said. I hoped to keep the conversation away from Hillary's fate. I had already told too many people. "Tell me what sort of mother she was to Hillary."

"Hanna was a wonderful mother." Martha seemed thoughtful. "Very careful. Now, I personally raised my children to be independent. Hanna kept little Hilly awfully close to her. Smothered her, to my way of thinking. Does that sound catty?"

I smiled. "If that's being catty, please, go ahead. I want to know what Hillary's home life was like."

"It was a good life by most measures. The Ramsdales certainly wanted for nothing. If Hanna smothered Hillary, well, perhaps no one could blame her. She wasn't a young mother, you see. Hillary was a blessing that came somewhat late in life. A surprise, after Hanna and Randy had given up on children. I think that being an only child of older parents can be a special burden, don't you?"

"Yes," I said. "I can see how it could be. Do you think Hillary was unhappy?"

"Good Lord, no," Martha snapped. "Randy would not permit his girls to be unhappy. He doted on Hanna and Hillary. He would move mountains for them."

"You said that Hillary was a surprise. Thinking back, do you think the baby was a welcome surprise?"

"Hanna always said so. She had some female problems. I don't remember what, exactly. Hanna did tell me that she had lost several pregnancies and had a little one who died very early on. Very sad for her. So of course, after that much heartache, a healthy child like Hillary would be something of a miracle, don't you think? Now, I only know what Hanna told me. The Ramsdales bought the house next door because of our school district. They moved in in time for Hillary to begin kindergarten. I didn't know her as a baby."

I was keeping two columns of figures in my head, Amy Metrano's age when she disappeared, Hillary's age when she entered the local picture. Four and a half and fivish. Could work.

"Was Randy as protective as Hanna?" I asked.

She pursed her thin lips. "Oh yes. More so, I believe. Poor man was desperately lost after Hanna died. And he worried so about Hillary. I am persuaded that's why he married again so soon. He wanted to find another Hanna."

"Was the second wife like Hanna?" I asked.

"Physically, very much so. As is Elizabeth." Martha looked at me. "Would you call that kinky?"

"I would, yes." My response seemed to please her.

"I always thought so, too. Poor Randy. You cannot judge a book by its cover."

"Meaning," I said, "that beyond their appearance, wives two and three were not like Hanna?"

"Precisely."

The telephone rang before Martha got into her wind up.

"Excuse me, please." She creaked to her feet and picked up the receiver. After hello, she did some listening. Then she told the caller, "It certainly wasn't me, sir. But I can offer you Regina Szal or Maggie MacGowen. What's your pleasure?"

I knew it was Mike returning my page. I had been standing beside Martha during most of this exchange. She seemed to be flirting a bit, so I waited. She was chuckling when she handed me the receiver.

"For you, dear," she said, and mouthed, "Man."

I put the receiver to my ear. "Mike?"

"I take it you're not in trouble," he said. "Who's the old girl?"

"She lives next door to the Ramsdales."

"Jesus Christ, Maggie," he exploded. "What the hell are you up to?"

"Hi, honey," I cooed. "Nice to hear your voice, too."

He drew a noisy breath. "Sorry. But someday you're going to get into a deeper hole than you can get yourself out of."

"That's why I keep your number in my pocket, cupcake."

Finally, he laughed. "Okay. What's up?"

"Are you still in Long Beach?"

"No. I'm home. Michael and I are watching the end of the ball game. Waiting for you."

"I'm leaving in a few minutes."

"Good. Who all have you talked to?"

"People at the yacht club, the next-door neighbor. Guido and I made some pictures. I showed them to Leslie Metrano."

"And?"

"Rang no bells."

"Seen any signs of the Ramsdales?"

"None."

"If you do run into either of them, Maggie . . ."

"Yes?"

"Stay away."

"You're as bossy as Lyle."

"The thing is," Mike went on, "if anyone hurt you, I'd have

to kill him. So far, I've had a clean week and I want to keep it that way."

"Bye, Mike," I said.

"Did you hear what I said?"

"I heard you. I gotta go."

"You gotta get home. We're hungry."

"Bye." I hung up and went back to Regina and Martha.

"Everything all right, dear?" Martha asked.

"Fine. But I'm out of time. May I come back and talk with you again later? Maybe tomorrow?"

"Certainly." She smiled sweetly. "I was wondering whether you knew when Hillary and Randy would be coming back."

Regina pulled in a breath, getting ready to spill the big news. I grabbed her arm and squeezed and she seemed to get the message.

"It seems that everyone believes Hillary and Randy are somewhere in Europe together," I said. "Do you know when they left? Or where they went?"

"I'm sorry. I don't know that. Randy moved out next door after an especially nasty fight, sometime last winter. Elizabeth told me he had gone abroad. And not long afterward, Hillary joined him."

"When did she join him?"

She drew in a squeaky breath as she thought. "March? Yes, I think it was the middle of March. Hillary brought me some shamrocks for St. Patrick's Day, as she always does. And that was the last I saw her."

"Did she say where her father had gone?"

"No. She did tell me she wasn't getting along well with Elizabeth and wanted to be with her father. Apparently, Elizabeth sent her right along. I enjoy gossiping with you, dear, but you really should ask Elizabeth."

"She isn't home," I said. "Any idea where she might be?"

"There was a policeman here earlier today, and he asked the same question of my housekeeper. We were trying to think. To be honest, I can't quite remember. Since Randy left, Elizabeth seems to come and go rather irregularly. I don't keep close tabs.

The boat has been gone for some time. A week perhaps. Maybe she's gone off to Catalina."

"If she comes back, will you call me?"

"That's what the policeman said, too. Who should I call first, you or him?"

I put my arm around her thin shoulders and whispered into her ear, "The policeman and I can be reached at the same number."

She brightened. "Oh! Oh, my. Yes, I certainly do wish to speak with you further. You must explain that to me."

We said our goodbyes. Regina dispensed some hugs and promises of her own to Martha. Martha seemed fatigued suddenly, and I worried that we had overstayed. We left her in the living room and saw ourselves out.

"What a dear," I said to Regina as we walked back toward the Zodiak.

"She is a dear. I've heard stories that she was quite a hell-raiser in her day."

"I hope she was," I said, chuckling at the image. It seemed fully consistent.

When I took a last look up at the Ramsdales' house, I noticed that an upstairs window was open enough for the breeze off the water to ruffle the sheer curtains. Mike's card was still stuck in the front door.

I was looking just about everywhere except where I was going. I walked right into the back of Regina. She had stopped dead on the walk.

"Sorry," I said.

Regina turned a pale face to me and pointed to the Ramsdales' dock, where we had left the Zodiak.

I saw nothing. No raft.

I ran, Regina close on my heels. Our feet clattered on the small wooden dock. We found the raft's line attached to the stanchion and taut. When I leaned over the edge I could see the gray rubber of the raft bobbing just under the surface of the dark water. I knelt and began to haul it in. Even with

Regina's help, it was too heavy. And the effort was pointless. There was no hope of refloating the Zodiak. Ever.

Through the murky water I could see the long slashes that had reduced the thick rubber sides to ribbons.

Regina had green fire in her eyes again.

"What the fuck is this supposed to mean?" She was steamed.

"It means," I said, "that we're having dinner in Long Beach after all."

CHAPTER
10

"I can swim," I said.

"With your throat cut?" Mike lifted a rubber ribbon that had recently been part of the Zodiak raft. City lifeguard divers had brought the raft up onto the dock and circled the area with yellow crime-scene tape. A chunk of the sidewalk had also been cordoned off to make room for some floodlights.

Mike had called in the Long Beach police and given them some of the pertinent history. A couple of carloads of men in uniform were drifting around somewhere, ogling the local talent with more energy, I thought, than they were giving the investigation. I guess we hadn't infected them with the serious implications of the sinking of a six-foot inflatable.

The lifeguards had jumped right on it, but only because the outboard motor had sunk and was leaking oil and gasoline into the waterway. Not that one more oil slick would alter that environment significantly. My impression was that they were having an awfully good time in the water, at time and a half.

I was gratified that I could provide entertainment for so many. Regina and Martha watched all the activity from lounge chairs up on the Ramsdales' terrace, baby-sitting the bottle of bourbon they had started at Martha's house.

"So, I say it again," Mike said. "I'm glad you weren't in this thing when it went down."

"Never happen." I raised the Nikon 35mm I had dragged along and snapped a few frames of Mike holding up the ruins of the raft like a fisherman's trophy. I needed the camera in front of my face so he couldn't see the sweat on my brow.

"I look at this as the work of a coward," I said. "If Regina and I had been out here, he wouldn't have dared to shred the Zodiak."

"Uh huh." Mike dropped the flap of rubber. "Think about this: little Hillary got it with a razor in broad daylight, in a public place. Just like the raft."

I had been thinking about little else for several hours. But, ever macho, I flexed my puny biceps for him. "Two competent women are hardly the same as a ninety-pound girl or a seagoing balloon."

"You think you could scare him away?"

"Absolutely."

Before I saw him coming, Mike somehow bumped his hip against me, grabbed me around the middle, and flipped me off my feet. If he had let go of me, I would have landed in the water. When my eyes stopped rattling, I was looking straight down at the lifeguard divers swimming around the dock pilings.

"Excuse me," Mike said, setting me back upright. "What were you saying?"

"I don't remember." I gasped for air. "Was it 'Fuck you'?"

He laughed. "The things that come out of your mouth."

The camera, dangling from its strap, had banged into my shoulder when he flipped me. It hurt. While I didn't want Mike to see me scared, I didn't mind letting him know I was pissed.

"Don't do that again, Michael Flint."

"Why? Because it shows you're not so tough? You've been having a lot of fun, poking around, asking questions. But don't forget for one little minute that someone is playing for keeps."

"I am not poking around."

"Call it what you like." Mike kicked at the ruins. "Our friend is as cocky as he is nasty. You just stay the fuck away from him."

"The things that come out of your mouth, Mike Flint."

He glanced up, somewhere between sheepish and peevish. "I meant what I said."

One of the divers bobbed up to toss another find onto the pile of deflated raft, bits of boats, and other interesting detritus he and his partner had recovered from the bottom of the canal.

"Found the outboard yet?" Mike asked him.

The diver cleared his mouthpiece. "Yeah. It's down there, all right, but it's fouled in a lot of crap. We're going to set up a block and tackle, bring it up here in a few minutes."

The second diver surfaced. He tossed a black wing-tip shoe, maybe a size twelve or thirteen, onto the heap.

"What's the matter with these people, they don't trust the city to haul away their trash?" he huffed. "Throw their shit into the canal. Must be a dozen bags of it down there."

Mike picked up the wing tip by its shoestring. "You're going to bring it all up, aren't you?"

"If you want it." The diver positioned his mask and pushed himself off the dock. His wrist light snaked down through the murky water like a dragon in a Chinese New Year parade.

I looked from the shoe to Mike's foot. Mike is a slender six-two. The shoe he held would have been much too big for him. I called out to Martha, "Any idea how tall Randy Ramsdale is?"

"He's tall." She started for the dock. "Taller than your friend. And much stouter. What did they find?"

"A shoe."

"A nice one?" she asked. "Randy likes nice things. Everything perfect."

"It looks bankerish." I leaned over for a closer look. "Mike, how long do you think it was in the water?"

He shrugged. "Bodies in water I know. Shoes I don't. It's in pretty good shape, though."

"Regina and Cynthia said that Elizabeth Ramsdale tossed

Randy's things into the canal the night she tossed him out."

"Sound like nice people."

Martha made slow progress off the terrace, talking as she came. "Rather vain about his appearance, I always thought."

A big, good-looking cop with sergeant's stripes on his sleeve overtook Martha just as she stepped into the bright circle made by the floodlights. The officer's nameplate read Mahakian.

"You Flint?" he asked Mike.

"I am." Mike set down the shoe and brushed his hands on his pants. "What's up?"

"Where's your witness?"

Mike nudged me forward. "Miz Maggie MacGowen here."

Mahakian seemed doubtful.

"Actually," I said, "I didn't see anything. I think I'm a victim, not a witness."

Mahakian frowned some more. "No one answers at the house. We thought, after what Flint here told our detectives, that maybe we ought to go in, have a look around. But the judge is sticking about signing a warrant. He says anybody could have cut the raft, kids maybe. We have to show him some connection between the house and the raft, or some tie-in to your other case, or he'll pass. If you can tell me you saw someone inside, and they're not responding to the police, maybe I can talk the judge into a barricaded suspect."

"All I saw was a curtain move," I said. "Before Mrs. Szal and I went into the neighbor's house, I thought that all of the Ramsdales' windows were closed. When we came out again, one upstairs window was open. It could have been open all the time and I didn't notice. This is a big house and there are lots of windows."

"So you didn't actually see anybody?"

"Right."

"You're sure?"

"Yes. But I'd be happy to make up something if it would help. I'm dying to see inside that place."

He chuckled in spite of himself. "You a decorator or something?"

"Not hardly. I met the girl who was murdered. I would very much like to see her room."

"Murdered," Mahakian parroted. "God, you'd think just saying that much would be enough for this old creep to sign for us. Goddam Jerry Brown appointee."

"Did you tell him the dead girl lived here?" I asked.

"He needs proof of ID." Mahakian turned to Mike. "Is that what LAPD is doing down here, establishing ID?"

"*Mas o menos*," Mike said, waffling his hand. "Most of the time I'm just trying to keep MacGowen here out of trouble. It's a tough job, and I couldn't get anyone else to do it."

Mike thought he was funny, but I turned away. That's when I saw the stricken expression on Martha's face. I had forgotten she was there, had forgotten what she didn't know about Hillary. Feeling that I had misspoken, I went over and put an arm around her.

"I'm sorry," I said.

She shook me off. "I knew it was something bad. But, oh, why did it have to be Hillary?"

"I'm sorry," I said again, at a loss for anything better.

Mahakian came between us. "You the neighbor?" he asked Martha.

"I am," she said briskly, tossing off her shock.

"I understand that Mr. Ramsdale is out of town. When was the last time you saw or spoke to Mrs. Ramsdale?"

"As I told Maggie, not since the boat sailed. Perhaps a week ago."

Mahakian nodded as if that meant something to him. Something he wasn't thrilled to know.

"What?" I asked.

"I asked the judge how nobody could be home if all the cars are in the garage. He had some ideas. A boat wasn't one of them."

I looked at Mike. "All the cars?"

Mike had my arm. "You'd better show us, sergeant."

I felt a hole open in the pit of my stomach, like just before you reach the top of a roller coaster and you haven't seen yet how far down the other side goes. It's the expectation that gets you, not the drop.

I gave Martha's shoulder another squeeze and fell in beside Mike, hustling to keep up with Mahakian. We went along a dark and narrow side yard overgrown with ivy, through a tall wooden gate, and out into an alley that ran between rows of garages. The Ramsdale garage was as wide as the house, room enough for four cars and some storage.

We went in through an unlocked side door. Before Sergeant Mahakian turned on the overhead light, I don't know what I expected to see, except that it had something to do with a man who was fast with a straight razor. What I saw was sufficiently scary.

Ranged in a row were a new black Mercedes 500SEL, a utilitarian minivan, a two-man Sabot sailboat on a trailer. And a shiny red Corvette.

Mike pulled me to him. "What do you think, Maggie?"

"Looks like the same Corvette. But I'm no car expert. Maybe the tape will help."

"Sergeant," Mike said, "did you run the cars?"

"Yessir." Mahakian pulled out his notebook. "They are all registered to Randall Ramsdale, this address. No wants, no warrants, no nothing on any of them."

Mike went over and felt the hood of the Corvette. "It's cool now. What time did you call me, Maggie?"

"About five."

"Three hours ago."

Mahakian felt the hood, too. "You want to tell me about it?"

"A witness to Hillary Ramsdale's killing identified the doer as a male, Cauc, fair complexion, six-two to six-four, drove a late-model red 'vette."

"Sly would know the car, Mike," I said. "Probably give you a better ID on the car than he would on the driver."

Mike nodded. "Tell the kid to talk to me, would you?"

"He'll talk to you," I said. "Without Hillary, he isn't so tough. He's scared."

Mahakian jotted something on his notepad and pocketed it.

"Detective Flint, sir, I need to go call my supervisor, take another shot at the judge. Would you mind securing the premises until I can send someone to relieve you?"

"Go ahead," Mike said. "We'll stay here and neck till you get back."

Poor Mahakian didn't quite know how to respond to that. He patted his notebook, sucked in his round tummy, and left us.

When he was gone, I grabbed Mike by the shirtfront. "You can hug me. But I'm really not in the mood for anything else."

"Come here." He held me against him and stroked my back. Mike gives good succor. "You got pretty tight with the locals. Tell me what you know."

I thought for a moment, my cheek resting on his chest. I didn't *know* very much at all. I only had scraps. That's where I started.

"Hillary was sweet to old ladies. Her father, a perfectionist when it came to pleasure, doted on her. Her stepmother was straight out of Grimm's. There was a lot of noisy fighting for the entertainment of the neighbors. It seems that Randy, true to his name, had another woman. He gave her a ring with a substantial rock for Valentine's day. As I put it together, that's just about the time that Randy took off for parts unknown. Alone. About a month later, Hillary followed him. But if Hillary was actually living on the streets up in L.A., where was Randy? And if a nice kid like her preferred the mean streets, how horrible must it have been at home with the stepmother?"

"Real bad." Mike rubbed his face, a tired, disdainful gesture. "I talked to my friend Art in juvenile records up in Sacramento this morning."

"And?"

"How come no one filed a missing-person report on Hillary?"

"You tell me," I said.

"Couple of possibilities come to mind. And I don't like any of them. Parents don't lose their kids for a month without reporting it. Not if they want them found again."

I took a step back from him. "Where's Michael?"

"He couldn't wait for us. Had some homework to finish."

"I'm sorry," I said. "I know getting us together is important
to you."

"It's not your fault. Shit happens, huh?"

I didn't have anything to say. We waited there in silence for
a few more minutes before we were relieved by a pair of uniformed Long Beach officers.

While his partner wiped squashed snail off his shoe, the less
picky of the two walked into the garage.

"Detective Flint?"

"Officer?"

"The sergeant said to tell you the warrant is on the way
down. The minute it gets here, he's going to boot the door."

"Sounds like fun," I said.

"After you," Mike said, bowing me through the door. Mike
and I picked our way back around front.

By the time we got there, the block and tackle had been set
up at the side of the dock where the raft had gone down. The
pile of waterlogged stuff had grown in mass, clusters of green
trash-bag bundles taking up most of the small dock.

A few of the bags were torn. What I saw spilled out seemed
to be mostly clothes—Neptune's garage sale. There was so
much of it that I marveled at the vastness of Elizabeth's rage
at Randy. Most of us would have been satisfied to toss out a
few prized things and watch them float away, or sink into
oblivion. But how many of us could sustain fury as long as
Elizabeth had? Very scary woman.

The bourbon bottle on the table between Regina and Martha
was empty. Martha still seemed chipper, but Regina had
reached capacity. She was sound asleep, looking a lot like the
sleeping toddler her friend had been holding at the yacht club.

Mahakian was at the front door with a couple of suits, holding
a long, slender tool. They knocked a few times, hit the bell a
few more, called out, "Police. Open up."

Mike joined them. I had another agenda.

Yellow police tape kept a growing number of spectators at a
distance. I wasn't a spectator. I ducked under the tape, un-
challenged, and went for a closer look at the junk on the dock.

The bags had been perforated, so they split when the divers manhandled them to the surface. I pulled a bag, heavy-gauge lawn and leaf size, into a clear space and ripped it open. No one stopped me.

The first garment I pulled out was a cream silk pajama top with RR embroidered on the breast pocket. The size on the label was XL. Seawater had surely ruined the fabric, but until they got wet, the pajamas had been in good shape, no tears or frayed areas. Further digging found more pajamas of similar style and quality, folded stacks of men's boxer underwear—also monogrammed—a couple of terry robes, and, bizarre, a few pounds of ironstone dishes. Expensive, heavy dishes that probably gave the bundle enough weight to send it to the bottom and keep it there.

I looted through a few more open bags, found more of the wardrobe belonging to RR.

I looked up and saw Martha leaning over the tape. "What did you find, dear?"

"Randy's clothes."

"So many?" She seemed worried. "He must have bought all new things for his trip."

Mahakian worked the tool between the front door and the jamb. With a sharp crack, the frame splintered and the latch and the deadbolt popped. The door swung open.

I dropped the clothes and went up to Mike on the terrace. Martha was right behind me.

I tugged his shirtfront again. "Can we go in?"

"Not until we're invited. Let them look around first, just to be safe."

Mahakian and his colleagues paused in the open doorway and seemed to be smelling the house air. I figured out why in a big hurry and my stomach took another roller-coaster ride. After a moment, they went in, hands poised on the weapons at their belts. I watched the lights come on at the windows, followed their progress around the first floor, then up the stairs.

After no more than five minutes, Sergeant Mahakian came

back out. Mike went up and huddled with him, then he gestured for me.

"Hey, Miz Victim, come on in," Mike said.

"What about me?" Martha demanded.

"Wait for the second tour bus," Mike told her.

I was up the terrace steps and in the door before Mike. Behind me, I heard Martha grousing, "Why her?"

"What did you find, Sergeant?" I asked.

"No one's home. Detective Flint thinks you might be able to tell us a few things if we let you look around. You know better than to touch anything. Right?"

"Of course." I walked past him and into the living room I had seen earlier through the windows.

The rooms were beautifully done, if rather too opulent for my taste: restored antiques, heavy brocades in jewel tones of amethyst, garnet, and emerald, drapes with velvet swags. I had the feeling that anything that seemed less than perfect looked that way by design. Here and there a down-filled sofa cushion was scrunched, a few books on an end table were stacked randomly, a cashmere afghan was tossed rather than folded over an ottoman. A very old brass spyglass rested on a chair next to the window.

The only flaw was the dust that dulled the shine on the mahogany tables and on the ebony concert grand piano. I suppose there are scientific ways to measure the passage of time by the accumulation of dust. My best guess was days rather than weeks had passed since the room had been cleaned. The important thing was, the dust was undisturbed.

The other rooms on the first floor were a formal dining room, the kitchen, a breakfast room, and maid's quarters. Each was as beautiful as the next, and all had the same fine, undisturbed layer of dust. I worried about the tracks we were all making in the dust on the white marble floor of the entry, even if no one else seemed to.

Odd as it may sound, I couldn't feel Hillary in those graceful yet somehow sterile rooms. I had seen her piano, and could imagine her in a stiff party frock playing for the entertainment of a roomful of stiff adults. Beethoven, not boogie-woogie. No place to let down her guard. That impression changed when Mike opened the door to what appeared to be Randy's study.

The dark and ornate gave way to scarred natural pine floors, threadbare rugs, a brick fireplace, and big comfy chairs pushed in front of a huge television set. The walls were covered with Hillary, from formal poses to fuzzy snapshots of goofy faces. Over the rolltop desk there were a framed finger painting and a crayon still life of a vaseful of flowers on either side of a huge, immensely ugly paint-by-the-numbers seascape. All were signed by the adored child artist.

I nearly lost it when I saw the penciled hash marks on one wall, Hillary, age five, Hillary, age six, marked all the way up to age fourteen. And all made on the same date, November 1. The worst part was the thick line a couple of inches higher than Mike's head. "Dad" was written next to the line, and below it were nine dates. Every year as Hillary grew, Dad had remained a measurable constant.

Mike was looking at the same marks, looking as sad as I felt. I put my arms around him.

"What do you think?" he said.

"Daddy doted on his little girl. Tough competition for a wife. Come to think of it, I don't see any wifey pictures here at all."

"Now that you mention it," Mike said.

"I'd sure like to talk to Randy."

"I have a real bad feeling about that."

"Would it hurt anything if we peeked in his desk?"

"Sorry, kid. Much as I'd like to take a shot at it myself. That's a private zone until we get a different warrant. But we can go upstairs. Want to see Hillary's room?"

I was still looking around the room.

"Maggie?"

"I keep thinking about Casey and her dad. We abandon children in so many ways. Why should they ever trust us?"

Mike caught my hand as I turned for the door.

"What?" I said.

"Trust me." He kissed me, a brush across the lips that left a cool streak.

"Try it again," I said. He's so cooperative. There was nothing cool about any part of me when I drew away.

"Ready now?" he said, cocksure.

"Stunned," I said, working to breathe normally. "Lead the way."

Once I had found Hillary in the house, she seemed to be everywhere. It was tough going, walking where she had walked, seeing her things. Mike had done a good deed when he embraced me.

As we approached the room where Hillary must always have slept between clean sheets, the bathroom where she could shower whenever she wanted to, I thought about the first time I had seen her. The street had been so noisy. A big contrast to the warm, quiet, orderly house.

I had to remind myself that danger comes in many guises. Sometimes wrapped in pretty packages.

I held on to Mike, because the contact made me feel better. And he made sure he was available to hold.

The carpet on the stairs was deep. It muffled the sound of our steps. All the way up I could hear the other police talking somewhere above us, and voices from outside coming in through an open window. They had grown very loud and excited, like a block party.

I looked up at Mike. "Do you think Martha has been passing around more bourbon?"

"Sounds like it."

We turned into the first doorway at the top of the stairs and nearly collided with Mahakian on his flight out.

"Sorry," he panted.

"In a hurry?" I asked.

"Yeah." He sidled past us and fled down the stairs. "The outboard is coming up."

"Oh," I said.

"It's bringing some shit up with it. Probably more trash bags. Those candy-ass lifeguards are screaming for help."

We went into the master bedroom, an enormous expanse done in peach and vanilla ice cream, like Randy's pajamas. The sheer silk draping the windows billowed in the breeze from the French doors. Very ethereal, very feminine. And very sexy.

The two detectives who had come in with Mahakian were outside the French doors, standing on a narrow balcony that overlooked the terrace below and the dock. Mike joined them.

I was far more interested in looking around Elizabeth's room than watching the lifeguards raise Regina's outboard motor.

The room was dramatic for its starkness. There was very little furniture to distract from the focal point: the high canopied bed covered with a puffy satin comforter. An oversize bed, with lots of room for rolling around, even for a man like Randy, who, by all accounts, was a big man.

No one was paying any attention to me, so I pillaged the night-table drawers. I was looking for something to humanize the place, define its inhabitants. The electric dildo I found helped a lot. I found it among a variety of interesting things: K-Y Jelly, many dime-store silk scarves, wrinkled as if they had been knotted, reading glasses.

In the dildo drawer I also found a copy of Daphne du Maurier's *Rebecca*. One of my favorite books. I flipped through the pages. Then I looked back at the window where the detectives were calling down to someone below. Just like a scene from *Rebecca*.

I tossed the book onto the bed and went on through the room to the adjoining dressing room and walk-in closets.

Her closet was bigger than his. Either closet could have been converted into a good-sized bedroom. The odd thing was, while her closet was crammed, his was absolutely empty. I knew where his things were, out there on the dock. That wasn't the puzzler.

When my ex, Scotty, moved out, it took me a while to decide to spread my things into his closet space. A week, maybe two. Elizabeth had had a couple of months. And she really needed more closet space. Unless she was expecting Randy to come back, what was her hang-up?

I was puzzling over this when I closed the closet door behind me. I walked back into the bedroom and saw the men still leaning over the balcony railing. Just as in *Rebecca* when her sailboat was found at the bottom of the sea. With her in it.

"Mike?" I picked up the book and walked toward the windows. "I want to show you something."

The noise outside crescendoed, a collective groan. The detective standing shoulder to shoulder with Mike covered his mouth, ducked away, and, green-faced, ran past me headed for the bathroom.

"Mike?" I started for the balcony.

Mike met me, blocking my way. He was green-faced, too.

"What is it?" I asked.

"I think we found Randy."

CHAPTER
11

Bloated, half his face eaten away by the fishes, poor Randy didn't have any looks left to be vain about when I finally met him. He was a big man, though. Puffed up even bigger by the gases that come with putrefaction.

The breeze off the water lifted his fine, light hair and ruffled through the shirt of his creamy silk pajamas, so that he looked as if he were panting after a hard swim. His last, best effort. Around his legs was still wound a shroud made from a luscious peach-colored satin sheet, accessorized with three anchors on chains.

When I looked down at him from the balcony, he had been a beached absurdity, a Macy's Parade balloon that had strayed. Up close, however, he was beyond grotesque. Poor Randy.

Mike had Mentholatum smeared under his nose, like the other police and the county coroner's people. I could smell it ten feet away. I could smell Randy, too, though he wasn't as bad as I had expected.

I wondered how many men leave home forever wearing their monogrammed pajamas.

Mike stayed with the locals until Randy was zipped into a green plastic body bag. Green about the same shade as the trash bags that held a few cubic yards of his personal treasures. Odd, the tomb he had been taken from. Like the pharaohs, buried with the junk that gave him pleasure in this world. Had he, like they, planned to take it with him? Or had someone simply done a very thorough housecleaning, emptied the closets along with the occupant snoring on the left side of the big satin-covered bed?

Mike stripped off surgical gloves, dropped them into a receptacle for contaminated waste. Then he got down on his belly at the edge of the dock and scrubbed his hands in the dark water. I wouldn't have done that. Randy had come out of the same water.

Martha had given me a vacuum bottle of coffee before she went inside to stay, to lie down she said. Regina had long since called her husband to pick her up.

I poured Mike the last of the coffee and carried it over to him. His hands were still wet when he took the china mug from me.

"Thanks," he said.

"What happened to Randy?"

Mike inhaled the steam rising from the cup. "Throat was cut. Deep. Severed the trachea."

"That makes three, if you count the raft. So, is it over? I mean, don't bad things come in threes?"

"Sure. Unless they come in fours or fives."

"I was looking for reassurance."

"I can't give you any, Maggie."

"So, tell me. What sort of madman would sink a raft right over the very spot where he had left one of his victims? A victim, need I say, he had gone to great lengths to keep on the bottom."

"Couple of possibilities. One, he didn't know Randy was down there. Two, he wanted us to find Randy. I'm inclined toward number two, because I don't believe in coincidence of the magnitude implied by number one. Two also makes this raft business a crime of opportunity, suggesting he didn't know who the hell you are."

"Meaning he didn't follow me here?"

"That's what I would like to believe." He filled his lungs. "I'm finished for now. Let's get the hell out of here."

"Sorry," I said. "I'm staying over with Martha tonight."

"I think that's a real bad idea."

"She's scared, Mike."

"She should be."

"I can't leave her alone."

"She must have family."

"She asked me."

"Is there any point in arguing with you?"

"Is there ever?"

Tired, stressed, he sighed.

I took Martha's empty cup from him and poured the coffee dregs into the water. "Why don't you stay with us?"

"No."

"Martha thinks you have a nice ass."

He wasn't ready to be jollied.

"She told me she takes her hearing aids out at night. Can't hear a thing."

He looked up at me from under furrowed brows. "Did she really say that?"

"Not exactly. She said it was pleasant to watch you walk away."

"Uh huh." He wasn't buying yet. "Sure she did."

"I can't leave her alone, Mike."

"She isn't expecting to climb into bed with us, is she?"

"Maybe." I smiled; he had come around. "You never know. She might be a lot of fun. Ben Franklin said all women are the same in the dark. And older ones are so much more appreciative."

"He was old his own damn self when he said it." Mike wiped at the Mentholatum under his nose. "I don't have any clothes."

I glanced over at the pile on the dock. "Maybe Randy will lend you something."

"Maybe I'll do without."

"Even better," I said.

Martha put us up in a downstairs guest room that faced out on the Ramsdale side of the house. As cheerful as her chatter was, I knew she was scared half to death. While her house was equipped with a state-of-the-art alarm system, it wasn't enough for her that night. She was immensely relieved to have our company. She walked around the house with Mike, checking every window and door with him. When we called a moratorium on fussing and saw her up to her room, she was still edgy.

"To think he was next door all the time. Right there under the dock." She had a grim thought that crossed her lined face like a gas pain. "What if he had floated up?"

"Then we would have known what we know now, just sooner," Mike said.

Martha shuddered.

"Try to sleep," I said. "We're right here if anything happens. Don't worry."

She wasn't so upset that she had lost her sense of humor. She stretched up to kiss my cheek. "I've always been one to believe that I could take care of myself. But, now and then, it is nice to have a man around the house, isn't it, dear?"

I had Mike by the hand. I gave it a pat. "It's nice to have *this* man around."

Martha had found toothbrushes for us, and a razor for Mike. He shaved, and then got into a hot shower.

I folded my clothes over a flowered chintz easy chair and slid, naked, between the crisp sheets.

According to my watch, it was just after eleven. I dialed my home from the bedside telephone to make sure Casey had gotten in from Denver on time and intact. The machine came on after the fourth ring.

"It's me," I said after the beep. Then I gave Martha's number. "Call me if you have a problem. Otherwise, I'll talk to you in the morning. Lyle, the muffins were wonderful, but I think you were too skimpy with the pineapple in this batch."

Mike had given me the code so I could check his answering machine for messages from Lyle. I called Mike's number, pushed the code, and listened.

Mike's ex had called to tell young Michael she would be home late. Michael called. He was home safely but had left his calculus book in Mike's car. He needed it for class Monday morning. Lyle called. Casey's plane had arrived on schedule at nine, but Casey wasn't on it. At ten-thirty he had called again. He was still at the airport. No Casey.

I quit breathing.

Shaking so hard I almost could not hit the buttons, I dialed the airline, and got nowhere. I called the San Francisco airport and had Lyle paged. He must have been listening for the call, because he came right on the line.

"Where is she?" I asked.

"I don't know," he said, his voice tight. "Except she's not here."

"Did you call Scotty?"

"Constantly. No one answers."

"Lyle, will you stay there? If she missed her plane, she knows to page you."

"I'm not going anywhere."

I gave him Martha's number. Then I hung up and dialed Denver. Scotty, my ex, answered just as his machine kicked on. He fumbled to shut off the outgoing message, muttering crankily. Finally, he said, "Hello."

"Scotty, where's Casey?"

"What the fuck?"

"She didn't arrive in San Francisco."

"Shit, Maggie. We put her on the plane. Where could she be?"

"It was a nonstop flight, Scotty. If you put her on, one way or another, she would have to get off at the other end. She didn't."

He blew off some air.

"Did you actually see her get on the plane?"

He blew again.

"Scotty, answer me now, or so help me, I will reach through this telephone and rip off your face."

"Calm down, Maggie."

"I will not. You lost my daughter."

"Everything has a rational explanation."

"Give me one."

"Well, we didn't actually see Casey get on the plane. We had a very pressing appointment. So we dropped her at the airport an hour or so early."

"At the curb or at the gate?"

"Maggie, this child has more flight time than most commercial pilots. She can get herself from the curb to the departure gate unassisted. She only had carryons."

"But she didn't make it," I shouted.

Mike came running out of the bathroom at that point. "Maggie, what?"

"Casey is missing," I gasped.

"Where?" He wanted more, but I still had the telephone to my ear.

Scotty demanded, "Who's there with you?"

"The best sex I ever had." I hissed it. "Where is our daughter?"

"I'll check it out. I'll call you."

"Damn right you will." I gave him Martha's number and slammed down the receiver. I needed to scream some more. When I looked up at Mike, all that came out was: "She's only fourteen."

The telephone rang under my hand. I snatched it up.

"Lyle?"

"There's one sorry little teenager here," he said. "Want to hear her last words on earth?"

"Lyle, have I ever told you I love you?"

"Too often. Here she is."

"Mom?" Casey was really sweating. I could hear it.

"What happened?"

"The flight was overbooked."

"But you had a preassigned seat. You're an unescorted kid. They couldn't bump you."

"I volunteered. They gave me coupons for two free tickets if I took the later plane. Round-trip coupons. The next two times I go to Denver, it won't cost anything."

"Oh my God." I fell back on the bed.

"I only had to wait two hours."

"And during those two hours Lyle died a thousand deaths. Didn't you call?"

"I left a message."

"If Lyle was at the airport, how would he know you called him at home? Why didn't you page him?"

"Mom." She was crying. "I've already gone through this with Lyle, okay?"

"Not okay. Have you learned something here?"

"Yes," she sobbed. "I'm never going to Denver again."

"Go home," I said. "I'll yell at you some more tomorrow. And Casey?"

"What?"

"After you drop down to your knees and kiss Lyle's feet and beg his forgiveness?"

"What?"

"Call your father."

"Bye," she said, and then she was gone.

Mike was standing by the bed, naked except for a damp towel, face worried. "So?"

"She took a later flight."

"So she's all right?"

"She's fine. The rest of us may die of apoplexy. But she's fine. Just another example of independent thinking."

"Gotta nip that in the bud."

I shook my head. "Gotta get both of us cellular phones. Little hand jobs."

"We'll go shopping tomorrow."

Mike turned off the lights and slipped into bed beside me. For the third night in a row. I was getting used to rolling up against him in the dark. Three nights in a row. Three different beds. I was still juiced with adrenaline. We lay quietly in the dark, parallel bumps under Martha's sheets, letting our minds slow down. It was very companionable.

I reached out for his towel on the nightstand and used it to cool my face. "My God, Mike. It's so easy to lose them."

He shook his head. "No it isn't. You raise them right, they know how to take care of themselves. Casey's okay."

"I was seeing her on the street, like Pisces."

"Never happen."

Mike coughed and I felt him turn onto his side to face me.

"Casey's a good kid," he said. "You just have to tell yourself that she's at one of those ditzy ages and roll with it. Give her a couple of years and she'll be a normal human again. Like Michael. Now he's seventeen, the worst is over. He can pretty well be trusted to take care of himself."

"Michael left a message for you." I was glad he couldn't see my face in the dark, the smug grin. "He left his calculus book in your car and he needs it before school tomorrow."

Mike laughed softly. "What I just said?"

"Yes?"

"Cancel it."

Mike left before sunrise. He had to deliver Michael's book, then go home and dress for work. His shift officially began at seven-thirty.

I remember kissing him goodbye, I think. The kiss may have been part of the dream I had about swimming with the Ramsdales, Randy and all of his women. Pisces was there, and so was Hillary, dressed in a stiff party frock. The water was red and full of fish. I was glad when I woke out of it and found myself in Martha's bright, flowered guest room.

When I went downstairs—showered, hair brushed, teeth brushed, but wearing day-old clothes—Martha was in the living room chatting with a fresh team of Long Beach detectives. They were both very good-looking, sharp in suits and ties. I thought she was flirting again. I hated to interrupt her.

"Good morning," I said, hovering near the door.

"Good morning, Maggie. There's coffee in the kitchen. Are you hungry?"

"Not yet. I need to go tend to business, but I'll check in on you before I leave town this afternoon."

"Lovely, dear." She dismissed me with a cheery wave and went back to her detectives.

It was another beautiful, clear morning, full of newly washed sidewalk smells. Wind whipped the empty sail lines of boats at anchor, snapping their metal lanyards against mast poles, making music like wind chimes. A very zen and soothing music. Filled with a longing to stay, I walked back to the yacht club where I had left Mike's car. I wished for my running shoes.

I wiped heavy dew off the Blazer's windshield and got in. First thing, I checked Sly's bundle of stuff to make sure it was still intact—it was. Then I drove into Belmont Shore, following the scent of fresh cinnamon rolls. I had several bakeries to choose from, so I settled on the first one with an open parking space in front.

Fortified with rolls and coffee, I walked down the street to The Gap for a change of clothes. According to the sign on the door, I had ten minutes to wait until opening. I found a news rack and used the time to scan the local paper, the *Press-Telegram*.

There was a brief stop press on the front page about Randy and Hillary. Grisly murders, they were labeled. A cliché, but apt. The salient point the paper passed over was that even though both of them had their throats slashed, there was perhaps a two-month space between them. And not a word about Elizabeth Ramsdale.

When The Gap opened I went in and found a shirt on the sale rack, a loose-fitting thing with green-and-red parrots all over it. Casey would like it. I changed in the fitting room, paid, and was back in Mike's car before my half-hour investment in the meter had expired.

As I drove along the waterfront toward downtown, I began to think that I had a handle on how Hillary had been misplaced.

Nothing I had learned came even close to explaining how she had ended up on the street, but it was clear enough that long before reaching that point, she had dropped into the crack between what she needed and what the adults around her wanted. A big crack.

She had a wicked stepmother. So what? A lot of kids do. My Casey says she does. Very few stepchildren end up trolling for tricks.

As I put the sequence together, after Randy supposedly went abroad, Hillary had been at home, alone, with Elizabeth from around Valentine's Day until perhaps St. Patrick's Day. About a month.

I tried to imagine what would happen to Casey if she were stuck with Linda for a month or so. I felt an old rage begin to bubble up from its hiding place. Linda—and Scotty—had lost Casey after only two days. And not for the first time. A year or so earlier, Casey had been so upset by the situation at her father's house that she had put herself on a plane and come home. I figured that this back-and-forth-to-Denver routine now had two strikes against it. Strike three and we were headed to the judge for an amended custody agreement.

As hard as everyone tried to make things work, Casey had never lasted more than seven days with her stepmother. Hillary had lasted over thirty.

The first pay phone I came to, I stopped and called Lyle.

"How are things this morning?" I asked.

"Status quo. And what do you mean, I skimped on the pineapple? I don't put pineapple in my bran muffins."

"No wonder," I said. "Did Casey get off to school okay?"

"Oh yeah. She's one repentant little tyke. Even made her bed before school."

"Lyle, did she tell you why Scotty dropped her at the airport so early?"

"If I tell you, are you going to scream in my ear?"

"Probably."

"Just be gentle. According to Casey, it seems that Linda was done in by the baptism party, pooped. So she talked old Scotty into taking her out for dinner to some special place. They could only get an early reservation, so . . ."

"So they dumped Casey."

"That's one way of looking at it."

"Thanks, Lyle. I'll call Casey after school."

"How come you're not yelling? What's the matter?"

"I have to think about it. When I'm ready to yell, I'll call back."

"Lookin' forward to it," he chuckled. "The grant administrator on your film called a couple of times. She wants a progress report before she releases the next check. We haven't paid bills yet this month."

"I'll get in touch with her."

"When are you coming home?"

"I'm not sure."

"Take care of yourself, Mag."

"You, too. I'll bring you home a pineapple. Bye, Lyle."

I got back into the Blazer and rejoined the stream of Monday-morning traffic.

Amazing, I was thinking, how easily an intelligent, normally careful, affectionate father like Scotty could be yanked around. As if Linda were magnetic north and his dick were a compass. All evidence suggested that Randy had also been a pushover in that department.

My plan was to do some research in the local library, find out what I could about Amy Elizabeth Metrano. According to my map, the city's main library was in the Civic Center. It took me a couple of passes to get myself oriented on the right one-way street, but I managed to find the entrance of the public lot. And a parking space.

When I walked up out of the lot and into the sunshine, I was in a brick courtyard between City Hall and the library. There were a few homeless types sunning themselves on benches, but for the most part the people I saw were city workers going about their business, and schoolchildren with picture books under their arms. No one panhandled me.

Once inside the library, I asked for directions to the periodicals section. I found the shelves of newspaper indexes and looked up Amy Elizabeth Metrano in both the *Los Angeles Times* and the *Long Beach Press-Telegram*.

Through October 1983, when Amy disappeared, and continuing well into November, there was at least one, and frequently several, Amy Metrano stories daily in the first section of both papers. Around Thanksgiving the frequency of the stories began to taper off and move toward the back pages. I found irregular listings, a month or so apart, over the next year. Progress updates.

I made a list of the newspaper editions I wanted to check. By the time I had pulled all of the pertinent spools of newspaper on microfilm from the files, I needed a basket to carry them.

Reading newspapers on microfilm is a bitch. The image on the projection screen quivers constantly and wears out the eyes in a hurry. I learned a long time ago that it's best to make hard copies of the text I want and then read it all later. I staked out a working projector, went out to the circulation desk for a couple of rolls of quarters, then set to the dismal task in the dim light of the reading room.

After two hours, I had a thick sheaf of slick photocopies on the table beside the spools of microfilm. In the process, I had also gleaned a fair outline of the major events surrounding the disappearance of little Amy Elizabeth Metrano and the comprehensive, heartbreaking search that went on for months afterward. And I had a massive headache.

I boxed the spools of film, put them in the basket for refiling, gathered up my notes and copies, and went back out into the light.

It seemed to me that the press had been hung up on the details of the search and the questioning of a legion of possible witnesses. Most of the ink was spent on speculation, covering a huge range: all the way from the kid got lost in the woods to she was snatched by aliens. I saw sparks of creativity, but very little hard information.

The reportage was space-filling puffery and human-interest

sidebar because, in the end, the only facts were these: Amy Elizabeth Metrano, age four and a half, on a family outing to Lake Arrowhead, vanished during a game of hide and seek with her four older sisters. Period.

I went downstairs to the city directories and looked up George Metrano. In 1983, the year Amy disappeared, the Metranos lived on Sixty-eighth Way in Long Beach, George and Leslie and five minor children. Mr. Metrano's occupation was listed as pipefitter, hers as waitress. The house was rented.

Over the following nine years, the Metranos moved three times. Their last listed address was on Cartagena Street. He was listed as self-employed, she as homemaker. They owned the house.

I found a table in a quiet corner of the stacks and sorted through my copies, looking for Metrano biography. Anything suggestive.

According to the *Press-Telegram*, at the time of Amy's disappearance her father was an unemployed shipworker, laid off when the Long Beach shipyards cut back. Money was tight. The patrons of Hof's Hut, "a popular local eatery" where Leslie Metrano worked, had contributed to the search fund. The management had given her time off at full pay to tend to her family. The pipefitters' union was helping with old bills. The community, it seemed, had embraced the grieving Metranos in a number of decent and generous ways. People can be good. It was nice to be reminded.

While I had the directories out, I had looked up Randall Ramsdale, too. There was no city listing until late 1984 when Randall, Hanna, and minor daughter were in residence at the address in Naples. The occupation listed for him was investments. I interpreted that to mean coupon clipping.

Usually when people talk about a man, his job is maybe the second or third thing mentioned about him, after his marital status. No one yet had even suggested that Randy was inconvenienced by the need to work. If the way he lived was a fair indication, Randy had money. Lots of it. Ergo and to whit, a sluggard scion of the idle rich, as my father would have defined him.

I walked across the library to the government documents section and looked up birth certificates for both Amy and Hillary. Amy's I found. Hillary's I didn't. But only births in California are recorded. No one had said where the Ramsdales lived before they moved to Long Beach. Could have been anywhere.

As I walked back out toward the parking lot I felt I had made some progress. I at least had some interesting avenues to pursue.

Back in the car, I took the list I had made of Metrano family addresses and looked them up on the map. Sixty-eighth Way, where Amy had last lived with her family, was in North Long Beach. Using that address as a starting point, I charted the Metrano family's moves, a jagged line heading south, toward the water.

In California cities generally, the closer to the ocean, the higher the rent. I was increasingly bothered by something George Metrano had said that day at the morgue. If he was renting and out of work when Amy disappeared, how had he acquired the house he'd said he'd mortgaged to hire a private detective? The implication of that story was that they had spent every nickel, and then some, looking for their little girl.

The average house in Long Beach sold for nearly two hundred thousand dollars. I had read that gem while waiting for The Gap to open. I didn't know when they might have bought a house, but I calculated on the assumption that housing prices had not risen very much since the late eighties, and in some areas had actually gone down. So, I was thinking that even at a meager 10 percent down, with the double-digit interest rates that prevailed during the last decade, the monthly payments on a modest starter house would still have to run maybe two thousand dollars a month. Principal and interest only.

Not to mention that somewhere along the way, the unemployed pipefitter and the waitress had become self-employed.

I supposed that could mean anything from running a catering truck to, well, anything. The point was, it takes money to start a business. Had the community been that generous? Had there ever been an accounting of donated funds?

My destination was a straight shot up the freeway from downtown. As soon as I left the narrow coastal strip, the scenery changed in a hurry. The new high rises were like a ridge that dropped suddenly into the ugly, flat gray industrial sameness that spreads north from the harbor to Los Angeles. The neighborhoods that slid by on my right were worn-out, ticky-tacky tracts and low-rent apartments covered with indecipherable graffiti. I decided I should have held off before I speculated on the low-end cost of the Metrano house.

The Sixty-eighth Way address turned out to be a tiny duplex tucked up against the freeway, almost in Compton. The construction was early postwar, a single-story stucco rectangle with a flat white rock roof. Some time ago, it had been painted lime-sherbet green and the small front yard had been paved over.

Every house on the street had bars on the windows. Ten years ago, when the Metranos lived there, it might have been a safer neighborhood. But never, even when the small houses had been new, could it have passed as a *nice* neighborhood. What I saw was fast, cheap construction, the barest possible amenities provided. Rentals for the profit of absentee landlords.

The Metrano family had numbered seven in 1983. If there were even two bedrooms in either half of the duplex, they would be minuscule. My mind boggled at five little girls living in such tight quarters.

Working-class families expect, I think, to start out in simple circumstances. But Amy's eldest sister had been sixteen back then. The Metranos were not just starting out.

I unpacked a videocamera, and, through the car window, aimed it at the house. Then I drove away slowly with the camera still hanging out the window, getting some of the rest of the neighborhood and the cars zinging by on the elevated freeway that marked the end of the street. I had no idea what I would do with it, but it looked like I was working. If I had to report to the grant administrator, at least I wouldn't have to lie too egregiously.

At the corner house, an old man lugged a green garden hose out into the middle of his small yard and aimed a puny stream of water at the grass, holding it low in front of him in parody of exaggerated manhood. He wore Sears-blue work pants and a white T-shirt that had been washed so many times it was little more than gauze draped over his concave chest. The politically correct label for him would be Dust Bowl refugee. He would call himself an Okie.

When I waved, he waved back. Taking that as a good sign, I parked at his curb and got out.

Shielding his eyes from the sun, he watched me approach.

"You a reporter or the police?" he asked in a tobacco-ravaged rasp.

"Neither one," I said. "Exactly."

"I just bet you want to ask me about the little girl, though, don't ya?"

"Amy Metrano? Did you know her?"

"Sure did, her and her family." A gentle breeze lifted the fine wisps of his white hair, standing them like feathers. He had red skin-cancer blotches on his face. "Pretty little thing, she was. Used to ride her trike over with her sisters to borry a cup of sugar or an egg from my wife. Real polite little girls, every one of them."

"George and Leslie were good parents?"

"Well now." He gazed down the street toward the Metranos' duplex. "If I was to tell you the God's honest truth, I'd say Leslie was a real hardworking woman. Kept her kids clean. Kept them out of trouble. There was a passel of kids in that family, and things was pretty tight. But she did her best by them."

"You said *she* did her best. What about him, George?"

The old neighbor gave me a canny leer. "You're a smart one, aren't you?"

"I can hold my own."

"You said you wasn't a reporter."

"I used to be," I said. "Now I make films. It's different from reporting news."

"Films, huh? There was another fella asking about Amy just the last week or so. Not many folks is interested in the little girl anymore, but now and then someone comes askin'. But I start to think something is happening when two people come peckin' around. I never thought someone was makin' a movie about it."

"Who was this man?"

"Didn't say. 'Course, I didn't ask, neither. Like I didn't ask you."

"Can we back up to the question about George? What sort of father was he?"

The neighbor raised a bony shoulder. "He didn't use the belt, never heard him raise his voice. I guess you would say he was easy. Real easy."

"Easy meaning calm?"

"Meaning that." He nodded, shifting his hose to dribble over another spot of lawn. "And meaning it was hard to light a fire under him for anything, including picking up his lunch bucket and heading out the door for work in the morning. He was a nice enough fella. But he sure let the little woman carry a full share."

"Do you ever see them anymore?" I asked.

He shook his head. "Not since they moved out. Place has too many bad memories, by my calculation."

"When did they move?"

He thought about it, playing the water in a crystal arc. "Not long after they lost the little one. 'Bout Christmas, as I recall. My wife used to make them girls all a big gingerbread boy for Christmas, all frosted up with their names on them. That year she didn't bake nothin'. She just sat in her big old chair and bawled."

"May I speak with your wife?"

"Yes you may." He smiled slyly. "But I wouldn't be in no

hurry to do it, if I was you. You'll find her sittin' up there next
to Jesus."

"My condolences," I said.

He had liked his joke. "Next time I talk to Jesus, I'll have
him send them along."

"Thanks for your time," I said.

"Come by again."

I chuckled to myself all the way back to the car.

Ten minutes later, I found the second Metrano house. I had
been expecting something on the same economic level as the
duplex. Modest though it was, the Metranos seemed to have
made a step up from Sixty-eighth Way. Perhaps with the help
of friends, I thought.

The new house was in a tract built around a large green
park, down the street from Jordan High School. It was a good
location for a family with two girls of high school age. The
house wasn't large, three, perhaps four bedrooms, with a yard
behind. I thought it must have been a great relief for all of
them to have some space, some privacy. They had more room
and one fewer family member.

George Metrano hadn't told us when he had mortgaged his
house to pay the detective. Maybe it was this one.

I videotaped the front for a few seconds, and then went on.
What if the extra loan had been too much? What if they had
lost this house?

On that depressing thought, I searched out house number
three.

My concern, it turned out, had been groundless. The third
house was a giant leap up, a large, lovely custom-built home
with a brick wishing well in front. The neighborhood was well
established, big trees, lush broad lawns. An air of graceful
living.

From hardscrabble to blue-collar to *House and Garden* in ten
years. Upward mobility, the American dream, come to full
flower.

I thought about what the old neighbor had said. So, maybe

someone or something had lit a fire under George. Maybe all he had needed was a hand up. Still, the dream was sustained by two paychecks, his business, her job.

I had a jolt trying to visualize Leslie coming home in her Bingo Burgers blazer. It didn't work. Unless . . .

I needed to know who owned the burger franchise.

In some parts of the world, I hear, when times are hard and nothing brings relief, in desperation folks have been known to throw the occasional virgin into the volcano.

CHAPTER
12

I got back to the sports bar in the Shore during the midafternoon lull. There were only a few diehards drinking at the tables next to the windows. Oprah was on the big TV screens talking about how to hang on to a man once you get one. Her token shrink was saying that knowing how to strip was rule number one. A couple of waitresses sat at the bar with coffee mugs and talked back to her, offered advice of their own.

I found Lacy at a back table, alone, refilling catsup bottles.

Lacy was very young and very pretty, with a heart-shaped face framed by soft light brown hair. She looked like a wholesome, straightforward young woman. Not at all what I had expected. When I pulled out a chair next to her, she looked up at me with eyes that were red and puffy from crying.

"May I talk with you?" I asked, not waiting for an answer before I sat down.

"Are you police?"

"No. My name is Maggie MacGowen."

She wiped the neck of a bottle and screwed a cap on it. "This is not a very good time. Maybe another day."

"I'm sorry. I know it was a double blow for you, both Hillary and your fiancé."

"My fiancé?" She was aghast. "You mean Randy? Jesus Christ, Randy was never my fiancé."

"I thought he gave you a ring."

"He tried, anyway. I turned it down every way I knew how, but he kept getting it back to me. God, he was such a pain."

"I'm lost," I said.

Her face was now more angry than sad. "You heard all the gossip, right? That I was Randy's new babe? Well, I wasn't. I didn't want anything to do with him. I know it's not nice to say mean things about dead people. But he was a pig. I wish people would just shut their mouths."

"You've been crying."

"It sure as hell isn't for Randy," she seethed. Then her shoulders sagged and her face softened. "Hilly was a sweet girl. She didn't deserve what happened to her."

"How did you know Hillary?"

"I was her math tutor. Now and then she used to come in just to talk. She really didn't have anyone else."

"She needed a tutor? Was Hillary having problems at school?"

Lacy shook her curls. "Not really. She was such a smart little girl. They had her involved in so many things—music and sports, dance. It was a lot of stress. She got behind a little, that's all."

"Would her father come in with her to visit you?"

"No. Who are you? Are you a reporter?"

"Not exactly. I'm asking as a friend. I met Hillary last week, up in Los Angeles."

"Oh, my God." Her voice caught. "I heard about that. It's not true what they're saying, is it?"

I pulled out Guido's pictures and showed them to Lacy. "When I met her, she had been living on the streets for a while. She called herself Pisces."

Lacy smiled sadly. "Hillary loved to swim. I used to tell her she was born under the wrong sign. She should have been a Pisces. You know, the sign of the fish."

"When was her birthday?" I asked.

"Sometime in the fall. She was a Scorpio."

The date on Amy Metrano's birth certificate was March 10. I didn't know what the sign was for March 10.

Lacy had the pictures lined up on the table in neat rows. In most of them Hillary looked like a Central Casting teen hooker, very hard and brassy. Except for maybe one or two. There was one shot of her when she was looking at me over her shoulder. The way the light hit her face, the expression I caught, she seemed vulnerable and frightened. It was my favorite among the pictures, because it was most like the child Guido and I had talked to at Langer's Deli. Lacy had set that shot aside when she handed back the others. She ran her finger along the contours of the pale face.

"May I have this?" she asked. "I don't have any pictures of Hilly."

"Go ahead," I said. "Maybe I can find you something better."

She shook her head. "I want this one."

"Lacy," I said, leaning in toward her, "tell me what happened. Help me understand how a kid like Hilly ended up the way she did. Was she abused at home? Was it so awful for her?"

Lacy took a stiff napkin from the holder on the table and dabbed at her nose. "No, she wasn't abused. I mean, not in the way I think you mean. No question, Randy loved Hillary. Maybe he loved her too much. Randy was like this big spoiled brat. And she was one of his toys."

"In what way?"

She thought about it. "I guess what I mean is, she was like his favorite toy and he overwound her. You know how kids will do?"

"That's a good description. He put a lot of pressure on her?"

"Definitely." She nodded. "I told him that he should lighten up on her, let her quit some of her extracurricular things. But Randy said, oh no, Hilly can handle it. He paid me a lot of money to help Hilly get A's. With Randy, anything he wanted, one way or another, he got it."

"Did Elizabeth push, too?"

"I wouldn't know. I never met Elizabeth. I think she basically pretended Hilly didn't exist."

"I was told that you and Randy planned to run away together. Where did the story come from?"

"I think Randy started it. And I think he kind of believed it. I don't mean to sound conceited, but he really was obsessed with me. He told me he thought I would make a better mother to Hilly than Elizabeth did. He said I was more of a family person than his wife was. Like he was Ozzie but she was no Harriet.

"Then he shows up here one night when I was in the middle of a dinner shift, and tries to give me this big diamond ring. I wouldn't accept it, so he Fed Ex'd it to me. I did everything I could to get that ring back to him. I mean, it got ridiculous. Everyone kept telling me I should just keep it, or sell it. But I knew that if I did accept it, he would think he had paid my price and I was his. To Randy, everyone had a price."

"I spoke with the jeweler across the street," I said. "He told me you tried to sell the ring back to him. What changed your mind about keeping it?"

"He just would not take it back. Then there was Hilly."

"She wanted you to marry her father?"

"No, of course not. I didn't try to sell the ring until after Randy was long gone. Hilly came to me and she was just desperate. It was awful between Elizabeth and her. She wanted to talk to Randy, but no one would tell her how to reach him. He never called and he never wrote. I think she was getting real scared about him. He left awfully suddenly." She looked up at me. "I guess now we know why."

"You said Hilly was scared."

"Randy was on her all the time. I think I would have been relieved to have some space. She wasn't. She missed him. I guess he had sort of protected her from Elizabeth. What a bitch."

"Did she call family? Aunts, uncles, grandparents?"

"There was no one for her to turn to. All she had, she told me, was a godfather somewhere. She didn't even know his name, just that sometimes he sent her presents. I told her to go through her father's files and things and see if she could find a name or something. She did it. She didn't find a name, just some old cards addressed to her, no return address. And some other little things. We looked up a private investigator in the phone book. His ad said he specialized in finding missing persons. No lead too small. Hilly liked that, so we went to see him. He said maybe he could help, but he was expensive. So I sold the ring and gave Hilly the money."

"I heard it was a big ring. How much did this investigator cost?"

"A couple of hundred dollars. I got a lot for the ring. Thousands. I put the rest of the money aside in case Hilly needed it."

I think the future hit her all of a sudden. Lacy looked as if she was going to break down on me.

"What is the investigator's name?" I asked.

She pulled herself together enough to manage a wry smile. "Smith. Can you believe it? John Smith. Are you going to call him?"

"Do you think I should?"

Lacy's eyes were glassy with tears. She must have seen me as a bright blur in my parrot shirt. Yet her gaze was intense. She pushed aside the tray of catsup bottles she had filled so that she could move closer to me.

"What are you after?" she asked. Not a challenge. More an offer.

"I want to know Hillary. I want to know how she got lost. I've talked to a lot of homeless kids over the years. Most of them come from horrible, abusive backgrounds. Rich and poor. Sometimes you can save the kid from the street, help him heal. The thing you usually cannot do is send him home again. The streets are too often better.

"Right from the beginning, I knew Hillary was different. It

wasn't abuse that exiled her. It was something traumatic. After we found Randy, I began to wonder if she was afraid for her life."

"Why didn't she come to me?" Lacy hissed through clenched teeth.

"Maybe to protect you."

"Oh, Hillary." She folded her hands, but it didn't stop them from shaking. I covered her hands with mine and held them tight.

"You said you put the money from the ring aside," I said.

She nodded.

"Is there very much?"

Again she nodded, with some vigor this time. "More than I earned all last year working here. Why?"

"There's something you can do for Hillary."

"Like what?"

"Take the money and go away until this is over. Until we find out what Hillary knew."

The suggestion startled her. "I can't go away. I'm in the middle of my last college semester."

"Think about it. But don't think too long, Lacy. Don't tell anyone where you're going. Just go farther away than Hillary did."

CHAPTER

13

Mike's car sat at a funny angle, as if the front end had fallen into a sinkhole. Holes open up all the time in California—earth tremors, leaky water pipes, oil-land subsidence. They regularly swallow up bigger things than borrowed cars.

Thinking enough already, I muttered something that wasn't a Hail Mary and started to jog across the public lot behind the sports bar to see what had happened. The Nikon in my bag bounced against my side.

I don't know which I saw first, the long clean cuts in the front tire or the bill of a dark cap poking out from under the back bumper. I took a quick hit of adrenaline.

"You there," I shouted, and opened my stride to sprint. I was maybe five car lengths away. "Get away from that car!"

The rear tires blew then, pop, pop, in quick succession. A man scuttled away like a crab running from under a rock, a big man with a cap pulled low over his face, a loose Dodgers windbreaker, jeans. He must have been a good runner once, the way he was pumping, but he was long past his prime. I lit out after him.

We played cat and mouse among the cars in the lot, then he broke into the open and jackrabbited down a side residential street. He opened a lead, stretching fifteen yards to twenty before I turned it on some more. I wanted to keep him in sight, but I didn't want to catch him. I hadn't seen him drop his razor.

He was already breathing hard. My strength is endurance, not speed. So I kept a space between us and let him wear himself out. As long as I didn't lose sight of him before he ran out of gas, I knew I could run him down.

He sidestepped a convention of tricycles on the sidewalk. I vaulted over them, gaining maybe six yards on him. He looked back a couple of times, but I was too busy to catch his face.

I had my bag slung in front. As I ran, I attached a long zoom lens to my Nikon. Focus is tricky with telephoto lenses. You need to be very steady, because the exposure has to be relatively slow. When I had a clear stretch of sidewalk in front of me— no lawn mowers, no Rollerbladers—I said a Hail Mary in atonement, never knowing how much help I might need, and raised the camera to my eye.

I whistled my Candlestick Park earsplitter. Startled, he turned, and I snapped. To make sure he had seen what he saw, he looked again, the jerk. And I got him again.

By then I was gaining on him. I had to drop back, because the only way I wanted to catch him was on film. I slowed to keep the distance between us at a safe fifteen yards. I photographed his back, zoomed in on the Dodger jacket, got the label on his jeans. When he turned into an alley, he gave me a beautiful profile. Barrymore couldn't have been more cooperative.

I got to the mouth of the alley, and I stopped. There had been people on the street watching us, gawking. Some of them had talked to me, but I was too involved to hear them. As long as we were in the open, I felt sufficiently safe. The alley was a different equation.

With the camera in front of my face, holding my breath, holding my hand steady, I finished the roll on his retreating back. He looked back at least one more time for me. Bless his heart.

By the time he got halfway down the alley, he was really puffing, dragging his left leg a little. He ducked between two houses and I let him disappear. I had what I needed: smoking gun, smoking camera, same thing.

On my way back to the parking lot, I rewound the film, took it out of the camera, and reloaded. I felt good. I wasn't even breathing hard. There were a few sticky details waiting for me in the parking lot, but overall, I thought things were looking up.

I know how to change a tire. My father taught me before I got my driver's license. There really is nothing to it, once you get the spare out of the trunk and figure out which part is the jack and which is the handle. I have changed a few tires since. One time in a jungle in Honduras. At night. No big deal.

When I looked at Mike's car, though, changing a tire was not the problem. The problem was, where did I begin when I had one spare and four flats?

I called the Long Beach police. Then I paged Mike.

"I think it's a sex thing with this guy," I said when Mike returned the call. I was at a public phone next to a dry cleaner's, watching the police hoist Mike's Blazer with its slashed tires onto a flatbed tow truck. "He's impotent, so he has to deflate anything that's blown up bigger and harder than he is. Rafts, tires, whatever."

"Uh huh," Mike growled. "I think it's your balloon he wants to burst."

"He just wants to scare me."

"How's he doing?"

"He's doing just fine. I'm scared. He was so close to me, Mike. If I hadn't seen his hat, I might have tripped over him. Now I'm afraid for Lacy. He followed me. He must know I talked to her."

"Stay with the local cops until I come and get you."

"Don't come. Everything's under control. The helicopters are still circling overhead, the neighborhood is sealed off. Maybe they won't catch him this time, but they'll force him to lie low for a while."

"How will you get home?"

"Sergeant Mahakian from last night? He told me about a

cheapy car-rental place just up Pacific Coast Highway. He'll drop me by there as soon as they've finished tagging and loading your car. Then he's taking Lacy to the airport. She's really shaken." I paused.

"Do me a favor?" I asked.

"What?"

"Find out what George Metrano does for a living."

"He's a restaurateur. As in he has a couple of Bingo Burgers franchises."

"Why didn't you tell me that sooner?"

"Why should you care?"

"It might be worth your while to find out where he got the money to buy his franchises. And when."

"Maggie," Mike sighed. "Enough, all right? Stay out of it. Let the police do their job."

"Mike, I'm only doing my job." I felt stung.

"Yeah? Your job is anything you want to make it."

"I know. That's what I like about it."

"Go home, Maggie." His voice broke. "If I lost you . . ."

I couldn't let him say it.

"Listen to this," I said. "The film opens with Pisces on the street. That whole clip only lasts a few minutes, but it will run through the entire piece, intercut with footage of kids raised in privileged circumstances, like her. I think there are some beautiful insights there. I'll slip in pictures of her murderer in full retreat, among brief interviews with the Ramsdales' friends and neighbors about how charmed her life seemed. We'll end with the autopsy stills. What do you think?"

"Whose autopsy? Hillary's or yours?"

"Mike, all I am trying to do is come to some clear understanding of why this dear child ended up as she did. I'm not looking for her killer. I'm not interfering with the investigation."

"You already said he's following you." Mike sounded like my father when he lectured me. "He saw you on the street with the kid. And now he sees you all over town. You couldn't have done a better job of baiting him if you had put a hook in your mouth and tossed him the line."

"He never got near me," I said, defensive. "I know how to take care of myself."

"Right. Like you've done such a good job so far? Maybe you should run an ad in the local paper. 'Dear Mr. Killer, I got your ugly face on film twice now, but don't worry about me. I'm only doing my job. Love, Miz Maggie MacGowen.' Jesus Christ, Maggie. Get out of it."

"I'm sorry about your car, Mike. I'm having the bills sent to me. I'll be by later for my things."

"What does that mean?"

"I don't know," I sighed. I hung up, hurting in the general region of my heart.

Before the tow truck left, I retrieved Sly's stuff from Mike's front seat.

For fourteen dollars, including fifty free miles a day, I got a used Toyota with eighty-five thousand miles on it. All I asked was that it be in running order. And that's all they delivered.

Martha had told me she planned to go stay with a daughter in Scottsdale until things cooled down next door. She had a reservation on a late flight out of John Wayne Airport. I buckled Sly's stuff into the front passenger seat of the rented car and drove back over the bridge to check on her. I was afraid for her to be alone.

"Maybe you shouldn't be seen out here with me," I said to Martha when we were settling into chaise lounges on her front terrace. "Seems I'm being followed by a mad slasher."

"Seems you are, indeed," she said, her eyes bright, excited. "The man does have an affinity for rubber, doesn't he? Were you frightened?"

"I didn't have time to be frightened." I laughed, but my hand covered the thin skin of my neck.

Martha had poured me a tall glass of iced tea from a big pitcher. I took a gulp and nearly gagged. She hadn't warned me she was serving Long Island iced tea, not Lipton's. I managed to keep it down, but my eyes watered and my throat closed up.

"Tea go down the wrong way, dear?"

"Mmmhmm," I mumbled.

"Such a shame about Mike's car." Martha crossed her thin ankles. "He wasn't angry, was he?"

I had some breath back. "Not about the car."

"I see." She had that wise look on her face. "I do like Mike, Maggie. There's no bullshit about him, is there?"

"None."

"What are you going to do next?"

"Well." The Ramsdale house drew me. Several times, while I talked with Martha, I felt my attention drift toward the terrace next door.

"Maggie?"

"I'd give anything for another peek inside that house. Without Mike."

"You would get into trouble."

"I'm sure I would." I turned back to Martha. "Tell you what. You have some time to kill before your plane. I wonder if you'd mind telling me again what you told me yesterday about the Ramsdales, only this time on videotape."

She patted her hair at the sides and crinkled her face into a smile. "I always wanted to be a movie star. Mother wouldn't hear of it."

"You'll hardly be a star from this gig. But I'll send along any fan mail you generate."

"When shall we begin?"

"Soon as I haul out the gear. I'll bring a crew around another time to do it right. But I want to make a rough cut to show the grant people where I'm headed. It might be fun."

While I fumbled with tapes and half-charged batteries, Martha went inside to fix her makeup and change into dark slacks; she had heard the camera added ten pounds. When she came out, she waved a cigarette in a foot-long holder. Like Garbo.

"Nice touch," I laughed.

"I thought you would appreciate it." She draped herself on

the chaise, deflated bosom thrust forward, cigarette poised aloft. All she needed was a fur boa and a palm fan. "Where do we begin?"

"I'm not quite ready," I said, waiting for the cigarette to burn out. "Talk to me. How long are you staying at your daughter's?"

"Only a few days, I hope. I have to take my cat to the kennel. He hates the kennel." She looked over at the Ramsdale palazzo. "My cat put me in mind of something, Maggie."

"What's that?"

"Hillary's birds. We used to trade off—she would feed my cat, I would feed her birds when she was away. What I was wondering was, where are Hillary's birds?"

"I didn't see any birds in the house last night. Where did she keep them?"

"In her room."

"We only got as far as the master bedroom."

Martha was calm. "We have to do something. She loved those birds."

"I can call the police."

"It would take too long. Elizabeth has been gone quite some time. Those birds must be hungry by now. Wait here."

Martha's legs couldn't keep up with her torso as she rushed inside. She was leaning so far forward I was afraid she would fall on her face. But she didn't. She came out again in a moment, waving a key this time.

"Hanna gave me a key for pet-feeding purposes and emergencies."

"Why didn't you tell the police about the key last night?" I asked, close on her heels. "They destroyed the front door."

"What, tell them and spoil their fun?"

She walked straight down the side of her house and up to the Ramsdales' back door. The front door had been boarded over and sealed by the police. Though there was no warning attached to the back, I knew better than to open the door. So I let Martha do it.

The house was as we had seen it the night before, except that it was even lovelier with bright sunlight flooding through the tall windows. Martha hardly gave anything a glance, she was so intent on getting upstairs. When we reached the top, she was out of breath and dangerously red in the face.

"Why don't you sit down," I said. "Point out Hillary's room. I can check on the birds."

She pulled in a breath, an effort. "End of the hall. Last door."

I waded through the thick carpet. At Hillary's door, I hesitated before I turned the knob. Casey's room was sacred, private territory. Mothers by invitation only. In ordinary circumstances, Hillary, I was sure, would not have liked this invasion.

The bird cage sat opposite the windows on a filigreed white wrought-iron stand. It was covered. And silent.

I lifted the cover and saw them, three dead parakeets, one white, one blue, and one yellow. They had been dead for a long time. There wasn't very much left of them except bright feathers and brown bones.

I put the cover back and went out to report to Martha.

She was gone. Thinking about the open window the day before, the man with the cap that very afternoon, I panicked.

"Martha!" I called, running down the hall.

There was no answer. Just as I reached the landing, I heard her. Snoring.

I turned into the master bedroom and found her fast asleep on the big canopied bed with her hearing aids beside her. Too much exertion, or too much Long Island iced tea, had done her in. I let her be, grateful for a little time alone to go back and look through Hillary's room. The thought occurred to me that Martha was playing possum to that very end.

I left Hillary's door open so I could hear Martha if she stirred. Then I began.

Hillary's room was tidy, but otherwise it was a typical teenager's dream room. The girl had fulfilled the entire alphabet of a youngster's wish list: TV, VCR, CD, AM/FM, PC, as well as cable for MTV. Casey, overindulged by her guilt-ridden father in my opinion, didn't have half the electronic junk Hillary had acquired.

All of her treasures, from media toys to an impressive collection of china dolls, were housed in custom-built cabinets with glass fronts. Her swimming medals and trophies were formally arranged in their own handsome case.

It was so puzzling. Everything I had heard, everything I saw, told me that Hillary had been taken seriously. Perhaps she had been spoiled. Perhaps she had been pushed to excel, as Lacy said. The important element I found was that she was treasured, adored even. The neighbors loved her. The community cared for her.

I thought about the birds moldering under the cover in the corner, and I felt prickly all over. It wasn't normal to have left them in the house, dead.

When I was Hillary's age, I used to hide comic books, Harold Robbins novels, and other contraband in my pillowcase. I checked Hillary's pillowcases, her coordinated ruffled shams, the double dust ruffle, between the mattress and the box springs. Nothing there.

Her desktop was overly neat: textbooks lined up between marble bookends, fresh blotter, school-lined paper and stationery in folders, pens and pencils in a slotted tray, computer covered. Everything in place.

The drawers, however, were promising. They were crammed, as I thought they should be. Hillary had stashed away half-full tissue packs, broken swimming goggles, chewing gum and old holiday candy, used lipsticks, illicit notes from girlfriends written in goofy codes, hair ties by the handful, teenage romance paperbacks, and magazines with pictures cut out of them. The desk held exactly what it should have—her real stuff. But none of it helped me.

The books in her case ran to leather-bound classics. Hardly a spine was broken. Among them were her middle-school yearbook, *The Mustang*, and a gold-and-brown photo album. I took those two down and carried them over to the bed.

In her yearbook photo Hillary still had braces on her teeth. Her seventh-grade class had elected her best athlete. I managed to spot her in the Junior Scholarship Federation group shot, recognizing her from the pictures hanging on the walls of Randy's study. Wholesome, tanned, athletic; she did not look very much like Pisces.

I put the yearbook aside and opened the album. The first picture was labeled "Hillary's first day at school." Her face shone with expectation. She had a ragged-looking stuffed dog under her arm, but everything she wore looked new, crisp plaid dress with a big bow under the collar, shiny oxfords and ankle socks with lace trim. Her dark hair was cut in a stylish shag that came low over her forehead and brushed her cheeks. A pretty, happy child embarking on a new adventure.

Hanna was in some of the album photos with her, and so was Randy. Someone had carefully preserved a record of family outings, holidays, other important events in their lives. Just the three of them. No friends, no relatives. They were attractive, and from appearances, they were happy. At least they smiled a lot.

The story in the album ended with a printed card from Hanna's funeral and a pressed rosebud. There was no other album, no later photographs in the room. Nothing before kindergarten. Nothing after Hanna. I found that profoundly sad.

I slipped the kindergarten picture out of the album and tucked it into my pocket. Everything else I put away before I went into the adjoining bathroom.

Hillary had a drawer full of teenage makeup, the usual curling irons and electric curlers. In her medicine chest I found, among the half-used bottles of cologne and tubes of Clearasil, an unopened L'Oréal hair-tint kit, medium brown. Had I found hair color in my daughter's bathroom, I would have taken a good look at her roots to see what she had done to her hair and what she was trying to cover.

When I met Hillary, her hair had been bleached white-blond. In her yearbook pictures her natural hair seemed to be a rather dark auburn. The dye kit in her bathroom was unopened. So maybe she had bleached her hair before she left home. Maybe she and Elizabeth had fought about it.

Hillary's closet was full of trendy brand-name clothes. Casey had pouted for two days because I would not give her sixty dollars for a plain white cotton blouse that had a particular tiny label sewn onto the pocket. Hillary had three of them. And everything that coordinated with them, right down to the socks. I was grateful Casey wasn't seeing this wardrobe; I would have taken heat for weeks.

I didn't know exactly what I was looking for. Hillary herself, I suspect. What I found was an indulged yet typical young girl. And a medium-brown hair color kit.

I closed the closet doors and went out to check on Martha again.

I found her sitting up on the bed, fiddling with one of her hearing aids. She smiled at me, not a bit sleepy-looking. I picked up the copy of *Rebecca* I had left on the bed the night before.

"Where is the maid?" I asked.

"Elizabeth fired her ages ago."

"How many ages?"

"Why, right after she married Randy and moved in. He didn't like the idea, but she insisted she could take better care of her house than a racist expletive deleted."

"She was like that, was she?" I chuckled.

"Indeed," she said gravely. "Elizabeth was no Hanna."

"When did Randy marry Elizabeth?"

"No more than a year ago. I suppose you might say Randy and Elizabeth were newlyweds."

"Ah." I was surprised. "I thought they had been together longer. You said they fought."

Martha gave me one of her wise, make that wise-ass, looks. "Elizabeth entertained."

"She had a lot of parties?"

"No, dear. During the day. When Randy was out."

"Men?"

She shook her head. "Man."

"Why didn't you tell me earlier?"

"Why, you spent an entire day with Regina Szal. I was certain she had told you. How could she have left out that gem?"

"You saw him, the other man?"

"In passing."

"Describe him."

"He's a bit heavy, I would say. Top-heavy. I don't care for his type. I would describe him as oily. He must be very rich for her to prefer him to Randy, because she didn't choose him for his looks."

"When did this affair start?"

"I don't know, dear. I do remember noticing him right after the honeymoon. The first time Randy left the house, the friend paid a call. A very long call. Of course, since February, he has been here almost constantly."

Sly had said, "Her mother fucks at home and her father fucks a broad." Accurate, it seemed. At least half of it.

CHAPTER
14

John Smith Investigations was a cubbyhole office in a handsome downtown high rise. No reception room, no receptionist, and no one waiting ahead of me. Sitting in the client chair by Smith's desk, if I angled my head just so, I could see a tease of ocean shimmer in the single window.

"I know your findings are confidential, Mr. Smith," I argued. "But your client is deceased. I believe that something Hillary Ramsdale told you, or perhaps gave to you, might be crucial to the investigation into her murder, and her father's murder as well."

Smith sighed and gazed away in search of that bit of ocean view. He was maybe fifty, a burly, balding former cop in a good gray suit. He had a bravery commendation certificate on his wall next to a dartboard with J. Edgar Hoover's face behind the target. There was also a framed diploma from a storefront law school. It was a cheesy law school, and a cheesy frame. I thought it could only help his credibility if he took it down. After a few minutes of conversation, I knew he was smarter than his alma mater suggested.

"I don't know what to tell you," he said after thinking over my proposition. "If I want to give information to anyone, it will be to the police. You're cute as a bug, Miss MacGowen, but so was Mata Hari. How do I know who you are or what you're up to?"

"My best local reference is a Los Angeles homicide detective," I said. "The one I told you would be very upset if he knew I was here. I can hardly have you call him."

He steepled his fingers and propped his fleshy chin on them. "You understand my position, don't you?"

Smith had a tooth-sucking smugness I didn't care for. He leaned back in his big swivel chair so he could sight down his nose at my breasts. I wondered if the printed parrots on my shirt might have eyes just there to meet his stare. I didn't look down to see.

My mother's Texan cleaning woman always told me sugar attracts more flies than vinegar. In that case, it was spelled *sugah*.

"Mr. Smith," I cooed, "be a sport."

He chuckled wryly, a no sale. "Sorry."

I nodded, looking around, appraising the Spartan furnishings.

"You're in a high-rent district," I said.

"Address is important."

"Uh huh. The police won't pay you a dime for what you have."

"And you will?" He leaned closer to me across the vinyl veneer desk. "What you're asking me to do is highly unethical, thoroughly immoral, and probably illegal. How much do you think my eternal soul might be worth?"

"What is your standard fee?"

"Two-fifty a day plus expenses."

"I see," I said, leaning closer myself. "What if I hired you to continue with Hillary Ramsdale's case?"

"What if?" he repeated.

"If I were your client, I would ask to see the progress you have made to date."

"Go on."

"That's it," I said, sitting back. "How many more days do you think you would need to complete the job?"

"Tell me one thing. Why is it so all-fired important for you to get into this? You're not a relative. You hardly knew the kid."

I raised my palms. "Who else does she have?"

"You tell me."

The pictures in my bag were showing some wear. One more time, I took them all out, Amy and Pisces both, and spread them on the desk facing Smith. This time, I added the snap of Hillary heading off to kindergarten.

"Amy Metrano. Hillary Ramsdale. One is missing. One is dead. Why do their names keep coming up together?"

Smith sucked his teeth some more, thinking hard, studying the girls. Finally, he straightened up and looked me in the eye.

"My client relationship with Hillary legally ended when she died. Now that I have been informed about her death, I feel obligated to offer to the police anything I have that pertains."

"So why did we go through this little exercise?" I asked, testy.

"Just hear me out," he said. "If someone happened to be sitting in my office when I perused any such materials preparatory to forwarding them to the police . . ."

"What fee would that someone be prepared to pay you?"

"There is no fee for sitting in that chair, Miss MacGowen." He opened his long desk drawer and took out a legal-size envelope. "If you will excuse me, I will now inventory certain documents. I will trust you to respect their confidential nature."

I sat up again and watched him open the envelope. He took out two items. The first was a United States passport. The second was a yellowed newspaper clipping.

I picked up the passport, and he didn't stop me. I read the name inside: Randall Ramsdale. The last visa stamp was two years old. A big discovery for a little girl.

Carefully, I unfolded the brittle clipping. It was an early news article about Amy Metrano's disappearance. There was a photograph of her, and a plea for information. A copy of that same photo was on the desk in front of me, of Amy looking up with a clearer gaze than the newsprint version. It was a standard studio portrait, maybe a school picture, of a little blond girl with tight ponytails and a high forehead. Someone had taken a brown felt pen and colored in a shag hairdo.

Smith creased the clipping photo down the center, bisecting Amy's face. Then he laid it on top of Hillary's kindergarten picture so that the face was now half Amy, half Hillary. The two halves didn't match exactly; they were different sizes and taken from different angles. Hillary had a small dimple in her chin that Amy did not. But the eyes and the lift at the edge of the smiles were very close.

"Who drew in the hair?" I asked.

"I could only guess. This is the way Hillary gave it to me."

"Did she think she was Amy?"

"Hillary was a very confused little girl," he said. "She told me when she was little she had nightmares about people calling her Amy. It bothered her enough she told her daddy. Daddy said it was an old baby name for her. *Amie*, French for girl-friend, 'cuz she was his girlfriend. Kids generally buy the shit their parents sell them. So she named one of her dolls Amy and forgot about it like he told her to. Until she found the clipping. That made her keep looking. When she found her father's passport, she got really scared."

"That's when she came to see you?"

"That's it."

"What did she expect you to do?"

"Find her daddy."

"Meaning Randy Ramsdale?"

He nodded. "I did what I could, given what I had. Tell you the truth, I didn't take her real serious when she walked in. Men take off after fights with their wives all the time. Pretty soon they show up again. When they do, they're generally car-rying one of two things, a big bouquet of flowers or the name of an attorney. That didn't satisfy her. She needed to know, and she had my fee, so I went through the drill. I changed my mind about things when I found out Randy hadn't been using his credit cards. A man with his credit history doesn't suddenly cut up his cards. Not when he's away from home."

"Did you tell the police?" I asked.

"Tell them what? The Ramsdales had a fight?"

"Randy was dead," I said.

"How were we to know?"

He was right. I shrugged off my annoyance.

"What about the clipping?" I asked.

He gave me a crooked smile. "Would you believe the Metranos still have an information hot line for Amy?"

"I know. I called it. Breaks your heart, doesn't it?"

"I guess. I called it, too. I asked Mr. George Metrano why Randy Ramsdale would keep an old news clipping about Amy. He said a lot of people had been interested. Maybe Randy just forgot to throw it away."

"He didn't jump on it?"

"Yes he did. With both feet. I set up a meeting with him and the girl at my office, but he didn't show. Called later and apologized. Said he wrote down the time wrong, or some such shit."

"Did they ever get together?"

"Not in my presence. I assume they both had access to the telephone directory, though. They could have set up something themselves. I warned Hillary not to see him alone for any reason. I also told her she needed an attorney, pronto. That stepmother seemed to have been left with custody of all the community assets. I thought the kid needed someone to look after her interests."

"Did she take your advice?"

"Don't know. I saw her exactly twice. I called to make a follow-up report. I got the stepmother. She told me Hillary's father had come and fetched her."

"You believed her?"

The question made him very uncomfortable. I was beginning to feel like the schoolmaster grilling a naughty child. Smith very obviously was being pricked by the topic, as if he hadn't done his homework and was being asked to recite from it.

He took in a deep breath and finally looked me in the eyes. "I didn't believe or disbelieve. From the very first, I had been expecting Daddy to come home. I thought, as soon as the old guy got his rocks off with the new woman, he would get back to the details. Like the kid."

"Small detail, huh?"

He shrugged. "Hillary called sometime after, left a message on my machine. She just said everything was cool, and thanks."

"You're sure it was Hillary?"

"At the time I was."

"And that was it?"

"The end."

"You have been a fount of information, Mr. Smith. I'm not sure what to do with it, but I'm sure it will help."

"Are you?" He had gazed off toward the window again. "To tell you the truth, I'm thinking I didn't earn the money Hillary gave me. I was looking for her daddy. But I'm thinking I should have given the Amy angle more attention. Where I let her down is, I didn't think a kid with her background could have a problem as big as hers was. I guess I never did take her sufficiently serious."

I gathered up the pictures again and put them away. "Just one more question."

"Shoot."

"When did Hillary first come to you?"

"I can tell you." He flipped through the appointment calendar beside his telephone. "March. March fifteenth."

"That fits."

He thought that over for a moment. Then he looked back at the parrots on my chest.

"May I call you Maggie?"

"Most people do."

"You're an attractive woman, Maggie," he said, seeming to have revived some spirits. "But more important, I think you have a fine mind. I admire a woman with brains."

"Thanks. The point is?"

"I'd like to kick this all around some more with you. Put together everything we have, and really get down and dirty. I thought that if you didn't have plans for dinner, we could go up to my place, order up a pizza. See what two good minds can do together."

I stood up and hefted my bag. "I appreciate the offer, Mr. Smith. If I may call you Mr. Smith. I'm sure we could come up with something if we put our heads together. But I must decline your kind invitation. I would not want to be responsible if something happened to you."

He stood up, too. "Don't worry about me. I think I could go head to head with this razor-happy asshole."

"Perhaps you could. That isn't where the danger lies, however, Mr. Smith. If I read you correctly—and my fine mind is a real good interpreter of innuendo, subtle or otherwise—the danger would come in the form of the homicide detective who is expecting me for dinner."

He had the grace to laugh.

CHAPTER

15

L.A. freeways don't have a true rush hour, only times when the engorgement of cars reaches critical mass. Like constricted bowels. I headed north too late in the day to fit in stops at MacLaren Hall and Guido's if I was going to see Mike at any reasonable hour. And getting to Mike was my first priority. As it was, the forty-mile trip took two hours and at least three years off my life.

When I opened the door of Mike's condo I was in desperate need of strong drink, a hot bath, and some quiet before we got into anything. Mike was generally fairly easygoing, but from the tone of our last conversation, I expected him to be angry. A reflex, I guess. I was still in recovery two years after a long marriage to a human powder keg, still walking around with a lot of protective armor, according to Mike.

The living-room lights were turned down low. Ray Charles was on the CD player, loud enough to appreciate, but only just. Mike was stretched out on his back on the gray carpet wearing white sweats, a black pillow under his silver head, his eyes closed, hands resting on his stomach with a glass of white wine balanced between them.

I closed the front door as softly as I could, not wanting to disturb him. I had disliked his ex-wife's gray-and-black decorating scheme until I saw Mike lying there in the middle of it. The tones of his hair and skin blended so perfectly with the room that I couldn't decide whether his wife had decorated to show him off or had tried to make him invisible among the furnishings. Domestic camouflage.

I had my camera in my hand without really thinking about taking it out. More light would have been nice, but I opened the aperture all the way and took a couple of hand-held time-release shots. The texture would be interesting, I thought, if the pictures came out at all.

I was leaning over Mike for a face shot when he wrapped his fingers around my ankle and opened his eyes.

"The late Maggie MacGowen," he said, mellow and smiling.

"Hold still," I said.

"When you're in the room, I can't hold still. You move me." His hand slid up my leg inside my jeans.

"Keep talking," I said.

"What are you doing?"

"We have Whistler's mother, *A Study in Gray*. I thought it was time for Whistler's father."

"My kid's name is Flint. Does that make a difference?"

"Not to the artist." I reached down for his glass of wine, but he held on to it.

"You want the wine? Make me an offer."

"How about a trade?" I took *Rebecca* out of my bag and showed it to him.

He sat up enough to look at the title, then he dropped back down. "No deal. I read it in grade school."

"Maybe it's a clue. Rebecca sailed away and never came home again. Like Elizabeth Ramsdale."

"Still no deal." He massaged my ankle. "We located Elizabeth down in Cabo San Lucas. Arrived two days ago."

"No lie?" I knelt on the floor next to him.

"No lie."

"Tell me about it." I reached for the glass again, but he held it away.

"One thing at a time here." He slid his hand into the crook

of my knee. "I believe the bidding is still open on this fine, vintage, supermarket plonk."

I leaned over him close enough to feel his warm breath on my cheek. "I bid one kiss."

"I'm bid one kiss. Do I hear two?"

"Nope. My offer stands at one."

"Sold. If it's a good one."

I kissed him. A good—no, a magnificent—one. His fingers moved slowly up the inside of my thigh, spreading uncontrollable heat like a pot boiling over on the stove. Reduced to a quivering mass, I sat back on my heels to catch my breath, trapping his hand between my legs. His eyes were still half rolled back in his head when he passed me up his glass.

"Thank you." My voice sounded husky, as if I had inhaled some of that heat. "What's the next item in your catalogue?"

He raised his head into my lap. "Our next offering will cost you."

"That's all right." I stroked his shiny hair and his fresh-shaved cheek. "In the currency of this auction, I'm loaded."

"Bidding opens at one shirt with birds all over it."

"How do I know what you're offering is worth even one button of this fabulous shirt?"

"It's worth it." He tugged out my shirttail and tickled my belly with his little cookie-duster mustache. I giggled, and he grinned up at me. "In point of fact, I think I started bidding too low. Now it will cost you the shirt and the pants, too."

"I don't bid on closed lots," I said. "Show me what you have."

His hands were soft on my bare abdomen. "I found Hanna Ramsdale's mother."

"Alive?"

"Alive as anyone can be in Pasadena." He pulled the shirt off over my head and bent forward to kiss the lace covering my left breast.

"Wait," I said, pushing against his shoulders.

"No." He grinned. "Prepayment required."

I stripped off my pants and handed them to him. "Payment in full. Now, talk to me."

"Maggie." He pulled me down onto the floor on top of him. On the way, he undid my bra. "Do you really want to talk now?"

"No," I whispered into his ear. He was hard against me. I wanted him so badly that the room around us disintegrated into a vague, warm blur and he was the only solid reality. He helped me slip off the bra.

"What I really want," I said, "is to make mad, passionate love to you. Right here. Right now."

"Bidding opens at one kiss."

I paid. He delivered.

Gathering clouds obscured the moon. The canyon below Guido's house was a velvet abyss that opened beyond the gravel shoulder of the road and swallowed Mike's high beams.

"It's quiet up here," Mike said.

"If I were ever to live in L.A., it would have to be somewhere like this. Somewhere away from the city."

In the green light from the dash, I saw the strangest look cross his face; pain, glee—I couldn't read it.

"What did I say?" I asked, touching his hand on the wheel.

"It's good to know you've given some thought to moving down."

"Just making conversation. I said 'If.' "

"There are a lot of canyons around L.A. We could probably find you one a helluva lot better than this."

I felt another sort of canyon open up under me.

"Guido's driveway is right there on the left," I said. "It's easy to miss. Go slow."

"Can't go any slower, Maggie." He turned up into the steep drive. "If we go any slower, we'll stop dead."

"I work long hours," I said. "Sometimes I'm away from home for a couple of months at a time."

"Guido seems happy with his nine-to-five. Casey would be real pleased to have you home more."

"We're fine with things as they are."

"Land somewhere, Maggie." He stopped in front of the garage

and turned off the lights. "Casey will only be with you four more years before she goes away to college. Make the best of it."

"What are you saying? I neglect her?"

"No. You've done a great job with her. What I want to say is, I retire in three years. It isn't so long. Come, you and Casey, stay here with me for three years. Then I'll go anywhere you say. I'll live with you in a tent in the middle of the Sahara, if that's what you want."

I turned around in my seat to face him. "Are you proposing?"

"Don't make it sound like a threat," he said, laughing softly. "The last six months have been the worst years of my life. Maggie, I don't ever want to lose you again. I know marriage scares you. As long as we're together, I don't care whether we're married or not."

"I would drive you crazy, Mike."

He laughed. "You already do."

"There are so many complications." I opened my car door, misjudged how far down the ground was, and stumbled a little. "So much to think about."

He shut his door after him. "If you want something bad enough, you can overcome the complications."

I saw Guido spying on us from the window in his front door. When I waved, he came out onto the porch.

"Hello, children," he said. "What's new?"

"This and that." Mike squeezed my hand. "What's new with you, Guido?"

"My friend the computer nerd generated an interesting picture for us." He led us inside. "Until I saw it, I hadn't realized the political implications of the case."

Guido was grinning. I knew we had to let him play his joke to the end before we could move forward. He winked at me.

"You look good, Maggie," he said. "Even better than yesterday. You been running or something?"

"Why?"

"Well, your hair's a little damp in the back there. Thought maybe you ran all the way over."

"I just got out of the shower, Guido," I said, glaring a little. "So did Mike. You want a play-by-play?"

He winked again. "Why should I care?"

"Indeed," I said. "Can we see the picture now?"

"On the table."

Mike lifted a file folder from the coffee table and opened it. He looked, grimaced, and passed it to me.

I looked. I sighed. "Very funny, Guido. Richard Nixon was driving the red Corvette I taped?"

"Sorta." He bounced up next to me and peered over my shoulder. With his thumbnail, he outlined the face. "See this furriness along the jaw, around the eye sockets, and around the hairline? The computer couldn't read it. My nerd and I speculate that your man—or your woman—was wearing a mask."

Mike put on his glasses to look closer. "Son of a bitch."

"Surely someone would have noticed," I said.

"I didn't. You didn't." Guido shrugged. "Anyway, this is L.A. If you saw some guy wearing a mask, you wouldn't think a lot about it. Especially a guy trolling for poontang in a car like that 'vette. Looking for a little anonymity."

"What do I owe your nerd?" I asked.

Guido shook his head. "*Nada.* He assigned this as a class project. They got a big yuk out of it. Helped his image a lot. If he gets a date with a student, I think he should owe you."

"Good, because I have something else you might pass along to him." I handed him the two rolls of exposed film I had in my bag. "I shot one of these rolls of the slasher this afternoon. The other one is Mike. I didn't mark them, so I don't know which is which. Would you develop them all for me?"

He frowned. "Okay. But there's a one-hour processor down on Cahuenga. Wouldn't that be faster?"

"Here's the problem," I said. "I never got the subject's full face."

"Mike's or the slasher's?" Guido grinned.

"I got all of Mike, Guido. Buck naked, in the moment of ecstasy."

"Maggie!" Mike blushed. "You did not."

I turned to him. "I was simply offering Guido some incentive. Next time, though, I am taking the camera to bed with us."

He laughed. "When was the last time we made it all the way to the bed?"

Guido was comically round-eyed.

"So, Guido," I said, "the program is this: I want you to go through every shot and isolate the face parts. Then I want you to reassemble them and make a whole face for me."

"Like a jigsaw puzzle?"

"Something like that. Can you do it?"

"We can do something, my computer nerd and I. Something beyond cut-and-paste." He looked down at the film in his hand, and I knew the film was talking back to him. Guido sometimes seems really hyper. He isn't, exactly. It's just that when his mind is working on overdrive, the excess electricity he generates makes him bounce. All the springs in his taut body cannot be stilled. He could never play poker.

I grabbed his hard forearm, anchoring him like the string on a helium balloon.

"It's interesting, isn't it, Guido?" I said.

"Interesting? God, there's an understatement."

Mike frowned. "I don't get it. I mean, it's pretty damned amazing Maggie might have this guy's face on film. But that isn't what you mean, is it?"

"What do you see, Guido?" I asked.

"Same as you. A collage. Fragments cut and pasted together. In the end, when you sort it all out, what will you have? The truth? Or another mask?"

"Or another sort of mask?" I said. "I believe the only naked truth lies under those blurry edges your computer nerd couldn't read. When you stitch me together a new face from this film, are you going to show me what's under the blur, or just more obfuscation? What'll it be, truth or a new lie?"

"Just don't mess up the negatives," Mike said. "They're evidence."

"Trust me," Guido said. "How much time do I have?"

"None," I said. "We need it now."

"Let me call my friend and see if I can lure him back to campus." Still bouncing on his springs, Guido went to the next room to use the telephone.

Mike was giving me a dark look. "You two were talking in some sort of code. What's up?"

"Basically, the structure of this film project. More than that, though, it's the whole question of what happened to Hillary." I let out a breath and studied the grotesque parody of a face lying on its manila folder on the table. Then I turned to Mike.

"When I moved into my house," I said, "there were ten layers of wallpaper on the kitchen walls. I was interested in seeing the old patterns, to get some idea what the kitchen used to look like, what I might try. I started stripping it. But every time I had cleared away a goodly patch and could almost get some effect, I would break through to the next layer, and the next. Each layer obscuring the others. So you know what I did?"

"Tell me."

"I said fuck it. I rented a steamer and stripped the walls down to the plaster."

"Seems consistent with the woman I know and love." He smiled. "What is the point of this story?"

"This Hillary thing is like that, layers. Peel one away, find another."

"Most police work is like that." He waved a dismissive hand. "You never get the whole picture. You just hope for enough pieces so you can put the bad guys away."

"We were set up, Mike."

"How?"

"You said it last night when Randy was found. We were meant to find him. There are two overlapping layers here, two chronologies of events. The first is the chronology of discovery: Hillary is found first, then Randy. Then there is the chronology of death: first Randy, then Hillary."

"Right. So?"

"So, it's time to rent a steamer, Mike. Find the bare walls."

"Where do you think you'll find this steamer?"

"Hanna Ramsdale's mother."

He nodded with a sort of weary resignation. "I have to talk to her. She probably hasn't been told her granddaughter is dead."

"She should know. What were you waiting for?"

"Daylight, I guess. I hate bringing bad news to old ladies."

Guido came back just then.

"All set," he said. "I'm meeting nerdo at the computer lab in fifteen minutes. It's a twenty-minute drive, so I'm out of here. Maggie, how do I reach you?"

"Mike's machine."

"*Mi casa es su casa.* Stay here if you like. Bye." He ran, or rather he sprang, out the front door and banged it behind him.

"Shall we raid the refrigerator?" Mike said.

"Let's get something on the way."

"On the way to?"

"Pasadena. Isn't that where Hanna's mother is?"

CHAPTER
16

Somewhere between Highland Park and South Pasadena, Mike's pager went off. He unclipped it from his belt and handed it to me.

"Can you read it?" he asked. If he put his reading glasses on, he wouldn't be able to see beyond the hood of the car.

I had to wipe double-cheese Bingo Burger slime from my hands before I could take it. I punched the read-out button. "Your office," I said.

He pulled off the freeway at the next exit and found a public telephone. I waited in the car.

Clouds had moved in off the ocean until the moon was only a glow above the dense canopy. The air was appreciably colder and damper than the bright day promised. I pulled my blazer close and snuggled down into the corner of my seat. "The Ride of the Valkyries" blasted from the radio.

I watched Mike's straight back under the blue light from the telephone booth. He shifted from one leg to the other, agitated as he spoke. I felt uneasy. The dark, I guess, and Mike so exposed in the one well-lighted spot on the block of industrial warehouses surrounded by razor wire. He made a good target for anyone so inclined. For no reason perhaps other than habit, his free hand covered the semiautomatic pistol at his belt, fiddled with the release snaps on the holster. Maybe it was just something to hold on to.

I worry about Casey all the time. A sort of free-floating maternal anxiety based on nothing more concrete than a wild imagination and too much experience with the range of possibilities the big world offers.

I don't know when it happened, but I realized I had started worrying about Mike, too. He's bigger than I am, and a whole lot tougher. That had nothing to do with how I felt. I wanted him to duck out of the light, make himself less vulnerable. Standing there with his silver hair shining, he reminded me of Pisces under the moonlight. The night before she died.

Mike made a second call, argued with whoever answered at the other end. I unwound my arms and had just stepped out into the chill night air to be with him when he turned and motioned for me to come.

"What is it?" I asked, shivering.

"Some card calling himself John Smith says he needs to talk to you. Says you gave him my number. You want me to shine him on?"

"No." I jogged over. "Honest to God, that's his name. He's the PI I told you Hillary hired."

Dubious, Mike handed me the receiver.

"Mr. Smith?" I said.

"Is that the cop who'll use me for target practice?" he asked.

"If you get out of line," I said. "What's up?"

"I earned a little of my retainer this evening, did some checking on the fortunes of George Metrano."

"And?"

"And there is no fortune. He's one step away from filing Chapter Eleven, bankruptcy."

"The Bingo Burgers I saw looked like a booming concern," I said.

"It is. Problem is, he blows it away faster than he rakes it in."

"Blows as in blows it up his nose?"

"No, worse. His addiction is the craps tables in Vegas. He

lost a bundle about four years ago and went into court-ordered reorganization that time, too. There were a couple of check-kiting charges in the mess. The judge gave him probation if he'd hitch his star to Gamblers Anonymous. Seems he's been AWOL from meetings, though. He's signed notes on everything he owns again to pay off the casinos. The family home is being foreclosed on."

"Did you talk to him?" I asked.

"No. The little woman says he's out. I don't know if that means he's out to creditors or he's gone away."

"Interesting. Very interesting. Anything else?"

"I'll let you know."

"Thank you, Mr. Smith," I said. "You're a gem."

I closed the connection and pulled out my notebook.

"What did he say?" Mike asked as I punched in my credit card numbers and dialed the Metranos.

"George gambles big-time. He's losing everything he owns," I said.

"Ah," he breathed. Mike is a quick study.

Leslie Metrano's soft voice came on the line, quavering. "Hello?"

"Hi, Leslie. It's Maggie MacGowen. Did you have a chance to show my pictures to George? I've been anxious to get his reaction."

"He isn't home, Maggie. He's away on a fishing trip."

"He's fishing now? With all that's going on?"

"He had to get away."

Away from what? I wanted to know. But she seemed rather fragile. I settled for: "When do you expect him?"

"I don't know." Her voice broke.

"Are you all right?" I felt like a heel, as if I were lying to her. She was a sweet woman. I was thinking she deserved a break.

"It's just . . ." She seemed to haul herself together sufficiently to speak. "I expected him back by now. Maybe he had trouble with the boat. I wish he would call me."

"Where did he go?"

"Off Baja, he said."

"Alone?"

"I don't know." She started to cry.

"When?"

"Saturday night."

"Is anyone there with you?"

"My daughter and her baby," she sobbed, so forlorn she sounded like a lost child herself.

"I'm sorry, Leslie," I said. "I'm really sorry."

"I have to go now. I have to go collect the night receipts."

"No." I reacted hard, nearly shouted. "Don't go. Get someone else to do it. Or call the police and get an escort."

"You're scaring me."

"I hope so. Is it a lot of money?"

"Yes."

"Does George need money?"

"George always needs money. What are you saying, that he would steal from me?"

"He's already stolen your house out from under you. What's left?"

"He wouldn't hurt me. I have to go, or I start paying my night manager overtime."

Mike had been listening to my end of the conversation. I handed him the receiver. "Make her understand."

"Understand what?"

"George took his boat and went fishing off Baja. She hasn't heard from him since Saturday. Now she's on her way to pick up the night receipts from her burger places. It's a lot of money."

Mike was persuasive. I hoped Leslie was as bright as she seemed. I heard him do his tough-cop windup to get her attention, then he gentled his pitch. By the time he hung up, he sounded like someone's dear old dad. Then he immediately dialed the Long Beach police. He should go on the stage. Without more than a breath between roles, he switched from Dad to one of the big guys, using police boy-talk to get a promise of an escort dispatched to the Metrano house, pronto.

When he hung up the second time, he turned and grabbed

me by the arm. "John Smith, huh? Met a guy by that name in a motel once."

"Should we go down to Long Beach?"

"And do what?" He walked me to the car and opened the door for me. "The locals will take good care of her."

"Elizabeth is in Cabo San Lucas. Cabo is at the southern tip of Baja."

"Yeah. And that's a long way from Long Beach."

"It begins to come together," I said.

"Let's go talk to Grandma."

The address Mike had for Hanna Ramsdale's mother was almost San Marino, in the rocky foothills of the San Gabriel Mountains. We found the house on a narrow, winding street of gracious old mansions set in vast grounds. Mike turned into the drive with Sinclair on the mailbox in shiny brass letters.

The house was old enough to be classic, 1920s I guessed. It had been built to conform to the rugged slope behind it, a spill of white Mission Revival cubes and turrets topped with red tile that rose out of a broad hollow, like a Moorish castle in a pop-up book. Up the bank behind the house, cacti and spidery sage were artfully planted among huge granite boulders, picked out by spotlights; gray-green sentinels in the night.

Mike pulled into the circular drive and stopped beside a massive saguaro.

Mrs. Sinclair—Virginia Sinclair, Mike told me—answered the door herself. I don't guess ages very well, but I figured she was at least as old as the house. Her body had outlived its hide: the thin, patchy skin was stretched so tight across the strong bones that a big smile would surely break it. But we seemed to be in no danger of that occurring. She reminded me of some of my mother's friends, stiff academic wives who shudder at slang and dance an even-sided box step at faculty teas without swaying their hips. I know from experience they make good targets for spit wads shot from under refreshment tables. They never react when they get hit.

Mrs. Sinclair did not know we were coming. It was ten o'clock and she wore a high-buttoned white blouse, a pleated skirt, and a cardigan with brass buttons. Her shoes were good leather, low heels. Not new but well-kept. Everything about her seemed old but well-kept. She was tall and imperious, leaning lightly on a dog-headed cane.

Mike showed her his ID. "We want to talk to you about your granddaughter," he said.

"My granddaughter?" Her voice was deep, almost masculine. She stood as if guarding the door against us. "You mean Hanna, my daughter. Hanna is deceased."

"Not Hanna," Mike said. "Hanna's daughter."

Virginia Sinclair seemed confused. "Hanna had no children," she said.

"Hillary Ramsdale," I said.

"Hillary," she said, a light coming on. "Of course. But Hillary wasn't Hanna's daughter. She was my son-in-law's cousin, I believe."

I looked over at Mike, feeling prickly all over.

"May we come in?" Mike said.

"Of course."

Mrs. Sinclair moved aside for us to enter. She led us through the turreted foyer and into a high-ceilinged sitting room furnished with dark Mediterranean antiques. The room was beautiful the way a museum room is beautiful. And, like a museum, it was oppressive, a monument to long-dead craftsmen. And perhaps occupants as well.

Over the mantel hung an almost life-size oil portrait of a younger Mrs. Sinclair, seated in the same ornately carved chair she now sat down on, sitting with the same straight posture, her hands resting on the head of the same cane, re-creating the pose. It was eerie, because Hanna was in the portrait with her, standing beside the chair with her hand on her mother's shoulder. Looking at Mrs. Sinclair, an older echo of the woman in oils, I had the sense that her daughter stood there beside her. Mike saw it, too, and squeezed my hand.

Hanna was beautiful. She resembled her mother, though the features in the second generation had been refined, the bones cast more delicately, the contours rounded. Perhaps the genes had been overrefined, and the softness about her was symptomatic of her precarious health.

I sat down opposite Mrs. Sinclair, on a high bench with a carved back and an unforgiving cushion. My feet did not quite reach the floor.

Mike stood beside me with his hand on my shoulder, mocking the scene she had set, perhaps to wrest control from her.

"Tell us about Hillary," he said.

"Where is the child?" she asked.

I felt sour acid rise in my throat. "Hillary is deceased."

"I see." Her high, smooth brow drew into a frown. "She seemed a healthy girl. A bit strong-willed, perhaps. But then that is a Ramsdale family trait."

"Hillary lived with Hanna and Randy," I said, drawing her back to the topic.

"Yes. I don't recall the exact circumstance of how that arrangement came to pass. Something about a boating accident involving her parents. The Ramsdales were boat builders, you know. Clipper ships originally, I believe. More recently, yachts."

"We didn't know," I said. "We had no idea what Randy did for a living."

She smiled behind her veined hand. "Randy played for a living. The family paid him handsomely to stay away from the business. Very wisely, in my opinion."

Mike sat down then beside me. "You didn't approve?"

"I did approve. Most fully. My Hanna had a heart problem, you see. We didn't expect her to live as long as she did. I give all credit to Randy. He was a man with uncommon determination. He would have done anything humanly possible to make her happy, to give her a life."

"Did Hanna want a child?" I asked.

"Oh, yes." She raised her sharp chin. "A child of her own was of course impossible. That's why Randy took on a little ward. Hanna doted on Hillary. And such a pet she was."

I looked at Mike. "A pet?"

"Pretty girl," Mrs. Sinclair said. "Very sweet. I'm sorry to hear she died."

"How old was Hillary when Randy brought her home?"

"Just school age. Otherwise it would have been impossible for Hanna to manage. An hour or two in the afternoon, stories after dinner. Anything more would have destroyed her."

I had finally reached the bottom of the roller-coaster ride, though my insides were still catching up. Virginia Sinclair was a spoiled woman, with the innate coldness that comes from getting one's way too often. She was the sort who bought their children live bunnies for Easter because they were charming. Then set them out for the coyotes when they crapped on the carpet.

"Your daughter was beautiful," I said.

She smiled with her eyes, very pleased by the compliment. "Yes, she was. Her beauty was far deeper than mere appearance. Hanna had a lovely spirit."

"After she died, what happened to Hillary?" Mike asked.

She frowned. "The girl was Randy's ward. She stayed on with him."

"Mrs. Sinclair," Mike said, "are you acquainted with a family by the name of Metrano? George and Leslie and their daughter Amy Elizabeth?"

"Metrano?" She thought hard for a moment. Then she shook her head slowly, serious, still thinking. "I can't say."

"Amy Elizabeth Metrano," Mike said again.

Again she shook her head.

My bottom had had enough of the hard cushion. And the hardness of Mrs. Sinclair. The old bench creaked when I stood up. The sound seemed to bother Mrs. Sinclair. She gave me a librarian glare. The air in the room was stale, musty. I felt claustrophobic and started to pace to shake it off. She watched me as I moved around the room, looking at the precious ornaments, the pictures on the walls.

Hanna's house in Long Beach was open and full of light and

air, alive. I wondered whether this room had ever had life. I was reminded again of the museum feel. The Hanna museum.

Mike was questioning Mrs. Sinclair. "You told us that Hillary's parents died in a boating accident. What do you know about it? Where did it happen? When did it happen? Maybe you remember their names. Anything you can tell us."

"Their names? Ramsdale, I assume. I never met Randy's family. They all live in the East. As to where, I believe it was in Mexico. I remember Randy went down there and brought the girl home. She was quite ill for a while. Very upset, until she had to be sedated. Of course, it must have been a frightful ordeal for her to lose both her parents. Hanna and Randy sat at her side for weeks, reassuring her, until she recovered.

"The doctors had long told Hanna that living by the sea would be more healthful for her than living up here. Cooler, you see. And much less smog. When the girl was strong enough, Randy moved them all into a lovely home down at the beach. Had his boat right in front."

"When was the last time you heard from Randy?" Mike asked.

"Christmas Eve. He took me to dinner—our little tradition."

"The two of you?" Mike asked. "Or wife and kid, too?"

"The two of us. It would have been awkward for his wife. You see, Randy is still mourning Hanna's passing."

I had stopped pacing to look up at the portrait. "Did he tell you he planned to divorce his wife?"

"He did. She was unfaithful."

"Divorce can be expensive," I said, turning to her. "Especially for a rich man."

She smiled slyly. "I said Randy likes to play. I did not mean to imply he is mindless. In fact, Randy is deceptively clever. He had prenuptial agreements with both of the wives who followed Hanna. They were entitled to very small settlements should they divorce. And no death benefits if he predeceased them. From a financial standpoint, it was to their advantage to stay married and keep Randy healthy for as long as possible."

"He told you this?" Mike asked.

"Indeed. I would say he even boasted about it. But why ask me? Speak with Randy."

Ah, I thought, tensing, time to pay the piper. Mike and I exchanged glances—whose turn this time? I turned back to the portrait, but Hanna told me nothing.

"Mrs. Sinclair," Mike said, the professionally bereaved mortician this time, "I am sad to inform you that Randy Ramsdale has passed away."

She was wordless for so long that I turned around to see if she was still upright. She was. Stiffly upright. So brittle I thought a quick jerk would snap her in half.

"I'm sorry," I said.

Her face was dangerously pale. "Was there an accident?"

"No," Mike again. "It happened at the hand of another."

She grasped her throat. "Murder?"

"Yes."

"Both of them?"

"Hillary and Randy, yes."

I stepped toward her. "Can I get you something? Some water?"

She shook me off and kept her eyes on Mike. "Is there a will?"

"I don't know." He was taken aback. People in shock do and say odd things. I thought it was a telling first reaction.

Mrs. Sinclair began to bend finally. She looked around her room with a longing that was ripe with goodbye.

"You see," she said, "this all belongs to Randy. This was their house. I am here at his sufferance."

"He supported you?" Mike asked.

She nodded.

"Are there friends you can call?" I asked. "You shouldn't be alone."

I saw her glance flick toward the portrait. Toward Hanna.

"I am not alone," she said.

I was spooked. She never got around to asking how and why either Randy or Hillary died. I guess to her those facts weren't the essentials. Mike got up from the creaky bench and edged toward the door.

"When you feel up to it, you can call me," he said. "I'll try to answer any questions."

"Thank you," she said.

"Will you be all right?" I tried again.

"Yes. Please excuse me. I need to lie down." She rose majestically, the starch returned to her spine, and walked slowly toward the door. As we followed her, I noticed she did not lean on the cane.

She didn't open the front door for us, but stood in the center of the round foyer, her narrow feet planted in the hub of the ornate circular pattern in the parquet floor. Rootless like an ornamental tree.

"Good night," I said, reaching for Mike's sleeve as he held the door.

Virginia Sinclair was staring off into the dark beyond the front steps. When we turned to walk out, I heard her gasp. I thought maybe she was waiting for us to leave before she wept. She cleared her throat.

"Just a moment," she said. "What was that name again?"

"Metrano," Mike said, going back.

She shook her head. "No, the first name."

"George? Leslie? Amy Elizabeth?"

"George. I know that was his name. It was some time ago, but I remember him. He worked for Randy, refurbishing a boat. Temporary work. He was quite handy. Randy had him do some repairs around here as well. A nice fellow. A family man down on his luck."

"When?" Mike asked.

"Years ago. I wouldn't have thought of him except that we were speaking of Hillary and how she came into the family. When Hillary was so sick, the only soul who could comfort her was George."

CHAPTER

17

"Got it?" Mike asked.

"I think so." I turned my face into the icy wind that whistled down through a pass in the mountains above Virginia Sinclair's mansion. A slice of moon slipped out from under the heavy clouds, casting long, moving shadows like lumbering giants on the slope. Coyotes on a crag nearby saw the moon and set up a howl. Had the coyotes scared little Hillary? Or had they scared Amy Elizabeth?

Mike's face was in shadow, too, but I knew the expression without seeing it, jaw set, eyes flashing. Controlled rage.

"The situation has changed," he said. "My people have to get with the federales in Baja, get them to bring in Elizabeth Ramsdale for a rubber-hose job, have them loosen her up for us. I would like to fly down there to talk to her, but I think we'll let Ma Bell reach out and touch her. Make that Mamacita Bell. I just hope she's still there. Right now, I'm going to take you home."

"What about George?"

"If he's on his boat, the Coast Guard will find him. If he's with Elizabeth, I will fly down. Him we'll just shoot, save the state some grief."

"You talk tough when you're upset. But it's still a good idea."

I put my cheek against his chest and squeezed my eyes shut. The air was clear and sweet, but I couldn't seem to get enough of it past the constriction in my chest. "He sold his daughter."

"Looks that way," Mike said.

"But did he kill her?" I asked. "Could a father be so depraved?"

"It happens all the time."

We held on to each other as we walked back to the car. After we had left Mrs. Sinclair's, I had only made it around the first curve in the road before I lost the double-cheese Bingo Burger we had picked up at a drive-through on the way to Pasadena. I had eaten it before I knew that a burger franchise was the going price for kindergarten-age blondes.

Times had been hard for the Metranos. I had seen where they lived, a lot of little girls packed into tight quarters. A lot of shoes to buy in that family, and food, and doctors, all on the earnings of a coffee-shop waitress. I'm sure there was a sense of desperation. A case could be made for a certain nobility in the gesture of handing over one of the children to a rich family to give her privileges and opportunities her parents could not provide. And giving more to the other four girls as part of the bargain. *Grimm's Fairy Tales* stuff again.

The wicked witch in this story was George Metrano's affair with a craps table. If it had been me, I would not have been able to swallow the bread a deal like that had put on the family table. Maybe that was why George had this compulsion to lose it all. I'm no Freud. I couldn't explain what he had done. Even thinking about it had made me ill. If he had any human feeling at all, he must have suffered. I only hoped that every waking moment for the last ten years had given him the same torment his wife had suffered when she lost her child. Her torment times ten.

Mike's city car rattled down the hill. The shocks were shot, the torsion bars worn. All the bouncing and swaying did my queasy stomach no good. I rolled down my window and gulped air, my hair blown back away from my face. I didn't remember closing my eyes, so it was a surprise when I opened them and found myself in the garage of Mike's condo. He was in my open car door, gently pulling me by the hand.

"Come on, baby," he said. "Let's put you to bed."

I got out, shaky when I stood up, still half asleep. We went into the condo through the connecting door between the garage and the kitchen and I walked straight to the answering machine on the counter next to Mr. Espresso for messages.

Lyle had called. Everything was fine. My grant administrator still wanted a report. Guido had called to say that he had a picture for us and was driving over to deliver it. If we weren't home, he would stick it in the front door. Before Guido's message had clicked off, Mike was on his way to the front door.

I stayed to listen to the rest of the messages. Casey called, bubbling. She had an audition with the Joffrey Ballet. She needed money for new toe shoes.

When Casey hung up, I heard the deadbolt on the front door clunk a second time and Mike came back waving an envelope with "Love, Guido" scrawled across the front.

"You ready to see this?" He slit open the envelope with a steak knife and pulled out a single four-by-six color snapshot. He showed me the face of the man who had slashed Mike's tires. It was almost cartoonish, this computer-manipulated composite, but the face was whole and recognizable. I had only seen George Metrano once, the afternoon in the morgue with Leslie, but I knew him.

"Son of a bitch," I said.

"Afraid so. George Metrano."

"At least now you know he's not in Baja with Elizabeth, not if he was in town this afternoon."

"Damn. It's so much easier to take out an asshole below the border. We'll just hope he rabbits when we catch him and we'll shoot him on the fly, huh?"

"I'll help you." My voice sounded thick. "What did he possibly have to gain by killing her?"

"*If. If* he killed her. Maybe the question is, what did he stand to lose if he didn't?" Mike rubbed his face wearily, rasping the whiskers on his chin.

I touched his face. "If Mrs. Sinclair was correct and Elizabeth inherits nothing, then who is Randy's heir?"

"I could make a pretty good guess."

"Check it out, will you?" I said.

"Yes, ma'am." He chuckled. "Anything else?"

I looked inside the envelope. "Guido only gave us one print."

"One's all we need. It stays with me. You're retiring."

"Retiring for the night, you mean?"

"You know what I mean." He slipped George back into the envelope. "I have to get on the horn and make arrangements. I'll come tuck you in later."

"Wake me if I fall asleep," I said, yawning. I kissed his cheek and headed for the bedroom. I was tired, but I knew I couldn't sleep; I had seen the face.

Mike had unpacked my duffel, hung up my two clean shirts with his, put my dirty clothes in a pillowcase on the closet floor, lined my shoes up next to his. I had never seen my shoes next to his before. Somehow, the sight touched me.

I fussed a bit, cleared away yesterday's newspapers from the bed, smoothed the quilt. This would make four nights in a row in the same bed. I liked the number.

With nothing else to do, I brushed my teeth, stripped off my clothes, and ran a hot shower. I was standing with my head against the tile, steamy water pounding on my spine, when Mike opened the shower door.

"We're waiting for the head shed to work its way through diplomatic channels," he said. "As soon as the connection is made with the federales, I'm going into the office to make the call."

"I want to go with you."

"You can't. The boss will be there."

"No fair." I tried to pout, but I had water pouring in my eyes. The best I could do was squint and puff out my lower lip.

He laughed. "Don't use all the hot water. I need a shower, too."

"You can get in here with me."

"I'd like to, but I wouldn't be able to hear the phone."

"Will you scrub my back?"

"Hand me the soap."

I gave him the soap and my back. He started with my shoulders, massaging with strong fingers slippery with lather. I felt the tight muscles release. It was so delicious and so relaxing it was all I could do to stand upright.

He worked down my back, occasionally letting his hot, soapy hands slip around front, teasing. He circled my waist so his thumbs could work the knots in the small of my back. I was saying bright things like ooh and aah, writhing to direct him. Then he was all of a sudden in the shower with me, in his clothes, his body pressed tight behind me.

His lips nipped along the base of my neck, giving me goose bumps despite the steam billowing around us. He ran his tongue along the back of my ear, followed the stream of water that sluiced over my collarbone and down my breast, where he held his hand like a dam.

I turned around then, and began working on the annoyingly small buttons of his wet shirt. He worked my buttons with amazingly skillful tongue and fingers. I thought suddenly of something Guido had said, about making love to a man as experienced as Mike. I didn't care where Mike had learned what he knew. As long as he kept doing it. With me.

Around one, the summons came from headquarters. We were dry by then, napping on top of the quilt when the phone jolted us awake. Elizabeth was being held in a Baja jail as a courtesy, but the federales in Cabo San Lucas wouldn't hold her for very long.

While he dressed, I made Mike coffee and a sandwich and then kissed him goodbye. Very Dolly Domestic. And sweet. Until I had a flash of life with Mike, but without Lyle. Leaving Lyle would be like leaving one's widowed mother alone. My stomach started to rumble again. I sat in the kitchen and stared back at the red light on Mr. Espresso, hoping for some revelation to come.

At two, when nothing had resolved itself, I slipped into a few more clothes and some shoes and went for a drive, a change of scenery to sort things through.

In the middle of the night, when there isn't construction going on, the freeways become free ways. Once I realized where I was headed, I was impatient to get there. I pushed the little rental Toyota up to ninety, slowed to maneuver around a slow drunk, then hit the pedal again.

I was in Long Beach in under thirty minutes.

My big regret was that I had never met Randy. Never would. He was the key player in all of this, and I thought it would have been awfully damned interesting to hear what he had to say, an addition to the My Most Memorable Character collection.

From what people had told me, Randy would go to just about any lengths to get his own way. If sheer force of his considerable charm, stubborn will, and cussed determination didn't work, he used money. Sometimes he used money for bribery, as I believe he had with George Metrano, as he had tried with Lacy. Sometimes he used the threat of withholding money, as he had with his ex-wives, to maintain control.

I keep telling Casey that she should be careful what she wishes for, because her wishes might come true. Apparently no one had ever warned Randy. Or maybe he hadn't listened very carefully, because what he wished for ended up killing him. Poor Randy.

At two-thirty, all the bars and clubs on Second Street were closed. All the chickies were in for the night. The narrow streets of Naples were deserted. I drove through the alley behind the Ramsdale house, saw no one about, and parked two houses farther down.

When I got out of the car, I had one of Mike's big, heavy Kel-Lite flashlights in my hand. I had picked it up on my way out of the kitchen.

Mike had told me one time that when he worked street patrol in uniform, back before his hair turned white, the Kel-Lite had been his compliance tool of choice during hand-to-hand brawling. Better than his service revolver as a cudgel. His stories always failed the political correctitude tests. Sometimes their brutality set my back molars on edge. Most of the time, they made me laugh, because I knew there was no malice in anything he had done. Times have changed. Acceptable police practices have changed. So has Mike.

Anyway, I carried the flashlight as a sort of talisman against anything that might be waiting in the dark. I lurked down the alley. If anyone had seen me, and been worried, he or she would have called in to report a burglar. I heard no sirens, so I lurked on.

The back door of the Ramsdale house was heavy oak. I longed for Martha's key. But I would have had to break into her house to get it. So I broke into the Ramsdales' instead.

Randy's study was on Martha's side of the house. I knew she was gone, so unless I made a big noise, no one was likely to hear me. I used the Kel-Lite on the pane in the French doors closest to the latch. The shattered glass made less noise than I had expected as it fell onto a doormat inside.

I tried the knob. It turned, but the door wouldn't give. I could see hardware for a floor bolt, so I broke another pane and I could pull up the bolt. The door opened smoothly, finally, and I slipped inside, stepping wide around the glass.

I stepped inside and waited for my heart to stop pounding, a wide spot in the checkerboard of shadows, trying to listen to the house. All was still except for the ticking of a clock somewhere. Relying on my imperfect recollection of the floor plan, I felt my way through the dark and up the stairs to Hillary's room.

I went straight to her bookcase and used the flashlight only long enough to make sure that I had taken down the right books—the photo album and the yearbook. Then I went back out into the hall. I listened to be sure all was quiet before I went back down.

Thinking it had all been too easy, I pulled the French doors shut behind me and rebolted them. I was so slick, I thought, I could reel in a little extra money as a cat burglar on the side. Send Casey to an Ivy League school if she wanted. Or to London for ballet. I felt more hyped than scared when I came out into the narrow passage between the houses.

I flattened myself against the wall beside a skinny juniper, and looked for trouble. The alley end, where I was headed, was clear. To be cautious, because my dad when he taught me to drive told me always to look both ways in case a comet, or whatever, came shooting up behind me, I looked down to the canal end, too.

On the water, things are always moving: lights, boats, ducks, gulls. What alarmed me was a block of dark stillness against the motion. I froze, tried to focus on it. I was closer to the canal than to the alley. I tried to figure whether I had a big enough head start to make it back to the car if that dark shape decided to chase me. I hated myself for being so anal that I had locked the car—my caution had added two or three seconds to my escape time.

I thought about the alternatives, and chose one. Clutching the books tight against my chest, the Kel-Lite straight in front, I stepped away from the wall and shot the light into the dark.

What I saw was an old wooden dinghy that had been hauled up out of the water. It leaned against one of the support pilings of the Ramsdale dock. Next to it was a can of caulking. Kids, I thought, doing some boat-repair work on a vacant dock.

Feeling relieved, if a bit of a jerk, I switched off the light, quickly reevaluated my future as a burglar, and turned toward the alley.

My dad also taught me to look three times, left right left, before committing to a turn into traffic. I forgot that part at the wrong time.

When I spun back, he was there, blocking the passage to the alley maybe four yards in front of me. I flashed the light on him.

He flinched, raised an arm to shield his eyes.

"Officer Flint," I shouted in the direction of the shattered French door. "Metrano is here. Have the alley sealed."

George Metrano smiled, monstrous in the beam of light. "I watched you go in. You were alone."

"Cops have had the place staked out."

"No, they haven't." He started toward me. "What did you take?"

"Not a goddam thing." I gripped my booty tighter, and screamed, "Flint, out here, now!"

"Shut up." He hissed as he lunged, moving fast for a big man.

I ran for the canal. Ivy vines snagged my shoes and ripped up from their roots—I didn't have time to aim for the artfully placed stepping stones. If I tripped, I knew he would be all over me.

I felt him reach for me, a push of air from behind. I ducked to the side, used my flashlight hand to right myself, and ran on. I didn't have time to find him back there. I only knew he was too close. My back arched away from him, giving me a few more inches of time.

I came out on the sidewalk, careened around the corner, and headed toward the nearest bridge. I miscalculated my speed at the turn and lost both my footing and my lead. As I scrambled to find solid ground underneath, he dove. And he got me.

Metrano's huge hand caught me just below the knee, flipped me, and sent me skidding face forward onto the concrete. I kept the books, but lost most of the skin on my knuckles.

He slid his hand up my leg for a better grip. I managed to roll onto my back. I cocked my free foot to flatten his smug face, but he caught it, too. He was on his knees, I was on my butt, struggling to get upright, straining to wrench free as he tried to get over me, dominate me, pin me down. I hate to be pinned. Especially by a guy with a thing for razors. Every time I tried to sit up, he yanked my legs and sent me backward again. One big jerk had sufficient force to knock me on my head hard enough to make my ears ring.

I was plain old mad. On my way up again, I swung the Kel-Lite with everything I had, a well-placed backhand stroke. He was turning to see where the blow was coming from when Kel-Lite and face bones connected. He screamed like something on *Wild Kingdom*. Warm blood sprayed through the air and hit my face. I retched at the smell of it.

The follow-up shot I gave him didn't have as much force as the first blow, sufficient to raise a dummy bump on his temple, but not enough to break the skin. It did motivate him to try something else on me. When he moved his hands higher on my calves, looking for a better grip, I found an instant of hesitation to slide through. I snatched one leg free and got some leverage to kick away from his hold. Like a scared bunny, I scooted the hell away.

I felt the wood of the dock under me. He never gave me more than a few inches of lead, but I used them to scramble to my feet. A yard from the edge of the dock, I sprang for the water, a high, off-balance dive. He snatched at my trailing foot. I felt the hard parts of his hand collide with my shoe as the black water rose to meet me.

I coursed down through frigid salt water so dark I could see nothing. I was worried about the bottom, about sharp obstacles among the boat trash that had been dumped into the canal. But I worried about George Metrano more. I felt him hit the water somewhere above me, felt the shock waves generate down from him.

When my dive lost its initial momentum, I pushed myself deeper, groping ahead for debris. My lungs ached, my head throbbed, but I still had the books against my chest. A reflex grip, probably. Not that a photo album was what he was after.

The sharp barnacles on the dock pilings snagged my sleeve, and I reached for them. I wrapped an arm around the piling long enough to kick off my heavy shoes. Then, with the barnacles cutting into my hands like embedded shards of glass, I used the piling to control my rise to the surface.

When I broke through to the still, dark night, I gulped sweet air, got my bearings, and ducked down again, pushing myself beneath the Ramsdale dock. I pressed my face up to the gaps between the planks and managed to find breathable air. I listened for George, but all I could hear was the water lapping around my ears. I was so cold I ached all over. The salt water burned my scraped knuckles, stung my eyes. But I waited.

It is nearly impossible to keep track of time under water.

After what seemed like hours but was probably only a few minutes, I located George. I had lost the flashlight somewhere in my flight. Apparently, George had found it. A shaft of light between the planks hit my eye, so I slid down deeper until it passed overhead.

I couldn't stay there. So I came up for a last gulp of air, then dove down again through the water, pushing myself deep into Randy Ramsdale's grave. Around me, the light cut through the water like thrusts of a sword, but I was so close under him that the light passed over me.

I felt my way along the slimy seawall until I came to Martha's dock. I rose again for air, dove again, and continued along for two more docks.

I passed under a bridge and found moss-covered stone steps that led up to the sidewalk. The steps were too slippery to use, but I hauled myself up by the metal rail. Sheltered, I hoped, by a cluster of potted geraniums, I lay curled into a ball on the rough concrete and filled my lungs, gasping, shaking with cold. Green slime clung to my clothes. I reeked of boat fuel.

I risked raising my head to see over the pots. George was still searching the canal for me. He scuttled down the sidewalk in the opposite direction, knifing the water with his beam again and again. When he headed back my way, I was still out of breath. I knew it was only a matter of moments before he gave up on the water and looked elsewhere, the most obvious place being the alley where I had left the car. I had to be history before George got there.

When he leaned out over the water to follow his light, I snaked across the sidewalk, staying low. I slipped between two houses barefoot, managed to scale a tall wooden gate without rousing the neighborhood, and dropped into the alley. I prised the car keys out of my pocket and held them in one hand, the dripping books in the other, and ran down the alley, leaving a wet trail behind me.

Old George was no dummy. I was just faster. He came out into the alley farther along, running hard, dragging that leg again. I had the key out and ready. I was still shivering, so my hand shook, but I got the key into the lock, me into the car, and the doors locked again before he could touch me.

His face contorted with purple rage, the sinews of his neck pulled taut with the force he used to hurl obscenities at me. I couldn't understand a word, though the gist was clear enough.

I cranked the ignition and pushed my face up to my window. "Motherfucking child-killer," I screamed, jamming the car into drive. As I accelerated away, the heavy Kel-Lite crashed through the window behind my head. Shards of glass sprayed around me, a thousand points of treacherous light. Ducking from flying glass, dodging trash cans and parked cars in the alley, I got away clean. All things considered.

I was looking for a phone booth to call the police when I heard the sirens pouring in off Second Street. Always a courteous driver—as Dad taught me—I pulled to the side and let them pass. The cavalry was riding in to handle things. I would handle the details later. The next item of business on my agenda was growing soggier by the second.

At red lights, I slowed enough to see oncoming cars, then blew through the intersections. George would need clean clothes, and I didn't want to be hiding in his closet should he come home looking for some.

I parked around the corner from the Metranos' house and jogged to their front door. My clothes were cold and heavy, the pavement hurt my feet. But I had my booty, and my agenda, intact.

I banged on the door, leaned on the bell until Leslie came and turned on the front light. She peered out at me through the living-room drapes. She wore a robe over pajamas, but she didn't look as if she had been sleeping. Her makeup and hair were waiting for company. Probably George.

"Leslie, let me in," I said, hoping she could read lips, because I didn't want to wake up another neighborhood. When she hesitated, I opened the sodden photo album and held it up for her. Perplexed, but with curiosity sufficiently aroused, she opened the door.

"What happened to you?" she asked, clutching her terry bathrobe at the throat.

"Midnight swim," I said. "Where are the police? I thought you had a guard."

"They took me to the night deposit, that's all."

"Do you have a towel?"

"Of course." She turned on the inside lights then and let me in. "Just wait here."

She had left me in a raised, tiled entry that was a sort of launching pad for the step-down living and dining rooms. While I waited, I paced its chilly length.

It appeared that the house was nearly stripped bare. In the dining room, the only furniture was a card table and two folding chairs. But there were indentations in the carpet left by a large table and maybe eight or ten chairs. There had been other furniture, long dents that would conform perhaps to a china cabinet. The living room held only boxes, taped shut and lined up against one wall. I had seen all there was to see before Leslie came back carrying a beach towel.

"Are you moving?" I asked.

"Unless there's a miracle," she sighed. "Everything's gone. We'll never build back up again. Not this time."

I handed her the photo album and the yearbook and used the towel on my face and hair, wiped down my feet. Then I took the towel into the dining room and spread it over the card table. Leslie came with me.

"I hope all of the pictures aren't ruined," I said, taking the album from her and opening it over the towel. "This is Hillary Ramsdale."

She pulled up one of the folding chairs, took reading glasses out of her robe pocket, and started with the first page. The pictures were wet but still clear. I knew most of the deterioration would come when they started to dry and the emulsion separated from the paper.

Leslie studied the pictures on the first page. Pried open the second page and studied it, too.

"So?" I asked, impatient, miserably cold.

"The hair is different. Amy didn't have that scar, or whatever it is, on her chin. But it's her. You want proof? Go look at my little granddaughter. She could be Amy's twin."

"When the coroner's office called you Saturday, who took the call?"

She frowned. "George did."

"Where were you?"

"At work. I'm almost always there, trying to hold things together as best I can."

"Are you going to lose the business as well?" I asked.

She shrugged. "George has been working on a deal. These things take time, though. So until it's final, we've been just hanging on, selling off what we found buyers for, scraping together every nickel we could find."

"He had gambling debts to pay?"

"Not this time." There was fierce certainty in her voice. "He swore to me this time it was bad investments, some real estate we couldn't dump in a bad market. Negative amortization and a high vacancy rate were eating us alive. He knows I would throw him out on the street if he ever placed another bet. I figured that's why he went out on the boat, to get clean away. When he gets real upset, he tends to want to go place a bet."

"He didn't go anywhere," I said. "I chased him down the street in Belmont Shore this afternoon, and he returned the favor tonight, not fifteen minutes ago."

She rose, involuntarily like a marionette on a string. "Then where the hell is he?"

"I don't know. And as long as he isn't here, I don't care." I began pulling pages out of the album and lining them up on the towel so they wouldn't start sticking together. "Maybe he's holed up in one of your vacant rentals."

"Could be."

I glanced at her. "So, how long has he been working on this deal?"

"Couple of months."

"Like, since February?"

She thought before she nodded. "About then. He went back East somewhere for a couple of weeks. Around Valentine's. I remember, because he mailed me a card."

"Where was he this past Thursday?"

"Thursday? We went down to San Diego for a Bingo Burgers sales meeting, stayed overnight." She looked over at me. "Is that when the girl died, Thursday?"

"Yes."

"And you thought George did it?"

I nodded. "Her throat was slashed, just like Randy Ramsdale's was two months ago. I caught George today slashing my tires."

"You're a liar."

"Sometimes. But not this time." I sat down on the other folding chair, because my knees shook. I was exhausted. And running out of time.

Leslie was staring at me.

"You told me you didn't know the Ramsdales," I said. "But it seems George worked for them for a while. He was working for them up in Pasadena at the time Amy disappeared. Does that ring any bells?"

She shook her head. "George did jobs for a lot of people back then, anything he could pick up. He went around the harbor, the marinas, getting what he could. And he did some handyman work, too. Anything."

"You don't remember him working for the Ramsdales?"

"I was pretty busy. Five kids and a job, that kept me occupied, all right."

"You didn't see the name on a paycheck?"

"I'm ashamed to say it, but George took his pay in cash so we could get out of paying taxes on it. We just used up every bit of it for essentials. I do remember him working in Pasadena, though. He did some boat work for a man, and the man asked him to come work around his house. The job was supposed to last a couple of months, but our old car conked out and George couldn't get up there. So they loaned him a real nice little pickup with a camper shell. When he finished the job, they gave him the truck as part of his pay."

She blinked rapidly, all of a sudden holding back tears. "If they hadn't given him that truck, we couldn't have gone up to the mountains that day with Amy."

I was reminded how thorough Randy was.

Leslie swiped at her nose with the cuff of her robe.

"But the name wasn't Ramsdale," she said.

"Was it Sinclair?"

The name caught her up short. "Yes, it was. Sinclair. I hadn't thought about that for a long time."

"I bet it was tough for George," I said. "Being out of work and having a big family. Feeling like a failure. That situation can make a lot of tension in the house."

"Yes, it can," she agreed, smiling just a little. "'Course, I always said George was more interested in making babies than raising them. He's just a big baby himself. I can't tell you how losing his little girl turned that man around, let him see what was important to him. Everyone always used to tell me George would never be able to hold down a job, never amount to a hill of beans. But I knew he had it in him. Then after Amy was gone, well, he just knuckled down. He sure proved them all wrong."

"That was a hard way to learn a lesson," I said. "Losing a child."

She looked around the empty room, seeming overwhelmed, depressed. Her eyes brimmed again. "I used to think getting thrown out of your house and living on the streets was the worst thing that could happen to people. But I was wrong. I would live on the streets any day to have my baby back for even one minute."

"Detective Flint tells me results of the DNA comparison tests they did on you and the girl will take another couple of weeks."

"I don't need the tests to know the child in these pictures is mine. You know, there hasn't been a day in the last ten years when every time the phone rings, or someone comes to the door, or I see a blond-headed girl go by, that I don't think, oh, it's Amy come back to me. Now I finally do find her, and it's too late."

"I'm sorry," I said, because there was nothing else to say.

"I know," she sighed.

"I have to go," I said. I stood up and began gathering the album pages together. "I don't want to be here if George comes back."

"Why?" She was helping me.

"I don't want to be the one to tell you."

"Tell me what? After what I've been through in my life, Maggie, there's not one thing you can say that I can't handle."

"I'm not so sure."

"You'd damn well better finish what you've started."

I stood there, knees knocking harder, imagining footsteps across the tile entry. "I don't have the sort of evidence a court would ask for—police will take care of that—so you can believe me or not. That's up to you. I told you how I got involved, trying to find out why a kid got lost. Not Amy, but the girl I knew as Hillary. This is what I believe happened."

"I want to hear it," she said, encouraging.

"A rich, spoiled man wanted a child for his wife; she was sick and couldn't have one of her own. He thought a baby would be too much trouble, so he found a little girl that was already housebroken, knew about please and thank you, and was ready to start school so she wouldn't be underfoot all day. He paid a lot for her. He dyed her blond hair brown, surgically he gave her a cute dimple in her chin. He called her his own."

"You're saying he bought Amy from her kidnappers?"

"How much does a Bingo Burgers franchise cost?"

Leslie didn't answer. She also did not rise up in righteous denial. Or defense of George. All she said was, "Go on."

"From there, it gets murky," I said. "I don't know everything yet, but the basic equation is: George was in debt and had a daughter, plus Randy was rich and wanted a child, equals George became solvent minus the daughter. The corollary is: George was in debt again, plus Randy was dead and he had a daughter, equals . . . what? That's as far as I can go with it.

You're a businesswoman. You must be pretty good at math. That's why I came here."

"I think you should go," she said.

"I think you're right." I picked up the pages, left the empty cover on the towel. I padded toward the door.

Leslie was still at the table in the empty room, staring at the empty album.

"Goodbye, Leslie," I said. "Lock the door after me."

She looked up. "I know I should hate you for saying all those things."

"I'm sorry," I said. "I wish I could spare you."

"One thing," she said. "Can I have one of those pictures?"

I held them out to her. She came to me, both of us standing on the cold tile of the entry in bare feet. With tentative hands, she found the one she wanted, Hillary in a life vest in the bow of a sailboat, smiling, showing missing front teeth.

"It's just, she looks so much like my granddaughter."

My hands were too full to hug her, and she probably would have shunned me anyway. She held herself with the same innate dignity that had drawn me to Pisces.

Leslie's gaze fell on the taped boxes in the living room.

"I meant what I said," she said, "about living on the street."

"I have a daughter," I said. "I know you meant it."

I drove home in the pre-rush-hour rush, big rigs and kamikaze commuters tearing up asphalt. The heater couldn't overcome the cold air streaming in through my broken window. I shivered all the way in my wet clothes, the car full of the smell of dead things from the sea despite all the fresh air.

Mike wasn't back yet when I got in. I spread a towel over his kitchen table and, still quaking with cold, laid out the album again.

I was in the shower, scalding water pounding my spine, when Mike came in. He opened the shower door.

"Jesus, Maggie," he said. "What are you doing in here all naked again? Some consideration, please. I'm an old white-haired man. Night after night, twice yesterday. You're going to kill me."

I laughed or cried, it was hard to tell—my face was already wet. But whichever it was, the release felt good.

I looked up through runnels of shampoo-y water. "Who invited you?" I said.

He showed me the bulge in the front of his slacks. "You did," he said.

Sly was sitting at the end of his MacLaren Hall bunk, waiting for me. The bed was neatly made with a bright red cotton spread. The child was neatly made as well. Long, skinny white legs dangled from new-looking shorts with a primo surfer logo on the belt. The way he kicked his high-top sneakers, I couldn't miss them. I wanted to snatch him up and squeeze him, but the proud smile still warned of spiky personal fences erected around him.

There were five other beds in the dorm room, each with a different, bright spread. Sly's roommates were all in class, so we were alone except for the counselor keeping an eye on things from the hall.

"Looking sharp, Sly," I said. I handed him a big Toys Я Us bag and a box of goldfish crackers.

"How come you're always bringing me stuff?" he asked.

"Because I like to. Does it bother you?"

"Doesn't bother me." He grinned, still the old con man. Out of the bag he took a Loktite kit for a scale-model Corvette and a set of enamel paints, with an extra jar of cherry red. He ran his fingers over the picture on the box, his eyes wide. "This is hot."

"Yeah, it is. You told me you like 'vettes. Sorry it had to be the snap-together kind of kit. They won't let you have model glue in here. Hope it's okay."

"I'll check it out." He never gave away much, but I thought he was pleased, as much by the attention as by the gift. He seemed happy to see me, the way friends are happy. Gave me a warm glow.

"Where'd you get the hot clothes?" I asked.

"That faggot cop. He and his kid took me to get some stuff on Sunday."

"Detective Flint?" Mike hadn't bothered to mention a thing.

"I guess that's his name. The one that you . . ." He made an appropriately obscene gesture.

"Well, you look great. Need anything else?"

He shook his head. "I'm set. They got me going to school in here."

"How is it?"

"Not too bad. Hilly used to teach me stuff, and I liked that better. But it's okay here. They don't let you watch TV in the daytime, so it's something to do."

"Stay with it, Sly. School is your rocket, you know."

"Somethin' to do." He set the kit on the bed behind him and gave me one of his wise appraisals.

"So?" he asked.

"So, what?"

"Everyone who comes to see me wants to talk about what went down, or they want me to identify some guy. So, what is it?"

"I just came by to see how you're hangin'. I tried to get by yesterday, but, well, things happened. Sorry I didn't make it. I heard you had a good time last night, though, when Detective Flint came and woke you up."

He grinned. "Yeah. I couldn't ID that weird picture he had. I mean, for sure I never saw that dude before. But the cop, he took me out for pancakes, anyway. It was like two o'clock in the morning. Hot, I mean really hot. Like, I ain't been out after dark since they put me in here."

"I think you're a night owl by nature."

"Not no more. I mean, anymore. They get real strict about how we say shit. Like Hilly, always correcting me."

"She corrected you because she cared for you."

He swallowed hard. "She was hot."

I touched his shoulder. "I told your teacher I would walk you to class. It was nice they let you sleep in this morning, Mr. Night Owl."

Sly put his kit back into the bag with the paints and stowed it all under his bed. When he stood up, he smoothed the spread with pride.

"I'll show you the way," he said, still serious.

We walked out of his bungalow and across the campus, this very serious and wounded little boy and I. He was, for all of his toughness, very dear. I was sure that Hillary had been drawn by the vulnerable quality he had, as I was.

In all of our conversations, Sly had refused steadfastly to say anything to me about his family. Mike had told me the family had a rap sheet with Child Protective Services that read like *Tales from the Dark Side*. I didn't need to see it. All that mattered was that Sly was retrievable, and for that, in large measure, we had Hillary to thank.

The only children playing in the hazy sunshine were preschoolers on the far side of the grounds, bouncing around in a small fenced-in play yard equipped with swings and a slide. Sly watched them with a cloudy face.

Mike had told me how disappointed Sly was when he could not recognize George Metrano as the man who had slit Hillary's throat. That's why the treat of pancakes in the middle of the night. Mike wanted the truth. Sly wanted the man.

The windows in the stucco classroom block were open. Voices from inside floated out across the empty asphalt yard like a haunting of children; too much energy to be peacefully interred on a warm day.

I touched Sly's shoulder again. "We'll get him."

"Damn straight."

"That man in the picture? He was Hilly's real father. For what it's worth, I'm glad he isn't the one."

"Mike said the same thing."

I smiled. "So, you do know the faggot cop's name."

He turned his head away so I couldn't see the wry grin.

I stopped with him at the entrance to the classroom block. "Got your homework finished?"

"Under control," he said.

"Then I'll see you later, Sly Ronald."

He tossed his head back in cocky acknowledgment. "Later."

With his hands in the pockets of his new shorts, he started inside. After a few steps, he hesitated, then he came back to me.

"Where is she?" he asked.

"Hillary is still in the morgue."

"Shouldn't there be a funeral?"

"There will be, as soon as we get this all straightened out. Will you sit with me?"

"Yeah. Don't forget."

"I promise."

He squared his skinny shoulders inside his bright shirt and walked on to his class, alone.

I didn't mind leaving him at MacLaren. But I had a sick feeling whenever I thought about Sly after MacLaren—they could keep him only so long. What would it be? A foster home? Another institution? Back on the streets?

In the ear of my memory, all the way out to the parking lot I heard Sly howl the way Bowser had the day I brought him home from the pound to sleep on my heirloom brocade sofa. There's a whole lot more to taking in a damaged child than an abandoned puppy. Even though I understood that, every time I saw Sly it was tougher to leave him behind.

I drove the clunker rental Toyota downtown and parked in a twelve-dollar-all-day lot in the Civic Center. I didn't have all day, and I didn't have twelve dollars in my pocket, either. As it was, I walked down to a little deli in the Civic Center Mall under City Hall and spent my last five on a chicken salad sandwich and a diet soda. The sandwich man threw in an extra kosher dill and a couple of cookies because I smiled at him. That's what he told me, anyway.

I carried the food in a brown bag across the street to the police administration building, Parker Center, and asked the desk officer, Rayetta Washington, to please page Detective Michael Flint, Sr., Robbery-Homicide Division, Major Crimes Section, third floor, last office on the right, second desk inside the door. And to tell him that his snitch was downstairs with new information. I gave Officer Washington a smile, too, because she looked as if she needed one. She was at least nine months pregnant under her midnight-blue maternity uniform.

Officer Washington and I were discussing hee-breathing when Mike came down to the desk. He hadn't had much sleep, and it showed in the chiseling under his cheekbones, the shadows under his eyes.

"Maggie?" he said, surprised, pleased, and cranky all at once. "What are you doing here?"

I held up the sandwich bag. "You forgot your lunch this morning, honey, and I was afraid you'd go hungry." I turned to Officer Washington. "You know how men get when they miss a meal. Too hard to live with."

"That's it?" he said. "You brought me lunch?"

I kissed his face. "And you forgot to pay me last night, buster. One deluxe blow job, that's twenty you owe me. I need it now, because I don't have enough money for the parking lot."

Expression dark, he took the bag and cautiously looked inside. "It's a sandwich."

"What did I tell you?"

"I'm waiting to hear the rest of it."

"What? You think I have ulterior motives?"

"Or you're drunk."

"Okay. I want to hear the tape of your conversation with Elizabeth."

He sighed.

"Please."

Officer Washington had been leaning on the counter with her

chin in her hand, listening to all this. "I think you better let her, detective. You say no, I don't want to be held responsible for what she might do."

"Thank you, Officer," I said. "I hope you have a lovely baby."

Mike sighed again. "What kind of sandwich?"

"Chicken salad."

"Washington," he said, "do you like chicken salad?"

"Yes, sir, I do."

He put the bag on the counter in front of her and took me by the elbow. "Upstairs. I'll set you up in an interrogation room."

"*Bon appétit*," I said to Officer Washington.

"Later, honey," she said, grinning. As Mike and I approached the elevator, I heard her laugh out loud.

We had the elevator to ourselves. I did what I always do when I have Mike captive in an elevator: I grabbed him and kissed the breath right out of him. He cooperated without getting creative about it.

"Hi, baby," I said when I released him.

"Jesus, Maggie." He was trying without much success to stay cranky.

I straightened his tie. "You never told me you took Sly shopping."

He waved it off. "Not a big one."

"To Sly it was. You have unplumbed depths, Mike Flint. Every discovery I make about you, I like you more."

"Oh yeah?"

The elevator doors opened on the third floor and I walked out ahead of him. As he fell in step beside me, I said, "The canyons are nice, but I could live at the beach, too."

"Is this by way of a proposal?" he asked, nudging me.

"Just polite conversation. You didn't seem very happy to see me downstairs. What's going on?"

"Had a worry-making phone call this morning. From Long Beach PD. You know we're cooperating on the Ramsdale case. So, they tell me the Ramsdale house was broken into last night. Neighbors didn't hear the break-in, but there was a disturbance in the alley that got reported. You wouldn't know anything about it, would you?"

"It was so late when you got home last night, Mike. I was going to tell you all about it, but, well, you were in the mood for something other than talk."

"Sure, blame me. I saw the pictures on the kitchen table this morning. Is that where you got them? Did you break in?"

"Me?" I learned to act watching silent movies.

"You'd better go through it for me." He showed me into a barren little interrogation room furnished with a scarred wooden table and four oak chairs. He looked grim. Weary and grim. "Take a seat. Take a deep breath. And get to it."

"Well." In the light of day, my escapade the night before seemed pretty lame. I did not want to go over it. But I did what Mike said. I pulled out one of the hard chairs and sat down. I smiled up at him. Mike, standing, hip propped against the table, hand resting on his pistol, did not smile back. Seems I had spent all of my magic at the deli.

"After you left last night," I began, "I couldn't sleep, so I went for a drive."

"Never mind the embroidery work. Give me the bare bones."

I squared my shoulders. "Is this conversation being taped?"

"Yes."

I gulped, and began again. "I broke a window in the Ramsdale house, went inside, took Hillary's photo album and her year-book. Nothing else. George Metrano was waiting outside for me. He grabbed me. I got away by diving into the canal. I encountered him a second time in the alley behind the Ramsdale house. He broke my car window with Detective Flint's Kel-Lite. I drove, then, to the Metrano house to show Leslie Metrano the photographs I had stolen. She identified Hillary Ramsdale as her missing daughter, Amy. I went home, and for the third time yesterday, made passionate love to Detective Mike Flint, badge number one-five-nine-nine-one. That's as bare as I can make it."

"Are you leaving out anything I should know?"

I shook my head. "Nothing. Except, for the record, considering that he's a white-haired old guy, Flint's pretty amazing."

"This is serious, Maggie."

"I am serious."

"Did he hurt you?"

"A couple of bumps and scrapes. That's all."

"You're sure?"

I smiled. "You saw all there was of me to see, Mike."

He was controlled, but furious. "Why the hell didn't you tell me about it last night?"

I slumped down in the chair, the hard back snagging my bra hooks. I was just as tired as he was, and muscle-sore on top of it. I had kept myself busy all morning because every time I gave myself some free space for thinking, the possibilities of what George Metrano had in mind for me took root. I pulled the long sleeve of my shirt down over my skinned knuckles and swallowed back delayed panic, letting it wait a little longer.

"The truth?" I said. "I didn't say anything because I was scared shitless. When you came home, all I wanted was for you to hold me and make it all go away. I didn't want to get into a big hassle."

"Jesus, Maggie."

I interrupted the lecture mode before he got it booted. "I think George had been waiting there for a long time—long enough to know there was no stakeout. He didn't break in. He didn't assault me until he saw I wasn't the person he was waiting for."

"Who was he waiting for?"

"There's only one person left from that household to have a conversation with. And that's Elizabeth. I'm thinking he must have been lying in wait for her for a long time, because almost every time I have gone near that house, I have run across George in some way. I want to hear what the woman said to you."

Mike straightened up, tucked in his starched shirt. "I'll go get the tape if you promise to sit right here and stay out of trouble for the entire minute I will be gone."

"No sweat," I said.

"Don't move," he said.

"I remembered one more thing."

"Yes?" He had his hand on the door.

"Leslie told me that just about the time Amy disappeared, George was working in Pasadena for some people named Sinclair."

"Once you find the right thread, it all unravels in a hurry, doesn't it?"

"To a point. Still doesn't explain why Hillary took off. Or why they killed her."

"No, it doesn't." Mike's eyes focused off into space somewhere. After a moment, he thumped the edge of the door with his palm. "Hang tight. I'll be back."

When I was alone, with the door closed, I crossed my arms on the table and put my head down on them, turning to the left side because there was a bump under my hair on the right. The foul smell of the canal water seemed to rise with every deep breath I took, like stirring fetid sediment. I closed my eyes and, dizzy, coursed down again in my memory through Randy Ramsdale's grave. I shivered with the cold and startled upright just as Mike opened the door again.

"Sorry," he said, setting a battered tape player on the table. "Didn't mean to scare you."

"Too late." I rubbed my eyes. "Let's hear it."

Mike punched play.

I listened through some preliminary arguing about why Elizabeth should talk to Mike at all. A terrific, accented baritone in the background on Elizabeth's end seemed to settle her qualms about talking when he promised to keep her locked up until her dark roots grew in, unless she cooperated.

From the description of Elizabeth given to me by the women at the yacht club, I was expecting maybe poor white trash. The woman's voice I heard was low-pitched yet full of honey, not finishing-school or highbrow, but well-modulated. Now and then, when her temper flared, she slipped into a more natural-sounding nasal whine.

Mike worked on her gently for a while, getting her own bare-bones story. According to Elizabeth, she and a friend had sailed south a week ago, just the two of them on a little vacation, she said. They had put in at Ensenada and taken on a Mexican crew of three so they could relax—the going had been more arduous than they had expected. With the crew, they had gone on to Cabo San Lucas, doing a little fishing on the way. The friend she identified as Ricco Zambotti, an actor by profession. He was still in Cabo with her, she said, watching over the boat while the federales harassed her.

When Mike informed her that her husband was dead, there was only silence on her end. I would have given anything to have seen her face at that moment. She expressed neither grief nor surprise, no sobs, no gagging with mirth. She also did not ask how, when, where.

After a respectful pause, Mike picked up the interrogation: "Mrs. Ramsdale, when did you last see or hear from your husband?"

Elizabeth's voice: "In February."

Mike: "You never filed a missing-persons report."

Elizabeth: "Why should I? I didn't want him back. He was leaving me for another woman."

Mike: "Weren't you worried something might have happened to him?"

Elizabeth: "I couldn't afford to be worried. You should see the prenup I signed. If he died or divorced me, I got nothing. *Nada*. If he was gone, fine. I could still use the bank accounts. I wasn't going to go looking for him."

Mike: "You also did not report Hillary Ramsdale missing."

Elizabeth, after a pause: "I assumed she was with her father."

Mike: "She didn't pack a bag."

Elizabeth: "So what? They were a real spooky pair. Nothing they did suprised me."

Mike: "How spooky?"

Elizabeth: "I think it's spooky when a natural-blond kid dyes her hair dark. Means she has something to hide."

Mike: "What did she have to hide?"

Elizabeth, cocky: "Ask her."

Mike: "You said you inherit nothing from Randy. Does Hillary?"

Elizabeth: "Yes. Everything. She's the million-dollar baby."

Mike: "And if she were to die, who would get it?"

Elizabeth: "Not me. Ask Randy's attorney."

Mike: "I have. I just wondered whether you knew."

Elizabeth: "I don't want to talk to you anymore."

Mike: "Did you argue with Hillary?"

Elizabeth: "Maybe the connection isn't very good. I said, I don't want to talk to you."

Mike: "What did you tell Hillary about her father? She must have asked about him."

Elizabeth, angry: "She asked, all right. She nagged me until I thought I would lose it."

Mike: "Did you lose it, Elizabeth?"

Elizabeth: "No."

Mike: "Did you know Randy was dead?"

Elizabeth: "I told you. No."

Mike: "You haven't asked about Hillary, Elizabeth. Do you know where she is?"

Elizabeth: "No."

Mike: "Tell me about your last conversation with her."

Elizabeth: "I don't remember."

Mike: "If Capitán Salazar is still there with you, ask him to take you on a tour of the jail. See how you like it. Because, Elizabeth? You're going to be there until we get ready to come and get you. If I feel like walking the papers around the Justice Department, I can have you back up here in twenty-four hours. If I don't feel like walking, you could be down there for a year, maybe two. How long does Capitán Salazar think it will take for your roots to grow out?"

Elizabeth: "You can't hold me down here."

Mike: "I absolutely can. Murder is an extraditable offense. You want to talk to me some more?"

Elizabeth: "I couldn't possibly have done it. I was in Ensenada."

Mike: "Wrong murder, Mrs. Ramsdale. We were still talking

about Randy. Did you forget? You're not supposed to know Hillary is dead. How could you know when she died?"

What followed was a string of obscenities and the sound of flying furniture, or something akin to it. Mike turned off the tape and looked down at me.

"Can you draw me a picture?" he asked.

I nodded. "Elizabeth and friend Ricco set sail from Long Beach, alone, a day or two before the murder in MacArthur Park. She puts him off somewhere down the coast. He makes his way back to L.A., kills Hillary, rejoins Elizabeth before Ensenada, where they take on a crew so they can kick back. Could work."

"Yes, it could."

"So," I said, impatient, feeling ill. "You never told me you talked to Ramsdale's attorney. Who inherits from Hillary?"

"Her mother and father. That's the way the will reads. Her mother and father, no names."

"Ah." The light bulbs flickered on, dimly, in my aching head. "Once Randy was dead, all George had to do was swoop in and claim her as his long lost to gain control of the estate."

"You can see him killing Randy?"

"If he was desperate enough," I said. "I think it would be easier for me to kill a man than to sell off my child. He had already done that. But if he killed Randy, wouldn't he want us to know? No body, no payoff. Eventually, he led us to the body when he sliced up Regina Szal's raft. But he needed cash, now. Why wait so long?"

"He had to be careful no one figured out he had sold Amy in the first place. He could find himself in deep shit."

"Still."

"What?" he said.

"Where does Elizabeth come in? She had every reason to keep Randy alive as long as possible. Or maintain the illusion that he was alive."

"Don't assume they were in it together. Say she finds her husband's body, and deep-sixes it. What's George to do?"

"Too weird, Mike." I had to rub my head, counteract the throbbing. "Crime according to Newton."

"Huh?"

"You remember—every action has an equal and opposite reaction."

"Guess I was absent from the police academy the day they did this Newton guy. What's the point?"

"He kills, she hides it. And so on, until they have ruined each other's programs. It scans well. I like it."

He nodded. "Still doesn't explain why Hillary took off."

"Maybe it begins to. The game they were playing was deadly from the beginning."

A knock on the door interrupted whatever Mike was going to say next.

"Come," Mike called out.

The door opened, a face appeared. "Long Beach PD on the line, Flint. They have your suspect in custody."

CHAPTER
19

I was persona non grata at the preliminary interrogation of George Metrano. So I was pissed. I made rude remarks to Mike about the ugly turquoiseness of the Long Beach Police Department headquarters when I dropped him off. Mike gave me his pager and told me he would buzz me when he was ready to be picked up. I said uh huh, and burned rubber when I peeled away from the curb.

My errands took about an hour. I dropped off the Toyota at the rental agency, argued halfheartedly about their extra mileage calculation, tried to explain about the broken window. The more I talked, the more the perky agent became confused. In the end I abandoned the discussion because I had known from point A that the window would come out of my pocket; my insurance deductible was higher than the repairs would be. The perky agent promised to bill me.

A guy who seemed to speak only Farsi drove me in the rental agency's van to the tire shop where Mike's Blazer had been towed. I gasped at the tire bill I was handed there—still below my deductible—but said nothing when I passed over my Visa. I hoped I wasn't so close to the credit limit that it wouldn't get approval.

After all that, I felt ballsy enough to call Leslie Metrano.

There was no answer, and neither her answering machine nor the Find Amy Foundation machine kicked on. Maybe they had been seized as evidence, I thought. While I was in the booth, I dialed John Smith's number and left a message about George on his machine.

I drove up to Bingo Burgers. I was surprised how disappointed I felt when Leslie wasn't there, either. The night before, I had dumped a huge load on her slender shoulders. I guess I wanted assurance that she was all right. And reassurance that whatever George had done, she had had no part in it.

I ordered a Coke and a side of fried zucchini, to go.

At loose ends, I drove down to Naples, to the scene of my own crime. Two police cars in the alley made passage tight, but I squeezed through without new bumps on Mike's paint job. As I drove by the spot where I had parked the night before, I could see little glittery bits of shattered glass. But then, there were glittery bits all over the alley. Some of them could have been from my window, but not all of them.

I headed down to the bay and found a parking place in front of the library on Bayshore Drive. The sun had burned off most of the morning haze, leaving only a thin yellow pall of smog that accumulated at the base of the San Gabriel Mountains in the distance. The air was clear enough that I could see Catalina in sharp outline across the water.

Barefoot, I walked along the damp sand, sipping Coke, tossing bits of zucchini high into the air for diving seagulls to catch. Water lapped gently against the arc of shore, rocking the big boats that were moored on the far side of the bay. On that far side, I could see the mouth of the canal where the Ramsdales, and Martha, lived. Or had lived. Bright red and pink geraniums and vivid trailing bougainvillea contrasted with the green moss that climbed the gray cement bridges and clung to the seawall. I dug my toes into the fine sand, remembering how slimy that moss felt below the waterline.

When the zucchini was all gone, a pair of gulls hovered overhead, ever greedy for more.

George killed Randy. Ever greedy for more.

I sat down on the sand, and the gulls landed nearby, watching me, creeping closer, eyeing my hands and pecking at each other the whole time. I found a broken shell and drew two columns in the sand, one for George, one for Elizabeth.

When I saw them as competitors, pecking at each other as the gulls did, it all began to make sense in a corrupt way.

George acted. Elizabeth reacted. And Hillary, caught between them, ran away in fear for her life. I could see how her running could work to Elizabeth's advantage. As long as she wasn't identified.

I was thinking about Randy, about how no one seemed to give a damn about him, when the pager on my belt buzzed. The readout said two, as in code two, come with lights and sirens. I stood and brushed off the sand. The gulls walked close beside me until I slam-dunked the Coke cup and the empty zucchini bag into a trash can. When it was clear I had no riches to offer, they abandoned me.

The drive back downtown, following the shoreline, took less than ten minutes. At the police station the desk officer had me escorted through a linoleum maze to a far and dingy remove from the bright water out front.

Mike and Sergeant Mahakian came out of a side cubicle, laughing, to greet me.

Mahakian looked me over with rude scrutiny. He turned to Mike. "You win. She looks fine."

"Why wouldn't I?" I asked, nonplussed to be the butt of something here.

Mike took my arm, squeezed my biceps. "Remind me not to tangle with you."

"Mike," I hissed. "What?"

"You neglected to tell me you broke George's nose last night."

"I knew I'd connected pretty well. I didn't think I'd broken anything. Is he okay?"

"His eyes are nearly puffed shut and he'll need to get wired together before he can smell the roses again. Other than that, he's okay."

"I'm sorry," I said, feeling the heat rise in my face. "I only wanted to get away. I didn't mean to maim him."

"What did you use?" Mahakian asked.

"Mike's flashlight."

It was Mike's turn to blush. "No war stories, okay?"

I shrugged. "Why did you page me?"

Mahakian moved a step closer. "I understand Metrano assaulted you last night."

"He grabbed me."

"Did he use a weapon of any kind?"

"Not really. He used the flashlight to break my car window."

"Were you in the car at the time?"

"Yes, I was."

Mahakian and Mike exchanged smiles. "Got it."

"Now what?" I demanded.

"We want you to file charges against Metrano under the new stalking law," Mahakian said. "We can make a case he's been following you around. We'll throw in assault with a deadly weapon, malicious mischief two counts—the boat and the tires—to see if we can talk the judge out of granting bail."

"Isn't murder enough?" I asked.

"We don't have enough to charge him with murder, or even manslaughter," Mahakian said. "Will you do it?"

"What if he files assault charges against me? I came out better than he did."

"Don't worry, Maggie." Mike put his big arm around me. "I'll come visit you."

"I really don't want to tell a judge what I was doing at the Ramsdales' last night," I said.

"Yeah, you might take some heat. But think of it as your social duty."

"Let me talk to George and I'll do it," I said.

"No way," Mike said with force. He walked back down the hall and closed the door of the cubicle they had come out of.

"Is he in there?" I asked.

Mike crossed his arms. "You can't talk to him."

"There's your answer, Mike. No way." I fluffed my hair away from my neck and turned on my heel. "I have things to do."

Mike followed me a few steps. "Do you want George back out on the streets?"

"Yes." I wheeled on him, and expressing the heat and frustration I felt, I said, "If that's what it takes. I want to know what happened to Hillary. I have had enough goddam standard police procedure. If I have to beat the crap out of George to get it, I want his story. It will be a whole lot easier to get at him on the streets than in here with all you fucking Boy Scouts."

"Tsk," Mike said, embarrassed by my outburst, I think, but keeping up his us-guys-know-it-all facade for Mahakian. "And she went to Berkeley with all the other liberals. We don't beat the crap out of suspects, Miss MacGowen."

I didn't say anything. I turned and marched down the hall toward the arrow that said rest rooms, looked for the door with the skirt picture on it, and burst through. In a white heat, muttering obscenities, I threw my bag on the counter and reached for a handful of paper towels. That's when I saw her reflection in the chrome towel holder: Leslie Metrano huddled on the floor with her back against the blue tile wall. Her face was mottled with patches of flaming red and dead white.

I wetted the towels and dropped down beside her on the cold tile floor.

"What are you doing in here, Leslie?"

"I have no place else to go," she said, raising her cheek from her knee. "The ladies' room downstairs is full of bag ladies."

"You waiting to see George?"

She shook her head.

"You can go home."

"Never. Thanks to you, I know how George got the money to buy that house."

I handed her the cool, wet towels, and she wiped her face with them, making it a uniform flame color. She wore her official Bingo slacks and a white shirt with a hand-knit sweater over it. She looked very young, and very frightened. And there was something else, some emotion that purred below the surface like a tiger stalking prey.

"Can I do anything for you?" I asked. "Get you some coffee?"

"No." She dried her face on the sleeve of her pink sweater, smearing what was left of her blush and mascara. "I'm okay. They asked George if he wanted a public defender, but he told me to go hire him some big hotshot. I called our business lawyer, and he only reminded me we haven't paid our bill. I thought I would sit in here for a while and think things over."

"Do you mind if I'm here?" I asked.

She shook her head again.

"I know some attorneys. Maybe I could give one a call."

She looked up at me with clear eyes set in puffy flesh. "You told me you have a daughter."

"Yes."

"If she was taken from you, would you help the thief?"

"I would castrate him first."

"My sentiments exactly."

"How can I help you, Leslie?"

She leaned her head back against the wall and smiled up toward the ceiling. "Got a knife?"

This encounter was so surreal, two angry women sitting on the bathroom floor of the police station, with the source of their anger in an interrogation room down the hall. I opened my bag and took out a pack of gum that had been there for God knows how long, and offered it to Leslie.

"Maybe we can help each other here," I said. "I'll tell you what I think I know. If it gets to be too much, you say so. Okay?"

"One thing first. Did you hit George last night?"

"In self-defense."

"Go ahead, then."

"Okay," I said. "It begins. Ten years ago, you were destitute. Five kids, no prospects. George was unhappy and desperate. Am I close?"

"Close enough."

"After Amy disappeared, things began to look up. Friends helped. The community was generous. You and I know now what happened, but back then didn't you wonder where all the money came from?"

"What if I didn't want to question it too much? I just thought George was skimming the donations that came in. Is that so bad?"

"I'm not big on moral judgment calls," I said. "Skip forward, now. After ten good years, you were looking destitution in the eye again. George felt that old desperation again. He went back to his earlier source, Randy Ramsdale. Maybe he asked for a loan."

She shook her head. "George tried to blackmail him."

"He told you that?"

"Round about daybreak this morning he did. He came home with blood pouring out of his nose, a big old black eye. Looked like a licked puppy. Tail between his legs, that's for sure. He needed help and I made him talk to me to get it."

"Are you going to tell me what he said?"

"Every word of it. From one mother to another." She shifted to get comfortable, then she began.

"George told me he went to this Ramsdale guy and asked him to help out, maybe take a second mortgage on our restaurant. But Ramsdale said no, and he was real upset George had come by his house. He was arguing with George, telling him to leave, when she came home from school. When Amy came home, George said it broke his heart to see her, so pretty and grown up.

"Then he lied to me and told me he couldn't stand for me to be apart from my little girl anymore. He was going to get her back. I know it was the money he wanted. But he said that he decided right then and there to tell Ramsdale to pay up, or he would go to the police and charge him with kidnapping, and he was taking Amy back. I'm not sure that last part wasn't a lie, too. According to George, there was a big fight."

"Amy was there? She heard them fight?"

"Part of it. Her daddy, Ramsdale that is, had sent her upstairs. He was trying to hush up George when Amy came back into the room where they were. She was crying this time, real upset. She went up to Ramsdale and asked him who George was, because she recognized him as the man she always saw in her nightmares. The man who chased her and called her Amy. She was real scared."

"I bet she was," I said, fighting back tears. Hillary had also told John Smith about her nightmares. How do you handle it when you're a kid and your nightmare walks in and picks a fight with your father and you can't wake up and make him go away? And then your daddy disappears?

I reached up to the towel dispenser for a dry towel and dabbed at my own face. "When did George kill Randy Ramsdale?"

"We never got to that," she said. Then she started to laugh, self-consciously covering her face with her hands.

"What's funny?"

"I have to apologize to you, Maggie." She peered at me over her fingertips, tears running from her eyes again. "I let him blame you. George was sitting there on the kitchen chair telling me all about seeing my little girl, and I was holding this ice pack on his eye, wiping his bloody nose, taking care of him as usual. Well, I'd stayed up all night waiting for him, keeping busy fixing a few little things he never seemed to get around to. The toolbox was right there on the table beside me. I guess I was pretty mad before he even came home. When he said he made Amy cry, well, I just picked up that great big old hammer . . ."

I laughed. I could see what happened next. "It was you! You broke George's nose."

"Yes, ma'am, I did. Just picked up that great big old hammer and let him have it. Mashed his nose flat. He was so scared he didn't even holler. Then I told him to get in the car, I'd take him to the hospital. But I drove him straight here, instead. His eyes were so swollen up he couldn't see a thing." She gave me a sidelong glance. "You going to tell on me?"

"I'm going to shake your hand."

She gave me her hand, and we sat there with our backs

against the wall, holding hands and laughing. That's when Mike burst in.

"What the hell is going on?" he said, seeming alarmed.

I wiped my streaming eyes. "You can't come in here, Detective Flint. Real women only."

"Hello, Mrs. Metrano," he said, sitting down beside me anyway. "We wondered where you had gone."

"Where else could I go?" she said. "Except the little girls' room. How's George?"

"I think he's felt better," Mike said. "They've booked him and now they're going to transport him over to St. Mary's Hospital to get his injuries tended to."

"What charge did you book him on?" I asked.

Mike smiled. "Avarice, with intent."

"Did he talk?"

"Not a peep."

I smiled at Leslie. "Well, lah dee dah. They should have beat it out of him."

Leslie squeezed my hand. Her expression grew serious. "Maggie, I guess I'm ready now. I kept thinking how much it was going to hurt my kids, and my little grandbaby, to have George put in jail. But I know he never gave us one thought when he did all those things. A wife doesn't have to testify against her husband. I know that. But I have a few things I want to say."

"I'm proud of you," I said.

"Me, too." There was still some hesitation. But she took a deep breath and got to her feet, and gave me a hand up.

Leslie looked down at Mike, who was scrambling to his feet. "Get out your little notebook, Detective Flint. Time to tell all. Just one condition."

"Name it," he said.

"I want Maggie in there with me."

I took her arm and turned to bat my eyes at Mike. "Hear that, detective? She wants me."

He rolled his eyes. "Well, lah dee dah."

CHAPTER

20

"The cockroaches in the Cabo jail were bigger than the rats?" I said, my third guess.

"Nope." Mike fiddled with the handcuffs dangling from his turn signal. We had driven back to downtown L.A. and traded the Blazer for his city car. Now we were exiting the San Bernardino Freeway, stalled behind an endless line of red brake lights. "Three strikes, you're out. No more guesses."

"Good. Because I don't like this game. Anyway, for delivering George to you, you owe me big-time. Tell me, why did Elizabeth agree to fly home?"

"Oldest story in the world." He made the handcuffs spin. "The boyfriend, Ricco Zambotti, bribed his guards to turn their backs, then took off with the boat while Elizabeth was still in custody. Last seen, he was headed due west, straight for the two-hundred-mile limit."

"So Elizabeth got mad and spilled her guts, right?"

"That's it. According to her, Ricco did it all. When she found Randy's body, she called Ricco for a little hand-holding. She said it was his idea to sink the corpse, give her a little time to loot the bank accounts. Who could blame her? she said. And it was Ricco who gave Hillary a bad time, telling her that Randy had abandoned her. That Randy wasn't her real father anyway.

Elizabeth said she was just awfully upset, and hurt, when Hillary took off. She said she sent Ricco out to find the kid and bring her home. Instead he slit her throat and tried to make it look like the same killer who had sliced Randy, in case Randy ever bobbed up."

"She was so upset with Ricco that she took him on a cruise?"

Mike gave me a sidelong leer. "I'm thinking maybe I should let you and Leslie get the truth out of her. There's a flashlight in my trunk."

"Anytime," I said. "Anytime."

I was thinking a great big old hammer might be helpful, too, when Mike pulled up in front of MacLaren Hall.

"I need the receipt for the tires," he said as he got out.

"I told you I'd take care of it."

"No need. I'll turn it in to the department. The boss said he can find funds to cover it."

Couldn't argue with that. I opened my bag and handed him the receipt. He didn't even look at it when he put it into his pocket.

In the last hour of daylight, the MacLaren play yard was full of kids and full of racket. At one end of the asphalt six or eight of the older boys were pitched against some of the teachers in a rowdy game of half-court basketball. A bruising round of dodge ball took up the other end of the pavement, with hopscotchers and jump-ropers filling the space between. The lines between the games slopped over now and then, but no one seemed to be bothered by proximity.

Sly, my little loner, was off on the grass away from the other children, playing hit-and-run softball with a single adult. The young man with him was tall and slender, with dark shoulder-length hair and a single stud earring that caught the low sun. I pegged him for a volunteer, or maybe a college student collecting clinic hours for class credit.

The young man pitched a slow, straight ball at Sly's bat, talking to Sly the whole time, encouraging, joking with him. Sly slugged the ball, a bouncing grounder, and took off on a shambling run toward the single base. The man snagged the ball barehanded and went after the boy, full out, giving him no slack. About halfway to the bag, man caught boy in an easy tackle around the legs and wrestled him to the ground.

"You're out," he said over and over, using the ball to tickle Sly's midsection.

Sly was screaming. With delight, I thought. Before I could stop Mike, he lit out toward the dog pile, his marathon-runner legs pumping for all they were worth, suitcoat flapping in the wind.

"Wait, Mike," I yelled, sprinting after him. I didn't want him to interfere. To me it looked like the sort of good-natured rough-housing Sly had doubtless missed out on. But Mike had left the starting blocks first, and he's just plain old faster than I am.

To my utter and absolute astonishment, when Mike reached the tussle on the grass, instead of breaking it up, he joined in. Mike pounced and somehow rolled up on his back with his legs locked around the young man's midsection. Sly squealed with joy.

"Tickle him, Sly," Mike urged. "Get him in the ribs. Atta boy. Now the other side."

I stopped at the edge of the fray. They all stopped and looked up at me, all three of them red in the face and sweaty and giggly. To my further astonishment, the young man relaxed his head back against Mike's chest and Mike kissed him, a wet one, square on the cheek.

"See?" Sly said to me with mock disgust. "I told you the cop was a faggot."

"Maggie," Mike said, panting, "meet Michael."

"Hi," I said, dumbfounded. Here, at last, was Mike's seventeen-year-old son. "I've heard a lot about you."

"Me, too," he gasped, looking at me through the same gray eyes as his father's. Very disconcerting.

Sly, who had collapsed atop Michael, started in tickling again. Mike released Michael and rolled away. The youth bounded to his feet holding the squirming, scrawny boy in a headlock.

"Save the energy for the arithmetic." Michael knuckled Sly's head, sending out a spray of grass clippings. "We have two whole pages of it to do, squirt. We'd better get started, because I have to go home and do my own homework."

Reluctantly, Sly settled down, still breathing hard, still grinning so big his face might have split. He looked up at Michael with absolute adoration. I didn't blame him.

Mike got up and brushed himself off, managing to shoulder-bump the others a few times as he rose. This was a new side of Mike. I roughhouse with my daughter, I tease with Mike. But it's pretty tame stuff in comparison.

They were all looking at me, as if I had come with some message. Or a wet blanket. I said, "We're going to get dinner, Michael. Will you two join us?"

"We already ate here," Michael said.

"Pig vomit," Sly confirmed.

"And bats' asses," Michael added. "It was great."

I couldn't laugh yet. Watching Michael gave me such a strange feeling. Here was a younger, probably more handsome, maybe more saintly version of Mike. Whatever, he was Mike's product. A magnificent product. Like a rush I was hit with how deeply I adored Mike and everything about him. I stood there as if stricken, gasping as if I had been wrestling. I think Mike mistook my quietude for disapproval.

"Girls," Mike said, grabbing me in a headlock. "Girls can't take it."

"Can too," I said, punching his hard backside. "Just not now."

He kissed my cheek then, and let go. "Can't take it, but they sure can dish it."

Michael was watching us. "We saw one of your films in sociology, something about old people who live alone. I told the class my dad's girlfriend made it and no one believed me."

"Want me to write a note to the teacher?" I asked, jangled by the sound of "my dad's girlfriend."

"No big thing." He shrugged. "Dad says you're working on a film now. I wouldn't mind tagging along on a shoot."

"Me, too," Sly chirped.

"Fine. I'll put you both to work."

Mike tucked in his shirt, straightened his tie. He said, "Sly, we brought you another picture. Want to see it?"

Sly's entire being lit up, given another chance to nail the girl's killer. I pulled a manila envelope out of my bag and handed it to Michael. There was a single eight-by-ten glossy inside that Guido had managed to get for us from the files of Central Casting. Elizabeth had told Mike that Ricco Zambotti was an actor.

Ricco had looks, big pale eyes with long Mel Gibson lashes, curly blond hair, big white teeth. The statistics printed under the face claimed he was six-three, 190 pounds, thirty-four-inch waist, forty-eight-inch chest. Martha had said Elizabeth's daytime sneak-in friend was beefy. Ricco qualified as beefy. Prime, maybe, but still beefy.

Ricco's coloring was a problem. When Sly first described the man he saw slit Pisces' throat, he had said the man had dark hair.

Michael sat back down on the grass, Sly tucked in beside him. Together they looked at Ricco for a long time.

Mike wandered over behind them. "What do you think, Sly?"

Sly squinted up his little fox face. "Dunno."

I fished some felt-tip pens out of the bottom of my bag and sat down beside Sly.

I offered him the pens. "One time, Hilly colored in the hair of a picture of a little blond girl to see if that would make her look more like Hilly."

"She told me." Sly took a black pen from my hand and took off the cap. "Only it wasn't her who done it. It was her mother. She told Hilly she was kidnapped and all these people were looking for her to get her."

Mike frowned. "Get her how?"

"Like, *do* her," Sly said. "Just like they done."

"Why didn't you tell us this sooner?" Mike asked.

Sly shrugged. "Guess I didn't think of it. Guess it just came to me now."

"Did she say who these people were?"

"No. Except that the only person in the world who knew and could save her from them was her father. And she didn't know where he was."

Sly bent over the picture and started to color in the hair. He had made only a couple of strokes before he looked up at Michael with anxiety. "I messed up. I can't color good. I can't do it."

"Tell you what, squirt." Michael took the pen from the tense little fingers. "You tell me what you want, and I'll do it with you. Okay?"

Relieved, Sly slumped against Michael's shoulder and gave him instructions: make the hair longer, fix the eyebrows, make him look mean.

"That's him," Sly triumphed as Michael filled in the blond hair with dark ink. "I swear it, that's the asshole I seen."

It was my turn to ruffle his spiky hair. "You're sure?"

"I said I swear, didn't I? That's him. That's the guy I seen. He was following us around for a couple of days, you know, cruising in that hot 'vette."

I said, "I'm surprised Hilly would go with a man who had been following her around if she thought someone was out to get her."

"We were gonna get him first, like I told you before," Sly said, his voice catching. "We had it all worked out. This guy kept tellin' us he had something to tell Hilly, like some message from her mom and dad. People would say that all the time to us to make us go over to them. Normally, we'd just keep walkin'. Hilly wanted to talk to that one guy 'cuz of his car. She wouldn't tell me why the car freaked her. She was gonna make him show her his ID or she wouldn't talk to him. The deal was, when he got out his wallet to show her, I was gonna grab it and get the hell out of there. Then she'd know who he was."

"If Hilly had told you her father had a car just like that Corvette," I said, "would you have believed her?"

"Shit, no. No one has a car like that."

"Maybe that's why she didn't tell you."

"Sly, my man," Mike said, "what you just told us is important. I think there may be other things you haven't gotten around to sharing yet. When they come to you, have your social worker call me, will ya? We need your help to fry this man."

Sly dropped the picture, like a contaminated thing, onto the grass in front of Michael. Mike picked it up and put it back into its envelope.

Michael got to his feet, lifted Sly like a bundle of sticks, and stood him on the asphalt. "Homework time, kid."

The sun had disappeared below the line of buildings across the street, leaving the play yard lashed with long blue shadows. Most of the games had dispersed, and the children were moving inside, in clumps of two and three, taking their shadows with them. We four linked arms, I with Mike, Mike with Michael, Michael with Sly, in an irregular sort of conga line, shadows water-dancing behind us.

At the dorms, Mike turned to his son. "How late will you be?"

"Maybe an hour. Mom wants her car by eight-thirty."

Mike squeezed Michael's shoulder. "Take care."

"Dad?"

"What?"

"I got my letter from Cornell today."

"And?"

"I'm accepted."

Mike grabbed him in a bear hug. "I'm proud of you."

Michael smiled as if he had a sudden pain. Mike saw it and drew back.

"It's what you wanted, isn't it?" Mike asked.

"I thought so." Michael looked over at Sly, who was swinging from the step railing. "There's a lot to think about."

"Take your time," Mike said. "You'll figure out what's right."

"I hate it when you say that, Dad. Just once I want you to tell me what I should do."

"I always tell you what you should do," Mike said.

"Yeah. You say I should do what's right."

"Exactly."

"Michael!" Sly called, hanging upside down from the railing. "Kiss the faggot and come on. We don't have all night."

"You'd better go," Mike chuckled. "Your destiny may be calling."

"Later," Michael said, giving Mike a quick hug. "Nice to meet you, Maggie."

"Bye," I said. I watched him jog off toward the lighted doorway, recognizing a lot of Mike in him. It gave me an odd sensation, as if I were peering through a window into the past and seeing a distorted image of young Mike.

As we walked out toward the car, I took Mike's hand.

"He's a great kid, Mike. You've done a good job."

"His mother gets a lot of the credit."

I reached up then and kissed his five-o'clock shadow. "I just plain old love you, Mike. But I still don't know what to do about you."

"Take your time," Mike said, smiling down at me. "You'll figure out what's right."

CHAPTER
21

The telephone rang in the middle of night. We both bolted upright, the reflex reactions of a cop on call and a mother. Mike picked up the receiver.

"Flint," he said in a clear voice, rubbing sleep-filled eyes with his fist. When I was sure the call had nothing to do with Casey, I fell back onto the pillows, still sizzling with adrenaline rush. I eavesdropped on a lot of uh huhs and Jesus Christs before Mike hung up.

"What is it?" I asked.

"Bad stuff. George Metrano was booked on a single charge of murder and processed into the city jail at eight." He reached through the dark for my hand. "An hour ago in his cell he made a noose out of his denims and hanged himself."

"Jesus," I moaned. I curled myself around Mike and held on. "He's dead?"

"Yes, dammit."

"Does Leslie know?"

"Yes. They're bringing her in. Throw on some clothes. We should hurry. Leslie won't feel much like waiting around for us."

"Back up," I said. "I must have missed something. Why would Leslie wait around for us? What does it have to do with us?"

"George left two letters on his bunk. One for Leslie. And one for you."

"For me?" I sat up again and snapped on the bedside light. "Why would he leave a letter for me?"

"Guess we'll find that out."

We drove through dark space, a hot jet of light moving too fast to connect with the night world outside. Transients from the daytime galaxy.

At the Long Beach police station, we were taken into a small interrogation room furnished with a table and a few odd chairs. There Leslie sat alone with her head resting on folded arms. The fluorescent lights overhead washed her face a pale milky gray, made her smeared lipstick too vivid in contrast. Her eyes seemed unfocused when she watched me walk in and pull out the chair beside her. She muttered something I could not decipher.

I touched her coat sleeve and repeated the same impotent words I had used at her house the night before. "I'm sorry."

"Me, too." She brought up her chin and rested it on her hands, staring at the wall in front of her. "Doctor gave me something so I wouldn't go off and do something wild. Wish I had said no to it. My mind is so full of mush I can't feel anything. You ever have that happen to you, you can't feel anything?"

Sergeant Mahakian came in then with a pair of men in suits, detectives, no doubt. Six people made tight quarters out of the small room.

Mahakian carried two folders.

"I know this is unpleasant," he said. "But I don't know a better way to do it. The letters Mr. Metrano left are evidence, so we can't release them to you. I need you both to read their contents carefully to help us verify that they were in fact written by George Metrano and do reflect his state of mind. Now, in light of the circumstances, Mrs. Metrano, you might want some privacy. If that is your wish, you just tell me so and the others will clear out."

Leslie pulled herself upright. "Did you all read my letter already?"

"Yes, ma'am."

"Then I guess there isn't much left that's private about it, is there?"

"No, ma'am." He smiled gently. He opened one of the folders, took out a single sheet of paper encased in a plastic sleeve, and placed it on the table in front of Leslie. She moved it so that I could see it.

Yellow lined paper that had been folded into quarters, with a single sentence scrawled in blue ink: "Forgive me."

Leslie read it, turned the sheet over, read her name printed there like an address on an envelope.

"That's all?" she said, looking at both sides again. "That's all he had to say to me?"

"We didn't find anything else with your name on it. The second letter is addressed to Miss MacGowen. I would like her to read it over first before she passes it on to you, Mrs. Metrano. If she thinks its contents are too hurtful, we may hold off showing you until we can get in a family member or a counselor."

Leslie gave me a glance that told me she was beginning to feel again. She was furious.

Mahakian handed me two sheets, both encased in plastic sleeves. Both were covered with close, precise printing done with a cheap, leaky ballpoint pen. I slumped back in the straight-back chair and, with Mike looking on over my shoulder, I read:

Maggie MacGowen,

I don't have anyone else to turn to. My wife trusts you so I am asking you to please help her understand. Tell her not to hate me.

Tell her I never meant to hurt anyone. Maybe what I did was wrong, but I was only trying to do what I thought was best for us.

I confess before God that I caused the death of Randall Ramsdale. He would not help me with a loan. We had a fight about it that got out of hand. I feel he must take some of the blame for what happened to him. If he had not been so stubborn the result would have been different.

I hope that when my wife understands why I had to give our little girl to Mr. Ramsdale she will forgive me. Amy had a good life with him and we had a good life because of the financial help he gave us. I found her a good home.

After Mr. Ramsdale was dead I tried to get Amy back for my wife. I took to showing myself to Amy. I wanted her to get used to seeing me and feel comfortable when the time came. But I guess it scared her to see me because she in a way recognized me from a long time ago. Mrs. Ramsdale had her own reasons for keeping Amy and she told Amy I was trying to kidnap her and hurt her.

You will have to ask Mrs. Ramsdale what all she did, but I know she had that child scared to death of me. I believe that was why Amy ran away, because she believed I was going to hurt her. There was a private investigator came around asking questions. I thought he would help Amy understand I was her real and true father and she could come to me on her own. But it did not work out that way. When she came to me herself, she only got more scared when she recognized me as the man she thought would hurt her.

The saddest day of my life was the day I learned from Mrs. Ramsdale that Amy was dead. You have got to make my wife believe that I had no part in the killing of that little girl. Alive or dead we would still get Amy's inheritance, so why would I harm her?

I know I did some hurtful things to you and you probably hate me for that. I do not believe I would have harmed you. I had to make you understand that I was serious, just like I had to make Mr. Ramsdale understand that I was serious and needed some assistance from him. I guess that what I want to say most is that I am sorry that all this got started. I am taking the only action I know of that will put an end to it all with some honor.

Tell my wife that I have paid my insurance premiums and she will be okay.

Sincerely,

George Metrano

I read it through a second time, vaguely disappointed. At one point in this affair, I had nearly ascribed some noble, altruistic motives to George—poor man, big family, desperate solution. The letter showed no hint of nobility. Inelegant prose, an ugly story, tawdry rationalization. Nowhere did I see the word "love." Nowhere did I get the idea he felt truly repentant, nor had he accepted full blame for anything he had done. The only remorse I saw was that nothing had worked out the way he wanted it to. Like a Vegas craps shoot.

The man had been dead less than two hours. He had addressed his last formal thoughts to me. I should have felt something more—at the very least some sense of tragedy. But I did not. To be sure, I was aggrieved for his wife, who sat next to me, waiting her turn to see the letter. In a way, I guess that what I felt most was relief.

For years, George had dumped one heavy burden after another on Leslie. Among other things, he had stolen her peace of mind—no small crime. In the end, even in writing, he hadn't had the guts to confess his transgressions directly to her. He had been as amoral as a newborn child. And in his way, nearly as dependent. I didn't know yet whether Leslie had figured out that she was going to be a whole lot better off without old George, but I did my part—I passed her the letter.

Mahakian started to reach out for the pages before Leslie took them, but he pulled his hand back. Along with Mike and me and the two men in suits, he watched Leslie read.

Tears ran down her face, and her jaw was set in angry knots. Good grief therapy, that letter, I thought. When she was finished, she pushed her chair back and slowly rose to her feet.

Leslie addressed Mahakian. "When a man dies in prison, how is he buried?"

"Well." Mahakian looked around for support. "The body is usually turned over to the family."

"Yes. But if he has no family to claim it, what happens?"

"I'm not real sure. Now and then cadavers are turned over to medical schools. Most of the time the county buries them in potter's field in a sort of mass grave with other indigents. Why? Your husband said there was insurance money."

"My husband?" Leslie handed Mahakian the letter, holding him in an eerily level gaze. "The man who wrote this shit is a complete stranger to me."

With back straight and head held high, she strode from the room.

"Should I go after her?" Mahakian asked, befuddled.

"Definitely," Mike said. "She's bombed on dope. I don't think she should drive herself."

Mahakian passed his files to one of the suits and dashed out. He was a nice man. Good-looking, about Leslie's age. A long heart-to-heart with him could be good grief therapy for her of another sort. I wondered whether he was married.

Leslie had said she couldn't feel anything because of the sedative. Her reactions were flat. I planned to call her when the sedative had had time to wear off, to hear what she really thought. I knew it would be a big-time flame-out.

We stepped into the hall just as the elevator doors closed behind Leslie and Mahakian.

Mike said to me, "Quite a letter."

"Quite," I said. "George wasn't about to take the fall alone, was he? Not even posthumously. I feel so awful for Leslie."

"She'll be okay." Mike pushed the elevator call button.

"Tweedledee and Tweedledum," I was saying as the doors slid open for us.

"What is?"

"George and Randy. To be sure, a deadlier combination than Tweedledee and Tweedledum, but as alike in their way."

"You mean stubborn?" Mike pushed the lobby button and we started down. "Isn't that what George kept saying about Randy, that he was stubborn?"

"I mean that if either of them wanted something, he thought any means to attain it was legit, even baby-selling and murder. What a couple of puds. My God, Attila the Hun had a finer moral code than those two."

"Well sure, but old Attila was a big old bleeding-heart liberal leftist."

I laughed. "What makes you think so?"

"He had to be as far left as you can go," Mike said, leading me out through the deserted lobby. "Have you ever heard anyone described as being to the *left* of Attila? Never. It's always 'He's further to the right than Attila the Hun.' Therefore, if everyone is to his right . . ."

"Take me home," I said.

Mike and I were both feeling the loss of two nights' sleep. Ever macho, Mike said he was fine to drive, but I had to keep him talking all the way up the freeway. He gave up the effort just about the time the first orange glow of dawn lit the sky over the San Gabriels. He pulled off the freeway in downtown L.A., weaving like a drunk up Figueroa, and parked in the lot across from the Original Pantry. The Pantry never closes—it can't, even in a riot, because there's no lock on the door.

Mugs of coffee helped a little. Looking without interest at a plate covered with eggs, bacon, hash browns, I suggested we get a room at the Hilton and crash for a while where the telephones couldn't reach us. Elizabeth was due to be brought in sometime during the midmorning, and there wasn't time to go home, sleep, and come back.

Instead, we went to Parker Center, where there are a few cots stashed around so that morning-watch troops—the patrol shift on duty from midnight to eight—can get a little sleep when they have court scheduled during the day.

Mike found me a cot in a sort of closet behind the third-floor offices. The bed was narrow and hard, and had a tiny hard pillow, like the headrest in a coffin. My sleep was as close to death as I think I've ever gotten. At least it felt that way. I wasn't out very long, two hours at the most, before I was awakened by the morning sounds of working people. I was sitting on the edge of the cot, running my fingers through my hair, when Mike came in to get me. I was rumpled and grouchy and in dire need of repair. Mike, on the other hand, had shaved and put on a fresh shirt.

"Feel better?" he asked, damnably chipper.

"I think so. You wouldn't just have another clean shirt in your locker, would you?"

"I might."

I went into the closest rest room and did the best I could with the materials I had to work with, liquid soap, water, and a borrowed comb. Mike knocked on the door and handed through a red cotton golf shirt with "Robbery-Homicide" and a cartoon gangster with a tommy gun embroidered on the left breast. I traded my wrinkled oxford-cloth for his shirt, tucking it into the top of my 501s as I opened the door.

Everyone I saw in the hall wore regulation button-down and flannel and had a gun riding a belt holster. I felt conspicuously civilian.

Mike said, with a gleam in his eye, "Elizabeth Ramsdale is on her way up."

"Her way up from where?"

"Guest registration. I want to talk to her before they book her."

"I want to be there," I said.

Mike took my arm. "I think you've earned that privilege. Just stand at the back and look menacing. For some reason, some women are more intimidated by another woman than by a man. Just go along with everything I say and don't ever look surprised. And for God's sake don't ever contradict me. Got it?"

"Got it." I felt suddenly energized.

We were waiting in an interrogation room when Elizabeth was led in, handcuffed, by a pair of uniformed women officers.

After a night in the Cabo jail, followed by an escorted flight north, Elizabeth was a bit mussed, though her expensive hair-cut was money well spent, and she had enough tan that she didn't need makeup. For a monster, she was very nice-looking, and smaller, more slender than I had expected. There was something about her that put me off, as if the exquisite frame beneath her face had been formed out of stainless steel instead of ordinary bone. She was slender inside a blue jail-issue jumper. She had turned up the collar, rolled the cuffs, pushed up the sleeves. With her haughty carriage, she could easily have passed among the yacht-club set. Except maybe for the handcuffs.

Mike pulled out a chair for her.

"I'm Detective Flint, Mrs. Ramsdale. We spoke night before last. And this is MacGowen. Have a seat."

He left the cuffs on her.

I leaned against the wall, maybe three feet to her side, with my arms crossed, doing my best woman-officer impression. Mike stood, too, facing Elizabeth across the table. First thing, Mike dropped the doctored photograph of Ricco Zambotti onto the table in front of her. I watched her face fade about two days' worth of tan when she saw it. She didn't say anything.

"Coast Guard flew in Mr. Zambotti last night, Mrs. Ramsdale."

"Did you say flew him in? Where's my boat?"

" 'Fraid you have to write off the boat." Mike shook his head, sympathetic. "Ricco's quite a talker when he gets going. You want to hear about it?"

"I want my attorney."

"Sure thing." Next to Ricco's picture, Mike laid down the enhanced image Guido had made of George. Elizabeth's big eyes grew wider. She drew her full bottom lip between her teeth and bit it.

"You should be more careful about the friends and enemies you make, Mrs. Ramsdale," he said, his voice friendly. He was being Uncle Ned out on the front porch. "You hooked yourself up with some real conversational folks. Now, I personally cannot see how one little bitty woman could have pushed around two great big men. So, I thought maybe you would like a chance to make your own statement. You know, correct any errors or false impressions they may have given."

"I want my lawyer," she said.

"No problem," he said. "Let's just clear up a few details while we're here. The big picture is obvious enough, it's just that I don't have a real good handle on who did what and when they did it. Goes around and around in my mind, stuck. That ever happen to you? You get something stuck in your head? I do, all the time. This ditty is stuck in there right now, going round and round:

> "About the Shark, the phlegmatical one,
>   Pale sot of the Maldive sea,
>   The sleek little pilot-fish, azure and slim,
>   How alert in attendance be.

"That's Melville," he said. "Herman Melville. You ever have to memorize little poems like that in school? Boy, I did. Every time I try to sort out this case, I start thinking about that poem. In a way, I guess it is like a bunch of fish swimming around down there. Only, you can't tell one fish from the other. Except for the shark. Even that is pretty murky, Mrs. Ramsdale. Maybe you can help me out. The waters are so stirred up, I can't tell for sure which one of you is the shark."

Elizabeth looked away from him, saw me, dropped her eyes. She said, "I won't talk to you."

"That's fine," he said, smiling. "Long as you don't mind listening. Too bad you're all alone, because the way I read it, the three of you are going to take the fall together. What you need to start worrying about is special circumstances. We have a multiple-murder situation here. Add to that a couple of counts of conspiracy, assault with intent, child-selling, abuse, and neglect. I could go on for a while, but you know what went down. In the end, it adds up to three lifetime passes with a mileage bonus upgrade for seats on death row."

Elizabeth had been biting that big lip during Mike's entire speech. I saw blood around the small, even teeth. She didn't say anything, and Mike went on:

"The state hasn't executed a woman for a lot of years." He was slipping away from Uncle Ned. "But the environment is getting ripe for it. Seems to me the murder of an innocent little girl by her stepmother might be just the case the public and the courts decide to jump on.

"There are a lot of ways this could go down, Mrs. Ramsdale. Make it easy on yourself, give the state a hand. Usually, the DA wants to fry the triggerman. Or, in this case, the slasher. My take on this is that you're the shark and the other two danced attendance. But they did the dirty deeds, not you. So do yourself a favor. Tell me a story."

"I want my attorney," she said.

"Absolutely." Mike smiled. "Soon as we get you booked. Give me a few more minutes and I'll have you taken right back downstairs." Mike leafed through the file that had come up with Elizabeth. "Did you have your strip search? I don't see that here."

She hissed through clenched jaws, "Yes. I did."

"I don't see the paperwork." He closed the file and smiled more. "Not a big thing. We can do it again."

I was biting my tongue. One more minute and I was going to go out and call her an attorney. I thought Mike was skating near the edge.

"Ricco and George," Mike said. "Hard to keep prisoners segregated downstairs. I hate it when they get together, work out their stories. Sure plays hell, especially if they decide to scapegoat a third person. The story we're getting goes something like this. Your husband was leaving you. With the prenuptial agreement you signed, you'd be back waiting tables. Then, lucky you, you found him with his throat cut. You sank him in the front yard so no one would find him until you had drained the Ramsdale assets. The delay pissed off George. He wanted Randy declared dead so he could reclaim his little girl and cash in on Randy's estate—that was all part of his original deal with Randy when he handed over his kid. She was his heir. Did you know Hillary's identity, Mrs. Ramsdale?"

"I have nothing to say."

"Okay. This is how I read it. You need the kid for a while longer. You do everything you can to scare the shit out of her so she'll stay away from George. You harass her night and day, tell her George wants to steal her back. This makes some sense to her, because she can remember being snatched—she was four—and she can remember George helping Randy take her. You use her nightmares, you give her some new ones. You go too far, though, because after a while she decides she's safer living on the streets than living with you. What did you do to her, Elizabeth? Did you tell her about Randy? Did you tell her his body was out in front of the house? Did you take her swimming and show her?"

Blood trickled from her lip, and she wiped it with the back of her hand. Looking down at the red smear, she said, "I want my attorney."

"Uh huh. You were okay as long as Hillary stayed away. To make sure she didn't come back at some inconvenient moment, you located her and canceled her return ticket for good. Just two weeks before Mother's Day. That ever occur to you, Mother's Day?"

She gave Mike a defiant glare. "I won't say anything."

"You don't have to." Mike kicked the chair next to her, making both of us jump. "We'll just let Ricco and George tell it their way, Elizabeth, if that's what you want."

"Ricco won't say anything." She looked Mike right in the eye. "He loves me."

"He loves you? Is that why he left you in a Mexican jail? His best shot is to make a deal, go state's evidence and testify against you. If he has any brains, that's what he'll do."

"You're trying to scare me."

Like a blackjack dealer, Mike laid down another card, the computer-enhanced picture of the driver of the Corvette. When Elizabeth saw the grotesque image of Richard Nixon, she began to have some trouble with regular breathing.

Mike leaned over the table, putting his face near hers. "You forgot to cover your hands that night, Elizabeth. You forgot to vacuum loose hair out of the mask when you took it off, wash out the traces of sweat and saliva. That was dumb. Really dumb. But you know where you really messed up?"

"Yes," she said, snapping her head up to confront Mike. "I know where I messed up." Angrily she swept away the pictures of Ricco and George, making a racket with her handcuffs: "I learned a long time ago that if you want something done right you've got to do it yourself. No matter how dirty it is. And that's all I have to say."

"If that's the way you want it." Mike pulled out a fourth picture, a group shot of junior-high-aged kids mugging for the camera. I recognized them, the journalism class at Hillary's school. Mike had torn a page from her yearbook. The paper was a bit wrinkled from being in salt water, but Hillary's happy face was absolutely clear in the front row center.

Mike put the page on the table in front of Elizabeth. "The individual I sincerely want to talk to is Hillary. Of course, that's impossible. But I really would like to hear what she has to say. She looks like one great kid."

Elizabeth suddenly lost all of her starch, and nearly collapsed from her chair.

Mike, with complete emotional detachment, grabbed Elizabeth and righted her. When she had herself in control again, he backed away from her. He stood shoulder to shoulder with me. With arms crossed, back against the wall, dramatically sad-faced, he said again, "One great kid."

"Please," she begged, "let me go lie down somewhere."

Mike frowned. "What did Hillary say to Ricco before he cut her? Think she asked him to let go of her? Think she told him he was hurting her? Think she wanted to go lie down somewhere?"

Each question caught her like a blow to the face. I wished I could deliver the real thing to her. No, I wished Leslie Metrano had five minutes alone with her. I tossed off any notion of calling her attorney for her. As if reading my thoughts, she said, "I want my attorney."

"Sure thing," Mike said. But he didn't move.

She took a moment's time out for hard thinking. Then she turned her lovely eyes on Mike, looking up at him through the curly lashes. "You have to believe me. I didn't intend for the child to get hurt."

Mike shook his head. "You did some detective work, or maybe she called you. You found where she was cooping on the street and you sent Ricco to get her."

"He was only supposed to pick her up," Elizabeth insisted. "I'm telling you the truth. We were going to take her to Mexico with us, put her in a boarding school there for a while."

"Doesn't work, Mrs. Ramsdale," Mike said. "If all he wanted was to pick her up, why did Ricco take a razor with him? You can't tell me he had to protect himself. She only weighed ninety pounds. What I think is this. He cut her on the street to make it look like a hooker-client thing, hoping no one would pay much attention to it. But just for insurance, he made the razor cut look a lot like the one across Randy's jugular. Then if George started to get froggy, you could use that little detail to settle him down. The way I put it together, George was a bigger problem for you than the cops. What were your plans for him? Guess I should ask, when were you planning to do him?"

Elizabeth reached up to fluff her hair, and the chain between the cuffs banged her chin. She rubbed the spot as she looked from me to Mike.

"The question is," she said, "when was George planning to kill me?"

"MacGowen," Mike said, nudging my shoulder. "You have an answer for that question?"

"Yes, I do," I said. "As soon as you showed up at your house. Metrano has been lying in wait for you ever since you told him his daughter was dead. Now that you're in custody, guess he's missed his shot."

"He hasn't missed anything," Mike said. "He's taking his shot right now. He's spilling his guts, Elizabeth. He finally got smart. He's going to let the state do his dirty work for him."

Elizabeth was more scared than she let on. The armpits of the jumpsuit were sweated through. I gave her credit for hanging tough, though. When Mike asked if she had anything to say, she said:

"Yes. Fuck you."

"Nice way to talk," Mike said.

"I want my attorney," she said.

"You got it." Mike stepped out into the hall and summoned the uniformed officers to come fetch Elizabeth. I saw disappointment in the faces of a couple of the detectives who had been keeping the young female officers entertained. They were both lively, hard-bodied types, apparently holding their own in the mandatory war-story swap.

I followed Elizabeth as far as the door.

"Nice meeting you," I said to her back.

She turned and glared at me. "Fuck you, too."

Mike laughed.

"Be careful, Flint," I said when we were alone. "I may beef you with the ACLU. I am sure that interrogation was not within guidelines."

"Fuck the ACLU," he said, shrugging.

"I pay dues to the ACLU."

He smiled his wry smile. "Figures."

"She's quite a babe, isn't she?" I said as we walked out toward the elevators. "You have to admit, she's strong on determination."

"Cold bitch. The woman knows what she wants and she's going to get it, no matter what the cost is to her or anyone else. Feels no guilt—complete sociopath. A lot of career criminals are like that. And politicians."

"Will she ever talk?" I asked.

"She just did," he exploded. "She told us she's going to let Ricco take the fall for killing Hillary. For the rest, did she deny anything? You saw her. Was any of this new information to her? No way. She told us plenty."

We stepped into the elevator.

"Where did you find the Nixon mask?" I asked.

"Did I say we'd found the mask?"

"Pictures of her hands?"

He just grinned.

In retaliation, I took a handful of his rear end just as the doors opened onto the lobby full of police. "You're such a good liar."

"When I need to be," he said, grabbing my hand away. "The important thing is to keep her off guard for a while. As soon as her attorney shows up, she's going to find out what we do and don't have, mainly, Ricco and George. Tell you what, though—I'd sure like to be there when she finds out she's going to take the dive all by herself. Our shark swims alone this time."

"Herman Melville," I laughed. "Give me a break. Where did that come from?"

"From you," he said. "You said you like Melville."

We walked outside into the hazy sunshine. I squinted against the glare as I looked out across the patchy brown lawn in front of Parker Center. Little family groups, some with picnics and toys to occupy the legions of tiny children, clustered here and there wearing the same solemn faces you see in hospital waiting rooms. A young Latino was passing out bright blue fliers for the bail bondsman down the street. I saw the edges of the fliers sticking out of several of the picnic bags and a couple of shirt pockets.

I took Mike's arm. "What you laid out for Elizabeth—except for the obvious bullshit—is the way it happened, isn't it?"

"Pretty much."

"I'm glad they self-destructed, but I still can't comprehend the terror they must have put Hillary through. And I don't mean the month Elizabeth had her alone. From the time George gave her up, I think she was doomed. I try to imagine what it must have been like for her. As you said, Mike, she was four and a half when they took her away from her mother. She would remember her family. In the beginning, she would have cried for them. Remember what Mrs. Sinclair said? George came and settled Amy down after she was supposed to be Hillary because she was so upset. What could he have told her? 'Mom and I don't want you anymore'? 'Mom is dead'? What?"

"Unless Mrs. Sinclair has more to tell us, we'll never know,"

Mike sighed. The bright sunlight was unkind to his fatigued face.

I turned away from the sun and started walking. "The big crime was forcing the child to abandon not only her family, but herself. They gave her new parents, changed her hair, her name, gave her a dimple. Even changed her birthday. Can a child survive that sort of uprooting intact?"

"Maybe." Mike turned up his palms. "Depends on the kid, I guess. And how they treated her. After a while, she probably settled in okay."

"Everyone said she was the kind of kid who was always trying to please. So maybe she seemed settled in, but she had nightmares. Or else she thought her memories of Amy were bad dreams. Whatever, she was afraid of those pictures in her mind, the pictures of George." We stopped at the corner, at the edge of a crowd waiting for the pedestrian light to change. "She could never feel really safe. How could she ever be sure that someone wouldn't snatch her away again, make her start all over as someone new? And the household itself was hardly settled. Hanna died and left her. After Hanna, there were two stepmothers, both disasters. Old Randy was a constant, but from what I hear, he was never very tightly wrapped. In the end, even he disappeared."

The light changed and walkers surged around us to get into the crosswalk. The light had turned red again before I thought to move. I pushed the walk button again.

"When Randy was gone," I said, "Hillary set off on an odyssey to find the truth. When what she found was her nightmares personified, she did for herself what Randy, Hanna, and George had done before. She re-created herself. Pisces, child of the streets. A kid with no history at all."

"You really liked her, didn't you?" he asked.

"I would have, if I'd had time to get to know her."

The light was green again. As I stepped off the curb, Mike reached for my arm and pulled me back.

"Where are you going?" he asked.

"Across the street."

"Why?"

I had no answer. I had simply followed the flow of the crowd. I looked at the opposite side of the street, at the columns of gray-suited city workers trekking down into the mall for lunch. I put my hand against Mike's tie and looked up into his face.

"Make me an offer," I said. "Where shall we go?"

"Time to take your bearings, Maggie," he said, covering my hand, pressing it against his chest. "Time to figure out where it is you really want to go."

"I've had that figured out for quite a while, Mike," I said. "I just don't know how to get there."

"Where is that?"

"I want to go home with you."

CHAPTER
22

Saturday morning dawned hot and bright, with a strong Santa Ana wind gusting through the canyons. We filed down the grassy slope from the chapel at the top of the hill, small groups in funeral clothes, following the pallbearers along a crooked path among the headstones. My heels dug into the soft ground, so I walked on tiptoes, awkwardly, to keep from falling or losing my shoes.

The child in the coffin had been dead nine days now. Only determined prodding by Mike and the influence of the right judge had effected her release from the county coroner.

In the chapel we had sat divided as wedding partisans would, Hillary's friends on one side of the aisle, the friends of Amy Elizabeth on the other. Outside, the groups blended with those who came to remember Pisces—Sly, Sister Agnes Peter, Guido, me—and by their sharing in some small way rejoined the dismembered parts of the young girl's life. At least, that's how it seemed to me.

Sly was a proud pallbearer, using both hands on his assigned handle, the middle position on the left side of the narrow gray coffin between Mike and Michael. He wore long pants and a new shirt, buttoned at the neck like Michael's. His little fox face was a study in concentration. He watched Mike ahead of him for clues, stepping when Mike stepped, stopping when Mike stopped. For assurance that he was doing his task properly, he kept looking back at Michael. He still broke my heart.

I walked arm in arm with Casey and Guido and Sister Agnes Peter. Halfway down to the gravesite the slope grew very steep and the footing was treacherous for the pallbearers. Even though the young deceased had been very small and her coffin was not full-sized, I saw them all struggle, Mike, Sly, and Michael on their side, and opposite them John Smith, Leslie Metrano's son-in-law, and the stalwart Sergeant Mahakian. The grave had been dug under the branches of an old chestnut tree, and a bier erected at its side, among the exposed roots. The coffin was set atop the bier and the pallbearers fell back into the growing circle of mourners who had come to say good-bye to the lost child.

When the mortuary priest raised his Bible and asked for the group to pray, I looked at the faces in the small knot around Sly. He chewed the sides of his cheeks, trying not to cry, until Michael put his hand on the boy's shoulder and gave it a squeeze. Sly dissolved into deep, mournful sobs that defined the huge hole that Pisces had tried to fill, the huge hole that was the history of his short life.

Michael knelt down on one knee and brought the child in close, giving him a shoulder to cry against. Mike put his hand on his son's cheek, completing a circuit of support.

I wasn't concentrating on what the minister was saying, something about children going directly to heaven to sit next to God. Maybe he forgot that children don't like to sit. My Casey never had.

Knowing better than to do it, I looked over at Leslie Metrano. I knew exactly what she was thinking—about every instant of her Amy's life that had been stolen from her. I saw the shadows of those images roll across her face, and I could not bear it. I leaned against Casey's burgeoning chest and bawled.

Guido held me. Agnes Peter held him. The minister could have been reciting "Baa Baa Black Sheep" for all we heard. When we grieve, what we mourn is lost possibility. The coffin beside us, covered with a blanket of tiny pink rosebuds, contained nothing so much as lost possibility. What was there for a stranger to say that we did not know?

The priest said amen, Leslie fainted, and the service was over.

With family attending to Leslie, the crowd began to disperse. Michael picked up Sly, all gangly arms and legs, and carried him back up the hill toward the line of cars parked above the chapel. As I watched them go, I wiped my nose on the back of my hand. Guido handed me a pack of lens papers. They were totally useless, so I gave them back and used my sleeve.

Mike had walked over to us. He put his arm around me, and I leaned my head against his hard chest.

"Ready?" I said. He only nodded. His eyes were rimmed with red.

As we walked up the hill, Casey grabbed the elbow of Mike's dark suit coat. "Do you believe in the death penalty, Mike?"

"Sometimes," he said.

"Mom doesn't."

"Oh yeah?" He glanced at me, lifting the corner of his mouth. "What do you think, Casey?"

"I used to think it was barbaric. I mean, killing is wrong no matter who does it, right? But I think this time it's different. I mean, it's so unfair that those people are alive and she isn't. I think that sucks."

"So do I." He put his other arm around her.

"What are you going to do to them?" she asked.

"It isn't up to me," he said. "The courts will decide."

"You have to do something." Her voice rose half an octave.

"I'll do my job, Casey," he said calmly. "My job is finding the evidence the court needs for conviction. Elizabeth and Ricco weren't planning on getting caught; they left us a pretty easy trail to follow. We've already learned that Elizabeth's boat was in Dana Point the day of the killing. She and Ricco could have driven up to L.A. in an hour, maybe an hour and a half. Ensenada, Cabo—all a bunch of bull. And we can prove it."

"Any word on Ricco?" I asked.

"We'll get him," Mike said, frowning.

"I want to go to the trial," Casey said.

"You'll probably be in school," I said. I looked up at my daughter. She had always been, in my life, the source of both my greatest satisfaction and the most maddening complications. Casey had auditioned for the Joffrey and been accepted. That meant ballet every day. In San Francisco. Thinking no time like the present, I pulled Mike closer.

"So, Mike," I said. "Casey has good news. She's been accepted into the young dancers' academy."

"Congratulations," he said. "What does that mean?"

Casey began to sparkle again. "It'll be like a high school for performing arts. I'll dance and take classes, and I'll start having parts with the ballet."

I watched his face fall as the big question came to him.

"Where is this academy?" he asked.

"Here." She did a small graceful leap, a reflex. "In L.A."

I pulled her back. "I didn't know that. I thought it was in San Francisco."

Casey looked over at Mike and laughed. "I may be just a kid, but I'm not stupid."

I heard my name called out and looked up to see Sly standing on the curb at the top of the slope, waving his arms at me. We picked up our pace and he ran down to meet us. By the time he reached us, his legs were going faster than his brakes could handle. Mike caught him around the middle and set him down on solid feet.

"What do you need?" I asked him.

"My stuff," he gasped. "Where's my stuff? I gotta take it to my new place."

I snapped my eyes up to Mike. "What new place?"

"Don't panic," Mike said. "Sly's going to a group home in Reseda. He doesn't need MacLaren anymore."

"Oh," I said. My first thought had been that Michael was taking Sly home. Or that Mike was. As fond as I was of Sly, he still needed more supervision and counseling than any of us, or all of us together, could offer him.

"Where's my stuff?" Sly asked again, antsy about it.

"It's in Mike's car," I said. "All locked up."

Sly hurried us the last few yards. Mike opened the back door of his Blazer and took out the brown-paper-wrapped bundle that was buckled into one of the seats. He made a show of dusting the thing off and smoothing down the tape before he finally handed it over.

Michael leaned against the open car door. "What's in that?"

"Just stuff." Sly shrugged and tucked the bundle under his arm. "Let's go. I don't want to be late for lunch."

"Hold the phone," Michael said. I thought he was posing a bit for Casey's sake. I didn't like the way she noticed his effort and responded in kind. He reached out his hand to Sly.

"I took you to my house and showed you all my stuff," Michael said. "Now you show me yours."

"No big one." Sly rolled his eyes, tried for coolness.

"Then show," Michael urged.

Again Sly shrugged, and then, to my great surprise, he began to unwrap the brown paper. I slipped my hand into Mike's and squeezed it. I don't know why I felt so expectant. I had thought of helping Sly say no, but this exchange seemed to be something between him and Michael.

Out of the leg-of-lamb-shaped package appeared first a brown furry ear, then shiny black button eyes and a red yarn nose. When he pulled the paper away, he was cuddling a much-loved stuffed dog of indeterminate breed.

"Cool," Michael said. "Where'd you get it, squirt?"

"From her." Sly's big dark eyes teared up, but he held the tears back. "Hilly brought it with her. She said I should take care of it for her."

"Cool," Michael said again.

"Yeah," Sly agreed, imitating the way Michael bobbed his head. "Its name is Amy."